The WORLD'S STRONGEST REARGUARD | Labyrinth C... Novice S...

The Islet of Illusion—one of the health resorts managed by the Guild and another perk of being an Advanced Seeker.
In my previous life, I never would've dreamed I'd get to visit a place like this.

An enormous chariot materialized around me, and I found myself sitting on the carriage between its wheels.
"As you wish."
"Full speed ahead, Alphecca!"

The WORLD'S STRONGEST REARGUARD
Labyrinth Country's Novice Seeker
5

Tôwa

Illustration by
Huuka Kazabana

YEN ON
New York

The WORLD'S STRONGEST REARGUARD | Labyrinth Country's Novice Seeker

5

Tôwa

Illustration by **Huuka Kazabana**

Translation by Alexandra McCullough-Garcia
Cover art by Huuka Kazabana

SEKAI SAIKYO NO KOEI -MEIKYUKOKU NO SHINJIN TANSAKUSHA- Volume 5
©Tôwa, Huuka Kazabana 2019
First published in Japan in 2019 by KADOKAWA CORPORATION, Tokyo.
English translation rights arranged with KADOKAWA CORPORATION, Tokyo through
TUTTLE-MORI AGENCY, INC., Tokyo.

English translation © 2021 by Yen Press, LLC

Yen On
150 West 30th Street, 19th Floor
New York, NY 10001

Visit us at yenpress.com
facebook.com/yenpress
twitter.com/yenpress
yenpress.tumblr.com
instagram.com/yenpress

First Yen On Edition: March 2021

Yen On is an imprint of Yen Press, LLC.
The Yen On name and logo are trademarks of Yen Press, LLC.

Library of Congress Cataloging-in-Publication Data
Names: Tôwa, author. | Kazabana, Huuka, illustrator. | Taylor, Jordan (Translator), translator. |
    McCullough-Garcia, Alexandra (Translator), translator.
Title: The world's strongest rearguard: labyrinth country's novice seeker / Tôwa ; illustration by
    Huuka Kazabana.
Other titles: Sekai saikyo no koei: meikyukoku no shinjin tansakusha. English
Description: First Yen On edition. | New York, NY : Yen ON, 2019– |v. 1–4 Translator,
    Jordan Taylor — v. 5 Translator, Alexandra McCullough-Garcia.
Identifiers: LCCN 2019030466 | ISBN 9781975331542 (v. 1 ; trade paperback) |
    ISBN 9781975331566 (v. 2 ; trade paperback) | ISBN 9781975331580 (v. 3 ; trade paperback) |
    ISBN 9781975315719 (v. 4 ; trade paperback) | ISBN 9781975315733 (v. 5 ; trade paperback)
Subjects: CYAC: Fantasy. | Future life—Fiction.
Classification: LCC PZ7.1.T676 Wo 2019 | DDC [Fic]—dc23
LC record available at https://lccn.loc.gov/2019030466

ISBNs: 978-1-9753-1573-3 (paperback)
        978-1-9753-1574-0 (ebook)

10 9 8 7 6 5 4 3 2 1

LSC-C

Printed in the United States of America

CONTENTS

Solitary White

I first joined the White Clan, the predecessor of the White Night Brigade, when I was still in District Seven.

"You have a bright future ahead of you. Would you like to join us?" our leader had asked me.

A bluish tint streaked his wavy hair. He wore glasses back then, and a gentle smile always played along his lips—that, at least, is still pretty much the same.

However, after a certain incident, he changed.

The White Clan became fixated on gathering strong members and soon amassed a cache of precious weapons found in the labyrinth by whatever means necessary.

People followed his orders, even if it meant committing a crime. I did anything he asked of me, too. Eventually, he renamed our group the White Night Brigade. I think only the leader himself and his father, and maybe some high-ranking officers of the Brigade close to them, know why.

I'm sure Elitia doesn't know. Our leader showered her with special treatment. He made sure she was first in line to receive the Scarlet Emperor, which a few Brigade members went to great lengths to get, and gave her permission to wield it. I think Elitia believes that decision ended in failure. But our leader couldn't have hoped for more. Only those who prove compatible can make a cursed weapon activate its powers.

You need certain qualifications for a cursed weapon to possess you. Since I lacked those qualifications, it was my duty to obtain them. That way, one day, every member of the White Night Brigade could take such a weapon in hand and call upon its powers to destroy the walls that confined us. We would need weapons far more powerful than those you could get through normal routes if we wanted to surge ahead of all those Seekers in District Four.

I eventually reached level 13 as a Dual Fencer, but that wasn't enough to earn our leader's trust, and he only ever asked me to do odd jobs. So I decided to look for another way. I thought maybe if I could switch to a job with skills related to curses, our leader might open up to me more.

Why did he change? What could have caused this man, who had talked about wanting nothing more than to spend his days seeking in peace with his family, to become so coldhearted?

I can't bring myself to hate him even after all that's happened. If it hadn't been for him, I would probably still be squatting in some back alley in District Seven, abandoned by my party, unable to go forward and with nowhere to return to.

I wanted to be irreplaceable so no one would ever abandon me again. It wasn't easy, changing to a line of work related to curses.

The training bleached my hair white, and it's never gone back. At first, people told me it looked hideous, but to be honest, I preferred it that way. I felt the white in my hair was a sign I'd gained permission to be a member of the White Night Brigade.

But my wishful thinking meant nothing to our leader.

"Changing your job does not guarantee you'll gain the right to wield a cursed weapon. It seems you're not among the chosen," he said without even looking in my direction, after calling me one day to the Brigade's hideout for the first time in a long while.

I told him I would find another job if this one didn't work out. I didn't care if I leveled down; I would work my way up again by myself if I had to. I begged him to let me stay in the Brigade.

"Retrieving a wayward lamb takes precedence over forcing another to change its nature... Do you understand my meaning?" he said softly, as he always spoke. It was nothing short of my final warning, but he sounded almost playful as he gave it. "You will call Elitia back. If that proves impossible, retrieve the sword she carries."

"...But that's..."

"You switched to your current job so you could work with curses, didn't you?"

I still didn't have any skills related to cursed weapons. Maybe I couldn't learn any through the Charm Master job as I'd hoped. I had nothing of value left to offer to keep my place in the Brigade. The only way I could possibly contribute was with my loyalty, by faithfully executing our leader's orders.

"I have no use for you here. You can either recruit new members or go bring back Elitia…or both."

A single shake of my head here and I would lose the only place I belonged. I never had any real choice. If the White Night Brigade—if our leader were to abandon me, I would lose my only reason for living in this Labyrinth Country.

CHAPTER 1

The Recovered and the Returned

Part I: Nickname

Our long-running conflict with the Alliance that started when we first arrived in District Seven had finally been put to rest. With everyone's help, we successfully overcame the formidable obstacles in our path, from disbanding the Beyond Liberty alliance that had been monopolizing the best hunting grounds to defeating the Merciless Guillotine responsible for great tragedies.

The Guild had arrested Gray, the man who had been secretly plotting to take over the Alliance. He'd also faced retribution, albeit in a rather unconventional way, for trying to force the members of Four Seasons to join the Alliance. He was going to undergo grueling reeducation at the training facility after his arrest. It was an intense punishment, but it still felt a little lenient considering everything he'd done; perhaps I should have gone tougher on him as the leader of my party for leering at my party members.

"Atobe, he's going to be okay, right? We did make it in time, didn't we...?"

"Yes, definitely. I'm sure Roland will be fine... Let's have some faith."

We hurried to the Healer clinic as soon as we left the Beach of the Setting Sun. I was confident he would regain consciousness as long as we had the soul prison stone that held Roland's soul captive.

I asked to see Roland at the front desk and was surprised by how easily the Receptionist let us through. The Doctor at the clinic had examined Roland and had also diagnosed he was in a lethal coma due to the loss of his soul. It seemed Daniella had explained to them ahead of time that she'd asked us to help retrieve it.

We climbed up the stairs and rushed to Roland's treatment room. The Nurse looked incredulous as she led the way. "Normally, when a patient's soul has been stolen, no one is able to defeat the monster that stole it in time, and the individual's soul is lost forever. And when that happens, they're even more likely to turn into a demi-human than if they had been defeated inside the labyrinth..."

"I see. So that's why he's in this room..." A particularly strong door secured the room allotted to Roland, possibly due to the risk that he could turn into a demi-human.

"I apologize for the wait, Mr. Atobe. Ms. Daniella has told us all about what happened. It seems you accepted a truly challenging request... Please allow me to first express how thankful we are that you have made it through safely."

The Doctor looked maybe a few years older than me. It felt a little strange to be thanked by someone I'd just met—but I didn't have time to dwell on that. We couldn't all enter the treatment room at once, so only Igarashi, Theresia, Suzuna, Misaki, and I went in.

"I must say, we never dreamed you would retrieve his soul the same day it was stolen... On behalf of the number one clinic in District Seven, we salute your heroism." At that, the Doctor and the Nurse both bowed their heads in unison. I appreciated the sentiment, but we weren't out of the woods yet. All of this would be pointless if we couldn't resuscitate Roland.

"Doctor, how is Roland's condition...?"

"It remains unchanged; he is still in a lethal coma. I have only ever seen three patients recover from soul loss in my ten years here. I only wish I had more experience to offer."

"No, it's a great comfort to know you've seen three successful recoveries. Now, what should I do with this stone?"

The Doctor's eyes opened wide as I pulled out the soul prison stone. He reached out to touch it but pulled back halfway. "It's as I feared... The binding that monster placed upon his soul remains intact. It must be purified with a Holy attribute. We will make arrangements for someone to come at once."

"A Holy attribute... Just a moment, Doctor. Suzuna, do you think you can purify this using your Handwash skill?"

Suzuna stepped closer and picked up the soul prison stone. Black, turbid markings clouded its surface as if trapping Roland's soul within.

"It looks like the impurities are still tightly bound around his soul," said Suzuna. "I think I might be able to purify it if I had some water..."

"We would greatly appreciate your help if you have such specialized purifying capabilities through your profession. I'm ashamed to admit that even though I am a Doctor, I don't possess any skills that can heal the soul."

"I understand. I will do my best to purify it. Do you have clean water I may use?" Suzuna asked the Nurse, who poured some into a glass vial for her. Suzuna activated Handwash, setting the entire vial aglow with a faint light.

◆Current Status◆
> Suzuna activated Handwash
> Impurity on Soul Prison Stone was lifted ⟶ Changed to Soul Stone

Suzuna scooped water into her hands and let it drip onto the soul prison stone I held. As she did, the murky pattern on the stone started to dissipate. Then it transformed into what must have been its true form and began to emit a translucent light from within.

I moved closer to where Roland had been laid to rest in the room. His chest showed no upward or downward movements whatsoever, and it looked like he wasn't even breathing—but he was still alive.

"…Roland. Daniella and your soon-to-be-born child are waiting for you," I said to him.

My friends watched on wordlessly. I brought the stone nearer to him, and his body began to shine with that same pale light, almost as if it were breathing. Then—

◆Current Status◆
> Arihito used Soul Stone ⟶ Target: Roland
> Roland recovered from Fatal Coma

—the soul stone left my hand and shone ever brighter. What had been a tangible stone only a moment ago transformed into an ethereal light, which then melted into Roland's body.

"…Thomas… Take over from here… Tell Daniella I'm sorry…" Roland spoke to his party as if still gazing up at the Merciless Guillotine, prepared to die.

I guess time must have stopped for him there—but he's got a new start now.

Eventually Roland's eyes fluttered open, and he turned toward me.

"Did I…? Didn't that Named Monster get me…?"

"…Thank goodness. I'm so glad you've come to."

Roland just stared at me, unable to immediately grasp the situation. His eyes widened slightly once he realized my party members were with me, and he began to try to say something.

"Mr. Roland, we are immensely relieved to see you've regained consciousness. We have Mr. Atobe and his party to thank for retrieving your stolen soul," the Doctor explained.

Roland closed his eyes and took a breath. His face trembled, but he looked relieved. "Atobe…why did you save me…?"

"Daniella asked us to defeat a monster, so we did. That's all there is to it."

"That's all it takes to motivate him to act. We simply followed his lead."

"Don't get the wrong idea, though! We didn't go out just to save you, y'know! …Juuust kidding."

Igarashi and Misaki stepped up in turn to speak, though I had a feeling that Misaki's tone was a little too light for the situation. Roland lifted the corners of his mouth a little and smiled, then closed his eyes and took a long breath.

"You got me fair and square, rookie. But I guess that doesn't mean much for you all. Who could've known you'd make it to the top of District Seven in just a few days…*cough, cough*…" The medical staff rushed to Roland's side as he started to cough. It looked like even a short conversation was too much for him so soon after regaining consciousness.

"Mr. Roland, it truly is a wonderful thing to see you've recovered from the Fatal Coma," said the Doctor. "However, you will require rehabilitation. We pledge to support you along the way, so let's work hard together to get you back on your feet."

This was going to be Roland's second setback: The first was when he fell ill, and now the recovery of his soul would keep him from advancing to District Six. Daniella had told us about how, back when his illness first struck and his companions abandoned him, Roland suffered so deeply he was plagued with nightmares. I couldn't even begin to imagine how difficult it must have been to recover from such a harrowing experience.

But a light still shone in Roland's eyes. His expression didn't betray the slightest hint of resignation. "...This all has taught me a lesson. I can't bring the Alliance down with me, so I know I'll have to start from scratch all over again. But it looks like I'm worse at giving up than even I knew."

"Roland, starting from scratch... Don't you think you're exaggerating a bit?"

Daniella stepped into the room as I finished speaking. Her eyes flew open, and she stopped dead in her tracks the instant she realized Roland was awake.

"...Daniella."

"...Roland...!" she cried as she flung her arms around him. The sight moved all of my companions to tears. I couldn't help but look up at the ceiling to keep my emotions from getting the better of me.

"......"

"...Wh-what's up, Theresia? Are you worried about me?"

Theresia didn't nod but held on to my sleeve. Maybe she was worried because I looked up so quickly.

"Thank goodness... If you... If you'd actually died, I don't know what I'd—I'd...!"

"...I was sure I was a goner, too. But it turns out that man in the suit is no death god. In fact, he's more like the exact opposite."

A death god in a suit—that was definitely a foreign movie. Do other people think the same thing when they see me? Roland was joking, though. Maybe I shouldn't read too much into it.

Theresia still looked worried about me. I leaned in close to her and said in a low voice only she could hear, "It's just, I'm a little old to be crying in public, you know?"

"……"

As I wondered if she'd understood what I meant, Theresia's mouth, visible under her mask, seemed to gasp, and she took a step back.

Hmm... T-Theresia...?

Her face beneath her mask turned red. Maybe it'd been careless of me to speak so close to her ear... No, even if that were the case, this felt like a bit of an overly sensitive reaction.

"Haaah... Well, I guess that takes care of that. Suzu, you got a handkerchief?"

"Oh...s-sorry, Misaki." Misaki went to borrow Suzuna's handkerchief, only to find Suzuna already dabbing her own eyes with it.

"Atobe, let's give these two some space," Igarashi said after turning her back to me so I wouldn't see her wipe the tears from her eyes, then she led Suzuna and Misaki out of the room. The Vorns looked a bit embarrassed to realize they'd made everyone cry.

"Mr. Atobe, thank you so much for everything. I promise I will arrange your reward for all your hard work through the Guild," said Daniella.

"No, that's really quite all right..."

"Sometimes the Guild provides a reward if you take on another party's request and manage to fulfill it. I couldn't tell you how much saving me might be worth, but you could get something out of it. I'll bet it'd be easier on your pride to take a reward from the Guild than from your former rival...right?"

Roland cared so much about reaching number one in District Seven and aspiring to move up to higher districts. I'd be trampling all over his pride if I said I didn't need a reward for saving him. In that case, maybe we should claim some kind of compensation. I was a little curious as to what the reward might be. Would we maybe get it after we reported back to Louisa with our expedition results?

"Okay, we'll be sure to accept any reward offered to us. Thank you. Please do take care, both of you. Roland, I think you have a long road ahead of you, but..."

"Yeah, I'll be all right. I can't stay this useless for long, for my wife...and our new family's sake."

Roland and Daniella beamed at each other. Looking at the smiling couple, I could tell we didn't have anything to worry about.

"Mr. Atobe, please do feel free to visit us again should you ever find yourself in need of medical attention," said the Doctor. "I'm afraid we did not prove terribly helpful today, but we would be happy to assist you in the future with any other medical needs that may arise."

"Thank you very much. At some point I'd like to arrange physical exams for my party and myself."

I bid the staff farewell, then joined my friends and departed the treatment room. At that moment, I saw a familiar group waiting in the lobby: the Beyond Liberty members.

"...I heard what happened. I don't know how we can thank you for saving our leader," said an emotional, teary-eyed man. He and Roland must go pretty far back. I could tell his gratitude was genuine.

"You got here so quickly. You must have been on standby to gather at a moment's notice," I replied.

"Yes... We all... When we heard what happened to Roland, we couldn't just go about our day like normal. I was worried some parties would take the chance to leave the Alliance, but nobody's jumped ship yet, aside from Gray, who the Guild Saviors took into custody. I also spoke with the three members of Triceratops and heard what happened. They won't be returning to the Alliance, but we've agreed to work together going forward."

"I'm glad to hear it. I'm sure it'll be a great comfort to Roland to know everyone has decided to stay in the Alliance."

Members of the party we'd never even spoken to started bowing to us.

Ever since we first learned of the Alliance and how they took over hunting grounds, we wound up having to compete against them. But now, Gray, the man who had turned us against each other, was out of the picture. Maybe one day we could hash things out between us, but we had to keep going. The Alliance most likely had their own matters to attend to as well.

"I hope we can meet again someday. And the rest of the

Alliance—I wish you all the best," I said and turned to leave the clinic. Just before I stepped outside, I heard several voices from behind me.

"Thanks! I gotta tell you, Suit Man, you're badass!"

"Thank you for saving our leader! We love you!"

"Mr. Atobe! I swear I'm gonna be a Seeker just like you one day!"

A whole host of Alliance members, from the guy looking a bit rough around the edges to the young ladies, were cheering me on. I was a bit embarrassed, but it nonetheless was nice to hear.

"...I've got a feeling you're going to keep blowing up, Atobe."

"At this rate, you might even get a nickname. I just hope it's better than mine."

"N-nickname, huh...? Seems like they already call me 'Suit Man.'"

Igarashi and Elitia looked happy. I felt incredibly blessed we could still cherish these little moments of joy with one another even after coming out of a vicious battle where we looked death right in the eye.

Not long after leaving the clinic, we spotted Seraphina. She was wearing some type of military attire, possibly her Guild Savior uniform, instead of her usual armor.

"Seraphina, great work out there. That really was an intense battle. Are you all right?"

"Thank you for your concern. Truth be told, I am a bit exhausted, but it's nothing to complain about. This is what I train for every day. Mr. Atobe, is Mr. Roland...?"

"Yes, he's regained consciousness, thanks to your help. I think he'll be perfectly fine."

"That's a great relief to hear. I shudder to imagine what might have happened if you and your party hadn't been there... It appears we Guild Saviors need to redouble our training efforts." Even Guild Saviors had proven no match for that monster. Higher-ranking officers probably would have been able to handle it, but I could imagine they'd be stationed in upper districts.

And yet, my party had defeated that very monster. I wondered what the Guild headquarters and Guild Saviors would think about that. Was it safe to assume it had something to do with what Third-Class Dragon Captain Kozelka had mentioned?

"Now...I shall escort you to Third-Class Dragon Captain Kozelka. Mr. Atobe, as your party's representative, would you please follow me?"

"Of course. Okay, everyone, I'll come back as soon as I'm done. Until then, you're free to do whatever."

"We'll head back home and rest up a bit. It might be a little later than usual, but we'll wait for you to have lunch. Does that sound okay, ladies?" Igarashi led the group off to the apartment, looking for all the world like a teacher with her students. It warmed my heart.

"......"

And of course, Theresia pitter-pattered over to my side. Igarashi and the others forced a smile, resigned to the fact that this was just how things were.

"I'm sorry. Ever since I met Theresia, she's stuck by me like a bodyguard..."

"Heh-heh… I see. Well, that shouldn't pose an issue." Seraphina laughed. That in itself shouldn't have been so surprising, but I was used to seeing her as a stern military officer, so it did catch me a little off guard.

"…So she's your bodyguard…," Seraphina murmured. "It appears Ms. Theresia has found her place."

"Huh…?"

"Never mind. Mr. Atobe, you came straight from the labyrinth and haven't had a chance to sit. Are you tired? If so, I would gladly carry you."

"N-no, thank you; I'm not that tired. Please don't worry about me."

"I see… Adeline tells me I give comfortable, reliable rides, but if that's what you prefer."

Maybe she just sees me like the large, heavy packs she has to carry long distances for her military training? I know I'm a rear-guard, but standing in for a backpack might be going one step too far. I'll pass.

Part II: Honorary Title

Upon our arrival at the Upper Guild's Green Hall, I was escorted to the back of the first floor as usual. This time, however, we didn't stop at the room with the nine stars painted on its door. The door to this particular room had some kind of gem embedded in it instead of a doorknob. Seraphina took a ring out of her pouch and held it up to the gem. A thin strip of light shot out from the ring and hit the gem, which began to sparkle. At that, the whole door shifted inward with a loud *clunk* and slid over to the side to open.

We saw something similar on Ariadne's floor, too. Looks like it's not the only place in the Labyrinth Country to use these mechanical devices. I wonder if they're related somehow...?

"Each Guild office in every district reserves a special floor for Guild Saviors. We'll find Third-Class Dragon Captain Kozelka there... Now, please watch your step and come this way."

The door led to a spiral staircase that descended underground. The only light came from the stairs themselves, which emitted a pale luminescence. It wasn't too dangerous, as long as you watched your step.

We'd been climbing down for a while when I got the feeling we'd teleported—Theresia must have felt it, too, and grabbed hold of my sleeve. "It's okay; don't worry," I reassured her.

"......"

"These mechanisms mystified me back when I first joined the Guild Saviors, too," said Seraphina.

We never would've known the Guild offices had these kinds of floors if we hadn't gotten involved with the Guild Saviors. Thinking about it that way, we really had gone through some pretty remarkable experiences, especially for novices.

Eventually, another door came into view at the end of the staircase. Seraphina used her ring once again to open it. I couldn't tell if we were in the Guild basement or if we'd been transported some-where entirely different. One thing was for sure, though—this place was nothing like the building aboveground.

The walls looked completely seamless, and the floor seemed to be made from a material similar to what we saw in Ariadne's Sanc-tuary, just as I'd suspected. It looked like reinforced linoleum, like something you'd see on an alien spaceship in a sci-fi movie. Uniformly spaced lamps emitting a pale blue light hung along the walls to our right and left. Another Guild Savior came walking our way from down the hall and saluted Seraphina as he passed.

At the end of the hall stood the man we'd seen with Kozelka in the Beach of the Setting Sun. He looked over at us and casually waved. He had a frank way about him, much like the impression I'd gathered from the way he spoke when we first met.

"Way to go out there. Captain Kozelka's inside, but could you give her a sec?"

"Yes, sir. Will you be joining us, Dragon Sergeant Khosrow?"

"Nah, I'm just manning the door. I'll find some other way to kill time after I show you in. Also, you're my superior, you know. No need to be so stiff with me, Lieutenant Seraphina."

"This is simply how I normally speak. Furthermore, you have been with the Guild Saviors much longer than I, Dragon Sergeant Khosrow."

Dragon sergeant sounded like it must be another rank in the Guild Saviors. Maybe something similar to a sergeant in the military?

Khosrow smiled wryly, a bit constricted by Seraphina's sincerity. Then he looked over at me, and his expression changed to one of genuine intrigue.

"Hey there, kid. I hear they call you Suit Man, eh? Looks like you've some pretty killer equipment, too. Gotta say, though, that gun is a bit much with the suit... I'm surprised you could even get your hands on one in District Seven."

At first glance, Khosrow's mostly white hair made him look quite a bit older, but he probably had just a few years on me. He may have even been younger than Ribault.

"It's nice to meet you again. I'm Arihito Atobe."

"The name's Josh Khosrow. I'm a dragon sergeant, as I'm sure you heard, in Third-Class Dragon Captain Kozelka's service. Just think of me as an old fart, slow to get ahead or climb up in the world."

"...Are you still saying such things, Sergeant Khosrow?" asked Seraphina.

"Hey now, don't you go spilling any beans to Atobe here. At my age, I'm better off going for the deep, mysterious look." He seemed pretty carefree, but judging by the way Seraphina spoke with him, I felt there was a lot more to him than he was letting on. It was also possible something had kept him from rising in the ranks, like Roland. But I wasn't about to pry into something so personal with a man I'd just met.

"That piece of crap Gray's awaiting judgment now. The most severe charge against him is letting that monster loose on you. He's suspected of a bunch of other crimes, too, but he's got this mean, sneaky little skill that won't even show up on most Seekers' licenses. 'Course, we do have Saviors who could cancel that out, but we can't just have them babysit this guy forever. In the end, he'll probably get hit with a temporary seal on that skill, on top of some remedial education courses. We've got a real hard-ass leading those. Give the little scoundrel half a year, and you'll see—they'll make an honest man of him."

"I see... Well, as long as he doesn't abuse that skill again."

"You know, you've got to stay cynical around these guys with skills that could really do some damage. Just look at the mess this guy left in his wake, and for what? Stop using the damn thing, for cryin' out loud. Considering all the women he's left in tears, I wish they'd throw him in jail and lock him up for a least a few good years."

He'd also put the Four Seasons ladies in danger—just one more reason I was glad we'd come to District Seven in record time.

"Oh... Looks like she's ready for you. See you around."

"Yes, thank you, Mr. Khosrow."

Khosrow stepped away from the door and walked off. He called out to another Guild member down the hall and floated the idea of grabbing drinks, probably trying to make the most of his time in District Seven.

Seraphina knocked and then opened the door. Captain Kozelka, dressed in a uniform like Seraphina's but of a different color, stood up from her seat and came to greet us.

"Lieutenant Edelbert, reporting with Mr. Arihito Atobe, ma'am."

"Good work. Sorry to keep you waiting."

"Thank you for your concern, ma'am, but we took the opportunity to speak with Sergeant Khosrow, who informed us of developments with Gray."

I had a feeling I could guess why Captain Kozelka had kept us waiting, but I wasn't about to say it out loud.

"……"

Theresia tugged on my sleeve as if to keep me in line, even though I hadn't been thinking anything inappropriate. Captain Kozelka looked like she'd just taken a bath and gotten redressed. A faint soapy fragrance wafted my way as if to prove my suspicions. Though again, it would be rather untoward of me to point out any of this.

"…Please, come this way."

She wavered for a moment, perhaps over whether to explain that she'd been bathing, although I didn't think she had any obligation to disclose that to us. She'd certainly caught me a bit off guard, however, and I couldn't really shake that feeling.

We arrived at some chairs reserved for guests. Theresia stood behind me to my right, and Seraphina sat down next to me, across from where Captain Kozelka sat. When we'd met in the Beach of the Setting Sun, I was blown away by how unbelievably gorgeous the captain was. She was a real stunner, which made it almost impossible for an average guy like me to get a read on her emotions. Just looking at her made me nervous, but she had this tranquil air about her that put me at ease soon enough.

She had traded her black armor for a military uniform, though even that couldn't hide that certain gentleness she exuded... But I couldn't keep staring at her forever, dumb as a doorknob. I forced myself to switch gears.

"First, allow me to reintroduce myself. My name is Kozelka, a third-class dragon captain in the Guild Saviors. And you are Mr. Arihito Atobe and Ms. Theresia, I presume?"

"Yes, that's correct."

"......"

"Is Ms. Theresia...? No, I'll leave that issue aside for the moment. I'd like to discuss the matters at hand in due order."

I wonder if she has something to say about Theresia being a demi-human? I'm curious to know, but I'll hold off asking for now.

"Before we go any further, I'd like to make one thing clear. Please dispense with any titles and simply call me by my name."

"A-all right...then I'll call you Kozelka, if I may."

Kozelka looked straight at me, without a hint of a smile, though I didn't feel any sort of reproach in her gaze. She seemed the type to be more comfortable with formal titles, but I decided to follow her lead.

"...Does *dragon captain* sound unfamiliar to you?"

I got the feeling her tone was a little more formal than when we'd first met. Maybe this was just how she naturally spoke.

"Yes, I can't say I've heard anything like it before."

"The *dragon* in the title comes from the name of the party responsible for founding the Guild Saviors. Dragons are incredibly powerful monsters of an entirely different caliber than all others. As Guild Saviors, we strive to attain the strength to oppose such mighty foes—that is our foundational principle."

It sounded like not even Third Class Dragon Captain Kozelka had actually faced a dragon in battle. All the Named Monsters we'd fought so far had been nightmarishly strong enough. I couldn't even imagine how much more powerful a dragon must be to qualify as a different caliber.

"That may sound rather alarming, but rest assured, there are very few true dragons in existence. We have only ever recorded sightings of a smaller subspecies in the labyrinths around here."

"No...I was just trying to picture what I would do if I ran into one and had no choice but to fight it. I suppose having an escape plan prepared might be the better part of valor."

"Fleeing would cost you contribution points. So long as you're aware of that, however, escape can certainly be a valid battle plan. I must admit, I find it difficult to relate to those who believe a party's strength is defined by how long it can stand its ground in the face of danger..." Kozelka then looked at me as if she'd realized something. I could only wait for her to continue to find out what that reaction meant.

"Nevertheless, I believe none of what I said applies to you and your party, Mr. Atobe. I have examined your records and seen for myself the astonishing speed at which you have climbed through the ranks, defeating every single Named Monster you've encountered along the way. The Guild's highest-ranking members have been particularly impressed with your performance."

Impressed with our performance—that must mean some group of people had been watching and evaluating everything we did. It'd be nice to just accept the compliment, but nothing was ever that simple. Great responsibility is never far behind high expectations.

"What exactly do you mean by that...?"

"First, consider this possibility: Mr. Atobe, would you be interested in joining the Guild Saviors in the future? That includes your party members as well, of course," Kozelka said, staring straight at me. It was clear she was genuinely trying to enlist us.

I could tell the first time I saw the Guild Saviors that these were strong Seekers with years of experience who had chosen the path of protecting others. I was still just a novice, so the thought of joining them myself had never even crossed my mind.

Still, I knew how I must respond. I wholly empathized with the Guild Saviors' mission, but I had other things I needed to do. Seraphina looked over at me and smiled slightly as if she already knew what I was going to say.

"I'm deeply honored to hear the Guild has such high expectations for us. Given the generous invitation, I fear this may be quite rude, but...I must politely decline your offer."

"...Understood. It is a pity, but I can appreciate how joining the Guild Saviors so soon after beginning your seeking career may only limit your potential. Every party has the right to independently decide their own goals without belonging to any organization. You are of course free to decline the invitation as you see fit."

"Thank you very much for saying that. My party and I have our hearts set on two important tasks, and I'd like to focus on those before anything else."

I had never discussed this with Seraphina, who turned her gaze toward me. I looked over at her in the same moment, and our eyes met.

"F-forgive me... I should not have let my personal curiosity interrupt your conversation..."

"Lieutenant Seraphina, I see in these records you have fought alongside Mr. Atobe and his party on multiple occasions. Shall I take this to mean there are still many matters concerning his party of which you are unaware?"

"Yes, ma'am... I am afraid so. Though I have had a few opportunities to join Mr. Atobe and his party in battle, I have not yet spent much time with them at all."

"And yet, in that brief time, you succeeded in defeating a Named Monster together... Parties usually need to work together over an extended period of time in order to polish their teamwork. However, your party, Mr. Atobe, has managed to bring out its members' true strengths quite rapidly."

Does this mean Kozelka hasn't found out about my skills...? I guess maybe you can't investigate a Seeker's individual skills without good cause. In that case, as long as I don't do anything to increase my karma and get arrested, I can continue keeping mine close to my chest... I'd better be careful.

"Mr. Atobe, does one of the tasks you mentioned relate to your party member Elitia Centrale?"

So the Guild had taken note of Elitia joining my party after leaving District Five after all. Maybe this was a good time to ask for help in saving Elitia's friend? Elitia wouldn't have gone all the way to District Eight to look for help if there was something they could've done, but I wanted to ask anyway.

"Elitia and I happened to meet in District Eight, and we've been in the same party ever since. We're now on a mission to save her friend, who was left behind in a labyrinth in District Five..."

"...I regret to inform you it may be very difficult to save Ms. Elitia's friend the way things currently stand. Due to some extenuating circumstances, even we Guild Saviors have abandoned all interventions past the second floor of that labyrinth. We do continually monitor it to ensure a stampede does not occur, but this is a special case in that there are particularly high risks associated with engaging the Named Monster there."

The Guild Saviors fulfilled their duties as long as they could prevent a stampede. It was not their responsibility to take undue risks and attempt to rescue those who had been captured.

Elitia had looked long and hard for someone to help save her friend. And yet she'd found no one in District Six, or District Seven, and had to go all the way down to District Eight. I was sure one day we'd make it up to District Five. But I couldn't shake the feeling our chances of saving her friend would slowly slip away if we kept making our way district by district.

"...Kozelka, is there any way you could allow us to enter District Five, if only temporarily?"

"As a rule of thumb, Seekers should generally be level ten or higher before they advance to District Five. Your party has proven yourselves to be the most powerful in District Seven, but you are likely not yet strong enough to fight in District Five."

"Yes... I know it will be dangerous. But when I think of how terrified Elitia's friend must be, held prisoner by a monster somewhere in that labyrinth, I can't help but hope to reach her as soon as possible."

Kozelka said nothing and gently closed her eyes. After some consideration, she pulled out her license and began to do some kind of operation on it.

"I cannot arrange for you to visit District Five immediately... However, I do have one possible avenue to propose."

"...Really...?!"

"Affirmative. In the event you declined to join our ranks, the Guild's commanding officers instructed me to appoint you and your party with the honorary title of Advanced Seekers."

"*Advanced*... Is that in reference to what we've done so far?"

Kozelka nodded in response and motioned for me to check my license. Then—

◆Current Status◆
> Arihito's party received a request to accept
  honorary title Advanced Seeker

"Is this...a request to accept the title?"

"Whether you decide to accept is a matter you should first

discuss with your party members. Should you choose to receive it, the Guild might occasionally request your cooperation with its missions. You would be free to take on or decline each request, though the Guild would compensate you for every mission you do assist with. You would also earn additional Prestige Points. I'll have one of our staff explain the finer details to you another time."

Even if we do accept the title, it's not like we have to agree to every request for help, so we wouldn't be putting ourselves at risk. Knowing us, I doubt we'd decline many requests, but I'll bet they don't come all that often anyway.

"In other words, does this mean we would be able to collaborate with the Guild Saviors without having to officially join your ranks?"

"Affirmative. We have only a limited number of personnel at our disposal, so no matter what, we Guild Saviors will always need to rely on Seekers for support. Your contribution in quelling the stampede in District Eight was invaluable. This title would provide us a more clearly defined vehicle through which to compensate you for similar assistance going forward."

That makes sense. I'll see when I can discuss this with the group—but I still haven't asked Kozelka about the "avenue" she proposed.

"So going back to how this title would help us get to District Five..."

"Anyone with the Advanced Seeker title can be called into service in districts up to two levels above or below where they currently reside. While such cases are exceptionally rare, there is a small possibility that your party could be called upon to assist with a mission in District Five before you leave District Seven."

Kozelka explained such a request would allow us to temporarily reside in an upper district for the duration of the corresponding mission. Our time would be limited, but it sounded like we'd have the chance to enter labyrinths within District Five should we be called to a mission there. That must be one way the Guild Saviors rewarded Advanced Seekers for agreeing to help with dangerous missions; it was risky, but you'd get to explore labyrinths in higher districts.

We'll have no way of knowing when we'd even be asked to go to District Five, but we might get lucky. If we could focus on leveling up as much as possible before then...it sounds like it'd be a risk well worth taking.

This proposal could even help us with our other goal: the cathedral in District Four. We'd heard the people there knew how to turn Theresia back into a human, and this Advanced Seeker title could potentially get us there more quickly.

I turned to look back at Theresia, standing in wait behind me. She returned my gaze, but her lips showed no signs of emotion.

"...Mr. Atobe, what is it you plan to do with this young demi-human?" asked Kozelka, her voice noticeably colder. I shuddered slightly as I turned to face her again. She continued: "I must inform you that attempting to change a demi-human back into a human would be a grave mistake. After all, demi-humans are resurrected beings who have already lost their lives once."

She knows something. She knows how to change them back to normal—and how difficult it is.

"...I..."

Kozelka fixed her stare on me as if determined not to miss a single flicker of movement as she waited for my answer.

Part III: The Mark of a Demi-Human

There had to be a way to return Theresia back to her human form. If it were easy, Rikerton's demi-human wife wouldn't need to be out seeking for as long as she was. But I couldn't give up before learning what must be done, no matter how difficult the task might be.

I turned to look at Theresia, who looked right back at me. The sight of her face, covered by that mask that never displayed any emotion, strengthened my resolve.

"...This might not be the answer you're hoping for, Kozelka, but...I want to know what Theresia's voice sounds like."

Kozelka's face stayed still as a stone. Her all but imperceptible changes in facial expression gave me a sense of déjà vu. But I couldn't focus on that. I needed to tell her what I was thinking. I needed to tell her I wanted to make Theresia human again—that my determination to do so would never waver.

"I learned Theresia couldn't speak the first time she joined my party as a mercenary. Back then, I thought that's just how demi-humans are. But she is human. People say demi-humans don't have hearts, but we know they do."

"……"

Theresia came over to my side, no longer on standby. She seemed to be trying to protect me. Kozelka lowered her gaze. I had no idea what she was thinking and no chance of trying to read her.

"…The cathedral used to shoulder the responsibility of ruling over the Labyrinth Country together with the royal family, which has now essentially become obsolete," Kozelka explained. "While the Bishop's power has also waned, it remains on par with that of the Guild."

"Oh… I didn't realize. I'm afraid I don't know much about the political affairs here. Though I do think the least I could do is learn a bit about the country where I live."

Those research centers they said were available to us in odd-numbered districts could probably come in handy in times like these. But it was hard to make time to visit one when you were seeking nonstop.

"I imagine the vast majority of Seekers in this area have never heard of these matters. Many do not even know the cathedral exists… Sometimes, when a Seeker suffers an injury so severe even the Doctors at the clinic cannot treat it, the cathedral dispatches one of their own Healers to help. Some people may learn of the cathedral's existence this way."

"…Would it be possible for one of those Healers to turn a demi-human back into a human?"

"We do not yet fully understand why monsters regenerate in

the labyrinth after a period of time. However, some say when a human loses their life in the labyrinth, they activate a similar phenomenon. The labyrinth regenerates their body as a demi-human... In other words, the theory goes, 'curing' them."

Monsters couldn't speak, and demi-humans were reborn via that same principle. Nevertheless, they were still different. Otherwise, demi-humans would display hostility toward Seekers. But Theresia, Takuma, and all the demi-humans I'd seen in town hired as mercenaries listened to and followed orders.

"In addition...even if a demi-human were to undergo the Separation Ritual at the cathedral, they would be forever marked as having once been demi-human—just as I once was."

"......!"

It took me a second to understand what Kozelka was saying. In that brief pause, she stood up from her seat.

"Wh-what are you...?"

"...I'd like to show you proof that I used to be a demi-human."

I had to stop her—or so I thought, but it was too late to intervene in what she herself had decided to do.

Kozelka turned around and slipped off her uniform to expose her naked back. That was where I saw a drawing, almost like a tattoo, of a monster resembling a wolf. Her white skin shone so brightly it appeared to gleam, even in the relatively dim room.

"You...you changed from a demi-human back into a human..."

"...At a cost of a great many sacrifices. Mr. Atobe, do you truly believe Ms. Theresia wishes you and your party to brave the dangers this plan will entail?"

"Well…" I couldn't speak for everyone without talking to them about it first, no matter how sure I was that they would agree with me.

"Let's say you make it to the cathedral and learn how to return Ms. Theresia to her human form. If the only possible method involved insurmountable danger, could you choose not to pursue it? At present, you and Ms. Theresia are able to seek together as a party. Is that not…?"

"…I know that you're trying to warn us because you know something we don't, Kozelka. And I believe you when you say that any demi-human who becomes human will have a mark like the one on your back… But if that means Theresia will be able to speak again just like you can, that'll be more than enough for me. In fact, your story has given me hope."

"…To be *just like me* is no victory. I still…," she started as she once again donned her uniform. She turned to face me with that same unchanging expression. "I still haven't finished what I must do now that I'm human once again. Yet here I am, telling you of things that a Guild Savior should not mention, when all I intended in having you come was to congratulate you for your remarkable achievements…and to encourage you to continue doing such exemplary work."

"I…don't know what you still have left to do. All I know is if one of my party members has a goal they must reach, I'll try to find a way to help them achieve it. Elitia's goals, Theresia's goals, they're all equally important to me. And if we garner any acclaim for our achievements as Seekers along the way, it's a wholly unexpected honor."

At first, I took her warning to mean the Guild Saviors did not look favorably on our plans. But as our conversation continued, I realized that wasn't exactly the case.

Simply getting to the cathedral was not going to change Theresia back into a human. Trials more severe than anything I could fathom lay in store for us. Kozelka had said she'd paid "*a great many sacrifices*" for her own transformation, and I refused to believe she'd lie about something like that just to change my mind.

"May I take that to mean that for you, gaining prestige as a Seeker…is merely a necessary part of the process in attaining your party's goals?"

"Y-yes. Although, if I think back to when I first arrived in the Labyrinth Country, I wonder if seeking in and of itself shouldn't come first."

"…I think I now understand a little of why that one person regards you so highly. Your perspective is entirely unique. What kind of life must you have led before reincarnating to gain such strength of mind? I cannot even venture a guess."

"Just your run-of-the-mill office worker life. The one thing I can say is I always tried to complete any work I got assigned to do. Now, I'm simply trying to follow my heart."

I had no idea who this "*one person*" Kozelka mentioned was, but I got the feeling she wouldn't tell me just yet. And I had some doubts as to whether *office worker* even meant anything to her. An almost imperceptibly small smile crept along her lips. I wondered, eyes transfixed, if it ever widened enough to light up her entire face.

"How curious, that the man whose deeds have people calling

him a rising star in the Labyrinth Country would call himself *run-of-the-mill*."

"A rising star... I've heard that used a few times, but I always took it as a joke. I never expected the Guild Saviors' top brass would say that, too..."

"Only certain members have expressed this view. But they did not wish me to reveal their identity to you at this juncture."

A few people we'd met had called us rising stars. As for any who might be related to the Guild Saviors, the woman who welcomed us to the Labyrinth Country, Yukari, jumped to mind.

"...I've said too much. I'd prefer you make no mention of the Monster's Mark on my back to anyone."

"Yes, of course... I'm sure it took a lot to share that with me."

She wouldn't show that mark to just anyone. That much went without saying—at least to me it did.

"Shall I take that to mean your impression of me as cold and unfeeling has changed?"

"...S-sorry, I suppose I could've worded that better...but I didn't know what else to say..."

Kozelka's cheeks blushed slightly. I'd thought these things didn't affect her, but it looked like that was another mistaken assumption. "It's nothing worth such thanks. Ms. Theresia may also see one appear on her back, should you succeed in returning her to her human form."

I knew it—Kozelka isn't trying to say our plan is crazy. I realize it won't be easy. But I'm gonna make Theresia human again, no matter what.

"I will make some inquiries regarding Ms. Elitia's friend as well. Should you accept the Advanced Seeker title, I will essentially serve as your supervising officer. I'll be in touch with you soon, but feel free to share information via Lieutenant Seraphina as well."

"...I suppose lieutenant and second-class dragon captain aren't exactly the same, right? The latter sounds more like a special class."

"Typical Guild Savior troops can only rise up to a captain's rank. I cannot comment on the meaning behind the dragon class ranking, but suffice it to say it entails a special kind of duty. If Lieutenant Seraphina were ever to achieve dragon class ranking, she would be a third-class dragon captain, like myself."

"I see... Then Seraphina is quite advanced in ranking, for such a young woman."

"Her excellent leadership qualities propelled her up the Guild Savior hierarchy quickly. To be quite frank, it surprised me greatly to hear she of all people had chosen to serve with you."

Seraphina's shield and the defensive powers she contributed as a level-11 Seeker were not strengths we would normally have been able to access in District Seven. I felt once again we should really count ourselves lucky to work with her.

"That was all I intended to tell you. Did you have any other questions?"

"Thank you for sharing so much with me. I'm even more motivated now."

"I expect great things from you, even after you ascend to

District Six. Of course, if you still have matters to attend to here, you are free to remain in District Seven."

"I'd like to discuss that with my party members before making any decisions. Thank you for your time today."

Kozelka didn't respond right away. She cast a glance at Theresia, then asked, "…Why have you not asked me about how to change her back into a human?"

"Because even if I did, it wouldn't change the fact that we need to go to the cathedral."

"…Understood. I apologize for criticizing you and your party's motivations. In principle, I would say it is an honorable goal."

This wasn't going to be easy. Even if we did make it to the cathedral, we'd have a ton of hard work waiting for us. But Kozelka didn't deny going there would be our first step, and that was all the encouragement I needed to keep moving forward.

"Thank you again for taking the time to speak with me. Theresia, let's get going." I got up from my seat and left the room. I bowed slightly before the door closed and caught a glimpse of Kozelka bowing in our direction as well.

I requested a meeting with Louisa directly after that and waited for her in the room we'd used before on the first floor at the back of Green Hall.

"Theresia, we just met a demi-human who became human again. It wasn't a rumor."

"……"

Kozelka's story gave us hope, but it also served as a harsh

warning. She had made sacrifices to regain her human body, and the significance of that weighed heavily in my mind. It didn't inspire much optimism, that's for sure.

"We *will* get you back your body, and we won't let any one of us get hurt. And we *will* save Elitia's friend, I promise. I'm not going to let anyone tell us differently."

Theresia walked closer to me, slowly reached out her hand, and touched my arm. I patted her head to reassure her. She said nothing but looked silently up at me.

"...I'm sorry. It sounds like I'm trying to convince myself, saying all this to you..."

Theresia pulled back her hand briefly, then stretched it up to toward my head, but even on her tiptoes, she couldn't reach. I stooped down a bit, and she patted me back.

"......"

There was no way demi-humans didn't have hearts. I didn't have to look for proof of that in my skill that increased our Trust Levels; I could see it in the way Shiori read her little brother's mind, too.

Just then, we heard a knock at the door, and Theresia lowered her hand. Louisa stepped in and smiled at the sight of us.

"Mr. Atobe... I have heard all about your latest success. They say you did a wonderful job saving Mr. Roland."

"Yes, we went up against a formidable monster, but we all worked together and made it through. We also had some others join in and help, so in the end, we made quite a large group."

"Oh my... Is that true? I would have rushed to join you as well, if only I had the strength to fight. Though it may be a bit impertinent of me as a Guild employee to say so..."

"I'm grateful just to hear it. Besides, monsters above level six can be very powerful."

Louisa's a Receptionist, so I can't imagine she has many skills that would be useful in battle. If she can level up, then I'd be curious to know what her job's capable of...but I'd better stop myself there, before I get lost in thought, as I tend to do when it comes to skills.

"So you all work together to fight such fearsome monsters... If I continue advancing through the districts with you, I'd love to find a way to contribute as well."

"We still haven't gotten to the bottom of why Madoka can't acquire any new skills, so perhaps you could join us when we go to help her level up? ...We'll be sure to keep you safe as well."

"The Guild has a designated 'training labyrinth,' which you might be able to use. The Guild Saviors and garrison go there to maintain their levels, and as an employee, I can access it as well, though others would need to obtain a special title to enter."

Speaking of titles, I needed to tell her about the one Kozelka just proposed. Would that be enough to let us use the training labyrinth?

"Louisa, I just had a discussion in the basement of the Guild with Third-Class Dragon Captain Kozelka... She told me the party had been granted this honorary title." I pulled up the screen with the title's information on my license and placed it on the table to show Louisa. She peered at it through her trusty monocle and blinked in surprise.

"Advanced Seekers... I—I do apologize, but I have only ever seen this title in our manual, so I am unfamiliar with the particulars. Regardless, this title is an honorary recognition the Guild Saviors award to exceptional parties. I believe it should grant you authorization to use the training labyrinth."

"Oh, that's great news. It may be a while yet before we go check it out, but I'd love it if you could join us when we start to train our noncombatant members. Would you mind?"

"...W-well, if it's not too much trouble for the rest of your party... But would that really be all right? Here I thought I might spend the rest of my days without ever stepping foot in a labyrinth again... Oh! That reminds me. With this Advanced Seeker title, you would also be granted access to our Guild's health resort. It comes with many privileges, so please keep it secret from other Seekers, all right?" she said, pressing her index finger up to her lips, her happiness clearly visible through the incredibly charming gesture.

"Now then," she added, "let's take a look at these contribution points, shall we?"

"Yes, please."

◆Expedition Results◆
> MELISSA grew to level 6: 60 points
> Defeated 16 SAND SCISSORS: 960 points
> Defeated 2 OCEAN MANTISES: 120 points
> Chased off 3 ARACHNOPHILIAS: 30 points
> Recovered ROLAND'S SOUL PRISON STONE: 300 points
> Defeated 1 bounty ★MERCILESS GUILLOTINE: 3,200 points

> Defeated 1 ★MERCILESS MOURNER: 3,600 points
> Subparty defeated 1 OCEAN MANTIS: 30 points
> Party members' Trust Levels increased:
  60 points
> Subparty members' Trust Levels increased:
  25 points
> Conducted a combined expedition with a total
  of 9 people: 45 points
> Fought alongside CERES's party: 10 points
> Returned with 1 WHITE TREASURE CHEST: 100 points
Seeker Contribution: 8,540 points
District Seven Contribution Ranking: 1

All those Named Monsters popping up one after the other really were worth a lot of contribution points.

"Congratulations, Mr. Atobe! Not only did you reach first place in District Seven rankings, you also defeated a grand total of four Named Monsters in the district. What an incredible accomplishment."

With the Alliance temporarily disbanded, we'd at last managed to move up to the top rank. We didn't necessarily need to reach first place in order to advance to District Six, but after clearing achievements like "Defeat Three Named Monsters in District Seven" and "Leader Accumulates 20,000 Points," most would wind up in first anyway.

Only Merciless Guillotine had a bounty on its head because the damage it caused was so extensive that Seekers had been forbidden from entering that labyrinth. We received six hundred gold as a reward, which I decided to have sent to the bank.

"As of today, you have accumulated just under seventeen

thousand contribution points since entering District Seven," said Louisa. "I'll now add the special contribution points to this total."

"Special contribution points... Does that mean we earn a different kind of points for saving Roland?"

"Yes. You accepted and completed Beyond Liberty's request for assistance. The Guild awards separate points for contributions you earn on behalf of other people and converts them into contribution points, though their value depends on the terms of each individual request. These points were included in your results after you helped quell the stampede in District Eight, for example. I do apologize for the wait—it appears the calculation is taking a bit longer than usual."

Taking care of a stampede was worth one thousand points, but I remembered that the calculation differed for whatever work we did outside a labyrinth.

"Monsters must never be allowed to appear in town outside of a stampede, so the Guild awards all the Seekers who come of their own volition to help the same number of contribution points. If I take into account all your activity of the past few days, it comes out to..."

◆Party Triumph Evaluation◆
> Assisted in defending District Eight: 1,000 points
> Assisted in capturing GRAY: 500 points
> Fulfilled request to defeat ★MERCILESS GUILLOTINE: 3,500 points
> Special Contribution Points: 5,000
> Prestige Points: +5

"Party Triumph" sounded a bit over the top, but I just couldn't get over the figures lined up on the screen.

"We already received three hundred points for retrieving Roland's soul prison stone, but the special contribution points for completing that request are more than ten times that amount...?"

"Correct. When Beyond Liberty failed to defeat the Named Monster, they acquired a two-thousand-contribution-point penalty. It is a heavy burden to bear, but a Named Monster must be vanquished or it will cause a stampede to occur. In principle, this duty usually falls to whichever Seekers discover the Named Monster. However, since your party defeated it as part of the request you accepted from Ms. Daniella, you are also entitled to a two-thousand-point Reliever's Reward. You received an additional one thousand five hundred special points for saving Mr. Roland, bringing the grand total to what you see here."

Roland had said he didn't know how much saving his life would be worth, but I bet neither of us could have imagined how strongly the Guild would commend Seekers helping one another out, or how highly they valued an individual Seeker's life. I had started to harbor dark suspicions about whether people were reincarnated here in the Labyrinth Country to replace those who lost their lives while seeking, but this response blew all that doubt away.

"Even the Guild does not have the power to rescue all Seekers in distress, though that is our goal. That's why we so deeply respect the work your party has accomplished."

"Th-thank you very much, Louisa. With these additional

special contribution points, would I be correct in assuming we have met all the criteria to advance to District Six...?"

"That's right. These contribution points do not expire, provided you don't cause any serious problems. They should be worth the same value in the higher districts as well. You'll enter each new district with five thousand base points. So if, for example, thirty thousand points were required to advance to the next district, you would only need to earn twenty-five thousand."

In other words, parties with more Triumphs had that much more of an edge over others in terms of advancing. Seeking was apparently not the only way to gain contribution points. Maybe helping out with whatever came our way could end up being a kind of shortcut for moving up.

"You have far more than the twenty thousand required contribution points, Mr. Atobe. Congratulations; you can advance to District Six whenever you'd like," Louisa said with a smile.

I knew it had only been a few days, but they'd been so jam-packed, I got this feeling like we'd *finally* made it. A delayed sense of accomplishment rose up within me, and I smiled back at Louisa. Still, after witnessing Merciless Mourner's strength for myself, I knew the party had to focus on getting stronger before going anywhere, or we were bound to trip up at some point.

"I promised everyone I'd schedule us all a day off. Part of me would like to move up immediately, but I'd also like to take time to consider any areas we need to improve and do all we can to prepare before we go."

"Of course... In fact, I had heard you would be taking a break, so I submitted a request to use one of my paid vacation days. I have a lighter load of general tasks since I'm assigned to you personally, so the Guild granted my request."

"That's great... I hope you can take this chance to really let your hair down as well."

"...As long as you'll be taking it easy, Mr. Atobe, then I'm sure everyone...m-myself included...will be able to relax..."

People were still worrying about me working too much, even in my reincarnated life. Louisa was shyly blushing, but she was thinking about my health. I wanted to thank her, and yet...

"It seems I've picked up a bad habit of running errands on my days off...even though I know I should really be better about work-life balance."

"Mr. Atobe, you truly are dedicated to your seeking career, aren't you...? Oh! What would you think about going to the health resort I mentioned earlier?"

I hadn't seen that one coming, but it would be nice to get some R and R once we went over all the materials we picked up and such. The others might prefer that, too. I looked over at Theresia, her lovable spiked mask tilted slightly to one side as if to say, *What in the world is a health resort?*

Part IV: Harmonious Respite / Fruits of Labor

I remembered I had one more question for Louisa before ending our meeting.

"Louisa, I wanted to ask you about this White Box. Would you be able to refer us to a specialist who can open this one, like you did with the Black Box?"

"...I—I do apologize. This White Box did appear on your results page, but it was my first time ever actually seeing such a listing..."

Louisa placed both hands on her brightly blushing cheeks as I showed her the box. She hadn't gotten around to the box itself since we'd spent most of our time discussing the point totals, but I didn't think she needed to be so embarrassed about it.

"Unfortunately, we don't have any support staff who have anything above Falma's Sleight of Hand 4. Chest Crackers with Sleight of Hand 1 can open a Wooden Box, while Sleight of Hand 2 will open a Red Box and Sleight of Hand 3 a Black Box. Falma has a comfortable advantage over the basic requirement, so she can open almost any Black Box successfully. However, a White Box may pose risks even for someone at her level if it proves more complicated to open than a Black Box... The Guild does not recommend Seekers take any undue risks when it comes to opening such boxes."

"So essentially, it's impossible to open... Is that what you're saying?"

That made me even more curious about what was inside, but such was human nature. Although from what I'd heard, failing to open a Black Box could cause great damage, making it potentially even more dangerous with a White Box.

We shouldn't take such unnecessary risks. We've made it

through so many battles with fierce monsters; I don't even want to think about us all meeting our end because of a hidden trap in some box. We could possibly use Misaki's Fortune Roll before Falma attempts to open it. That would put a heavy burden on Falma, though, so I'll keep it in mind only as a last resort.

"In that case, all we can do now is ask someone who may know more about it...correct?"

"Yes... Precisely...," replied Louisa, racking her brain with her hands still on her cheeks. I felt bad for putting her on the spot, but I could really use any clues she might have.

"You know, Ms. Ceres might be familiar with these boxes," she then added. "She opened her blacksmith shop in District Eight, but she originally resided in a higher district."

"Huh... All right, I'll ask Ceres. Thank you, Louisa."

"On the contrary, I'm sorry I couldn't be of more help... I'll make sure to reduce my general workload going forward and put more time into studying matters that may be of any use to you." But she was a great enough help as it was, meeting me at a moment's notice. I stood up and shook her hand, then she saw us off to the entrance, and Theresia and I left the Green Hall.

Upon returning to the suite, I learned Melissa had thought of some recipes for lunch and picked up the ingredients on her way back. A spread of freshly made dishes greeted me in the dining room where Ceres and Steiner, who had also dropped by, were chatting pleasantly with Igarashi as they all waited for the meal. They'd said they would join us again to eat when we parted ways after leaving the labyrinth. Igarashi got up to greet me as soon as she saw me walk in.

"Welcome back, Atobe. We were prepared to wait a bit longer, but your timing's perfect."

"Arihito, you sure you didn't wanna eat out? Anyway, I managed to score some really tasty-looking sake. Check out this suuuper fancy Dwarf Killer sake!"

Misaki came in her apron and showed me a glass bottle full of what looked like sake. A weathered label bearing the likeness of a little man with a dwarf's build was wrapped around the bottle.

"That name sounds dangerous...but I'll take it, thank you. It's still pretty early in the day, though, so I'll hold off for now. I'm not *that* big of a drinker, you know."

"How dare you! Just kidding. I figured you'd say that but picked it up anyway. Looks like we've got another secret nighttime weapon, huh, Suzu?"

"...I—I don't think we should use alcohol like that..."

"You could probably turn that sake into water, Suzuna...but I guess that's not really what your skill is for, is it?" With Handwash, Suzuna could purify any water she scooped up with her hands. I wondered if it would work on alcohol as well. There was only one way to find out.

"...Having you drink the sake from my hands could be a little... Oh, um, but if that's what you would like, Arihito, then of course..."

"Don't worry your head about that... Arihito, keep that kind of joke to a minimum, would you? Suzuna is a very earnest girl," Elitia chided.

"S-sorry. I'll be a bit more careful."

"Hmph, I personally think you'd do well to lighten up a bit more, Arihito. But I must say, that young lady sure serves up a scrumptious-looking feast," said Ceres.

It sounded like Melissa, with her Cooking 1 skill, had been the driving force behind the meal. She came out of the kitchen carrying a large frying pan and transferred the stewed, Mediterranean-style seafood dish it contained onto a big platter in the middle of the table.

"This looks almost Italian... Are these kinds of recipes popular in the Labyrinth Country?" I asked.

"...Some reincarnates know how to make lots of different dishes. Some are chefs, too. They can do fighting and supporting roles fifty-fifty, so it's a popular job... That's what my dad says," Melissa replied. Maybe Dissectors had access to cooking-related skills because they fell under the same big umbrella as chefs.

Madoka came walking my way, holding a pot with what looked like Cion's food, and started heading for the front door as I was thinking that over. They did sell food specifically made for guard dogs, but Falma had given us some recipes tailored to Cion, so we followed those and fed her homemade meatballs and things made with a mix of meat and vegetables.

"Madoka, do you mind if I give her some?" I asked. "Cion's worked so hard, and I want to thank her."

"Of course, if that's what you'd like, Arihito. I'm sure Cion would love that," replied Madoka, beaming up at me as she handed over the pot.

I went out to the yard, figuring Cion would be waiting in her doghouse, but I found her sitting patiently right outside the door. She was panting frantically with her tongue hanging from her mouth. Did that mean she was hot? Silver hounds were apparently better suited for colder climates and had the long, fluffy fur to match. They were wild animals by nature, used to living outdoors, and so could shed their undercoats to some degree on their own, but it looked like she could use a little grooming.

Cion gobbled up the meatballs, which had been left to cool, as soon as I put them in her bowl. We had just been through a pretty fierce battle, so she must've used up a lot of energy.

"...Cion, are you hot? Maybe we should give you a trim."

"...Bow!" she replied after first licking her snout to ensure she didn't send any food flying. She was wagging her tail—was that her way of saying she wanted me to cut her fur? Melissa had mentioned she could give Cion a trim if she acquired the Groom skill. She did seem to really like Cion, so maybe it'd be better to let her choose whether to take it or not. It was probably about time to sit down with her and go over her new skills now that she'd leveled up.

After Cion finished eating, I got the idea to check her mouth for cavities. I'd taken care of a large dog once before and knew dental health was very important for them. We hadn't done much to take care of her teeth, but they looked healthy.

"All right, looking good. I'll give your teeth a good brush one of these days."

"...Aroo."

Cion didn't know exactly what I was planning to do, but she'd guessed she was in for something, and her ears drooped. I started petting her to cheer her up, and eventually they pricked back up again.

"...You're even more of a dog lover than me, aren't you, Atobe?"

"...N-no, it's just, we used to...sort of have one at the orphanage. I wouldn't say I have a favorite animal, but I guess I do know a bit more about dogs..."

Igarashi walked over from the front door—where she had been watching me for who knows how long—crouched down in front of Cion, and started to pat her head. Cion had also grown quite fond of Igarashi and wagged her tail furiously.

"Remember how I told you back when we'd first come to this country that I used to have a dog? I know we're just renting this place from the Guild, but it's like I got another chance to do that now without even realizing it. I feel so lucky..."

"Yes, I remember," I said, standing up. "Was that when we moved into the Lady Ollerus Mansion?" Igarashi smiled up at me and tucked a little hair behind her ear in a gesture that made her seem all the more refined.

"But our little Cion will have to go back to Falma one day, won't she? I can't help but feel sad when I think of that...though I know it's pretty selfish to even mention it."

"I'm afraid we'll have to... But her mother is also there, you know. And someday, if she finds a good partner... Well, I guess she is a big girl, but age-wise she's still a puppy, isn't she?"

"Bow!"

I couldn't speak dog, so I had no idea what that meant. Maybe she was happy she was getting pets, or maybe her belly was full. She looked so cheerful, maybe she even wanted to go for a walk.

"How lovely it would be if we could take care of her pups one day, too... But it's probably far too early to be thinking about settling down now."

"When that day comes, I'd certainly love to have them join our family."

"Yes, our family... W-wait, since when have you been such a smooth talker?"

"Huh? ...O-oh, no, I mean, I did say family but not because everyone's been calling us a couple or anything..."

"Because you wouldn't want me as your partner...?"

"...N-no, not at all. I wasn't trying to say anything about wanting or not wanting you..."

Even I knew telling her she was too good for me would be a mistake. Then again, if I told her I didn't mind others seeing us as partners, that might open its own can of worms... I stood there desperately searching for the best way to respond, and Igarashi laughed.

"...Igarashi, that's not fair; you know I'm no good at that sort of thing." She was still my weak spot. Not to say that was entirely a bad thing, but I still crumbled under her pressure.

"Hee-hee… Sorry. I saw the chance to make you squirm and couldn't help myself."

"Well, I guess I should've seen that coming, but…it's still bad for my heart."

"I guess we all tend to go pretty hard on you, not just me. Suzu's not like that, though. I imagine you feel pretty at ease with her, right?"

"You could say we're on a similar wavelength, or at least that's how I feel. But I'm pretty comfortable with everyone in the party."

"That's true… Although I'm pretty sure I give you the hardest time."

That's definitely not… Well, I guess relatively speaking, she does make me the most nervous.

"This kind of self-deprecating talk is only going to put you on the spot. Maybe we should head in…"

Just as we were about to go back inside, Cion turned to face Igarashi.

"…What the—?"

Igarashi was crouched down next to Cion in a knee-length skirt she'd changed into after returning to the apartment. For a second, I couldn't tell what was happening—but then realized that Cion had burrowed her head deep into Igarashi's skirt.

"C-Cion…! S-stop, this is so embarrassing…!"

I suppose it made sense for a dog to try to get any kind of affection they could from a person they'd come to care for, but I couldn't understand this at all. Maybe silver hounds liked sticking their noses into dark places?

"Wait, I shouldn't just be standing here... C-Cion! Don't dig around in there!"

"A-Atobe, go over there! And don't you dare look back here!"

"O-okay...!"

Igarashi scolded me, nearly in tears, and I turned to go through the door—only to find Misaki, Melissa, and Madoka peering out at us through the cracks.

"Wooow... What a scene! Doesn't Kyouka look sooo cute when she's flustered?"

"...You should eat before the food gets cold."

"Cion looks like she's having a great time... She really loves you, Kyouka. I'm so jealous."

Igarashi looked at the girls as if to say, *Stop staring and help me!* It seemed like she'd need to be a bit more careful the next time she crouched down in front of Cion in a skirt. I walked into the house, trying to act like nothing had happened, only to have Suzuna and Elitia ask me why my face was so red.

We helped clean up the dishes after lunch and moved into teatime. Ceres held up her saucer and tilted her cup to her lips ever so gracefully. Steiner had dined in another room, and I thought maybe they'd removed their helmet and armor to eat, but it looked like they wouldn't be showing us what hid beneath anytime soon. Now they had returned in their usual gear and stood waiting behind Ceres.

"Arihito, knowing you, I'll bet you want to take care of business before settling down for a day off. Do you have any work for me?"

"Before we get to that, I'd like to ask you something, Ceres... Have you ever seen this kind of White Box before?" I said, placing it on top of the table. Ceres donned a glove Steiner handed her, pulled out a magnifying glass that was clearly some kind of magical tool, and set to examining the box.

"...I have heard of boxes such as these, yes. They say only exceptionally rare Named Monsters carry them, and they only ever fall into the hands of the first person to defeat those monsters. Hmm... This is..."

"Can you make anything out?"

"Hmph. As a jade, I pride myself on knowing more about the secret phenomena and legends of this country than you. These markings on the surface may look like a simple pattern, but they are in fact letters of what is called the Logos Runes. You must meet the conditions written on here before you can open the box."

"Logos Runes... Are you able to read it because you're a Runemaker?"

Ceres nodded. She placed her saucer and cup on the table, then readjusted the brim of her tricorn hat slightly.

"This one should be relatively easy to open... At least, that's my rather optimistic expectation. It says you must carry it with you and fight a strong opponent... That is, if I am interpreting it correctly. Someone else may read it and take it to mean something entirely different."

"No, we'll trust your interpretation... Thank you very much. So for the time being, all we need to do is take it with us whenever we seek?"

"I would say so…though I'm afraid reading the Logos Runes is slightly beyond my expertise. It's moments like these that make me want to level up, but unfortunately, it's not that easy. I have to work hard at it every day."

"Master, you looked terribly pleased when you went after Mr. Atobe and his party in the labyrinth. Might you possibly be interested in returning to your seeking activities?"

Ceres pushed her hat down firmly on her head.

"…It's not that simple. I just couldn't sit back and watch, that's all. My place is at home, taking care of the shop."

"Well, you two really helped us out. Is that flame-throwing magic a Runemaker skill? It looked incredibly powerful."

"Oh… Y-yes, yes it is… I'm surprised you noticed that. Though in the end, I'd say Takuma and Luca contributed more to the battle after you used your powers to strengthen their skills."

"Your skills were also slightly improved thanks to Mr. Atobe's skills, Master."

The only skill I could think of that could've strengthened magic attacks would be the Wolf Pack activated by Complete Mutual Support. Is that what they meant? I bet if I acquired Magic Support 1, I'd be able to see a clear increase in total strength whenever I activated it.

"…I-it's all your fault. You made me feel this way…"

"What? …C-Ceres, did I do something wrong…?"

Her face half-hidden, Ceres peeked up at me from beneath the brim of her hat with one hand on her chest as if to keep it from beating too quickly.

"You made me want to go seeking again, with you… I've tried waiting for this feeling to pass, but I simply cannot sit still. How do you intend to make that up to me?"

"U-ummm… About that. I've actually been planning to take out Madoka and Louisa so they can train to an appropriate level since they might have a difficult time joining us in battles. What would you two think about joining us when we do…?"

"…R-really? I can no longer use all the magic I had at my peak, and I've lost the ability to increase attack power, but…w-would it still be okay if I went? Just to be clear, I'm a level four. And Steiner acts tough, but they're actually only level three."

"Th-that's not my fault. We went on so many challenging seeking expeditions together just to maintain this level… Are you saying those precious memories were for nothing?" They were arguing. I guess it was true what they say: The closer you are, the more you fight.

"…Ahem. My apologies, what an unsightly display."

"Ha-ha… No, don't worry about it. But I feel a bit anxious now, hearing you came to help us out at your levels. The vanguard Takuma seemed to be pretty high level, so it was good he came, too."

"Hmph… I suppose you can't help but care about battle formations, member compositions, and the like, even for other parties. You're a true leader, right down to the core, Arihito."

We were still on a break, but Misaki looked over from the other room to see what the three of us were talking about, then waved at me. She was probably making fun of how self-conscious I was acting.

"Well then, we'll take you up on your offer, leader. If we have the chance, we'll go with you to the labyrinth."

"I'm looking forward to it, Mr. Atobe."

With that settled, I called Madoka over and asked her about the materials we'd gotten the Carriers to take back for us.

"The materials from the big crab wouldn't all fit in the storage container we had, so I rented a new storehouse and had them put everything in there... I hope that was okay?"

"Yeah, it's better to have a separate container reserved for all the materials we get from larger monsters. If it's in a storehouse, then that crab was...?"

"Yes, I asked Mr. Rikerton to take a look, and it seems it has some edible parts. Its shell and legs are too big, so they're normally used as building materials, but apparently we can use at least some of it for armaments."

It felt odd to think that ghostly, translucent crab was edible. At the same time, I was also genuinely curious about how it might taste, which I guess went to show how used to this country I'd gotten.

"How about that Merciless Mourner? It looked like an empty husk on the inside..."

"U-ummm... Mr. Rikerton mentioned something about Samurai Chainmail. He said the shell that wrapped around its body is kind of like the armor samurai used to wear and that it can be fitted as armor the way it is as long as the measurements are right. It's in the storage container, but he recommended we have it appraised before we use it. We also found a rune among the dropped loot."

Madoka was really helping us out by handling all this inventory business. It must have taken a lot of courage to even look at that gigantic crab, not to mention that empty husk from the Merciless Mourner. I needed to tell her to make sure she didn't push herself too far.

"We couldn't get any materials from the defeated sand crabs, but they did leave eight pieces of dropped loot instead. The praying mantis had turned to stone before the Carriers could bring it back, so they only managed to remove its scythes and wings, as well as two magic stones. You can see everything on this page if you'll take a look... Oh, um, Arihito, is my report okay so far...?"

"It's so perfect, I'm speechless. Really great work, Madoka."

"Th-thank you! ...This is all I can really do, so... Also, I heard back from one of the stores that works with Bargain, and I think they'll knock down their prices if we submit our request by the end of the day."

I couldn't get over how capable this young girl was proving herself to be. I was actually a little concerned she'd work herself too hard. For once, it was my turn to be the worrier.

"All right, could you show me later what they have in stock? You're doing such a great job, Madoka. Make sure you take breaks and relax, okay? And just let me know if there's anything you'd like to get for yourself. You've earned it."

"N-no, I couldn't... I haven't really done all that much..."

"Madoka, didn't you have your eye on that cart for magic tools? That sure is useful, you know," Ceres piped in.

"That would complement your skills, too," I agreed. "What do you say we get one?"

"...A-are you really sure...?"

"Of course. I'll have to see how much it costs, but I'm hoping it's not too far out of our budget..."

"U-ummm... It's about one thousand two hundred gold... Th-that's really expensive, isn't it...?"

I'd put Madoka in charge of handling all our finances, but I felt like I could trust her with everything after seeing her take such great care with expenses. She hadn't said anything back when I bought the Owl Scope for a thousand gold. I thought it'd probably be better to carefully consider each purchase from here on out and spend money only when necessary.

I told Madoka we could afford the cost of the cart, and we agreed to go buy one in the next few days. We figured it'd be best to see something that expensive in person before making any decisions.

Rikerton hadn't finished dissecting the huge crab yet, so I decided to take a look at what materials we knew we could use and the items we'd gotten so far.

◆Dissection Center Report — Mr. Arihito Atobe◆
> 2 Ocean Mantis Sickle Blades

> 4 Translucent Ocean Mantis Wings

> 1 ?Gauntlet discovered while dissecting ★Merciless Mourner

> 1 ?Helmet discovered while dissecting ★Merciless Mourner

> 1 ?Armor discovered while dissecting ★Merciless Mourner

> 1 pair of ?Greaves discovered while dissecting ★Merciless Mourner

◆Newest Acquisitions◆

> Sand Scissors dropped 1 Manipulation Stone

> Sand Scissors dropped 1 ?Bracelet-like Item

> Sand Scissors dropped 6 ?Rusted Metal Ingots

> 2 Blade Edge Stones discovered while dissecting Ocean Mantis

> ★Merciless Mourner dropped 1 Battle Rune

It looked like we'd acquired some usable materials on top of the yet-to-be appraised armaments from Merciless Mourner. Those must've come from the full-body armor husk it left, no question about it. A few other dropped items needed appraising as well. I decided I'd ask Madoka to use her Appraise 1 where she could, then see if I could handle the rest with a Mid-grade Appraisal Scroll.

"Hmm... We should probably take a look at these materials in the workshop before you decide how you want them processed after all," said Ceres.

"Ceres, you and Steiner have a right to your share of the

materials we've acquired from the monster you helped us defeat," I told her.

"We'll take your business in the processing bit, so you can keep our share. I'm sure Luca, Takuma, and Shiori would feel the same. Shiori had mentioned she wanted to go out for drinks with you lot before you move up to District Six. That should be thanks enough for her," Ceres replied, most likely counting herself among the participants of that outing and looking very pleased.

I was pretty sure Shiori would bring Takuma along, and I wanted to invite Luca, too. It looked like dinner would be lively again tonight. With that thought in mind, I called out to the others so we could make our way to the workshop.

CHAPTER 2

New Powers and a Friendly Gathering

Part I: Translucent Wings

We made our way to Ceres and Steiner's rented workshop and began to discuss how to use the materials we had collected.

"Madoka, could you first bring out the monster resources?" I asked.

"Sure, I'll put them on this counter," she replied. According to Madoka's license, her Unpack Goods skill allowed her to access items not only in the storage container but, apparently, materials in the storehouse as well. When I mentioned this to the group, Ceres pulled out a short pointing stick—perhaps she used it to cast magic?—and began to lecture us in a professorial tone.

"The explanations that appear on one's license are not absolute, you see. They cannot properly describe any phenomena the Guild has not observed for themselves. Some skills or armament effects may also warrant a more expansive interpretation of what is recorded. Furthermore, your license cannot reflect any hidden powers that have not been completely evaluated."

"Professor Ceres! I think I only kinda caught that, but as long as Arihito gets it, we're all good!" said Misaki.

"I don't know if that was worth raising your hand to say… Misaki, what's gotten into you?" asked Elitia. "You're bouncing off the walls."

"I know we're gonna take a break after we finish up work, so it kinda feels like we're going on summer vacation… Arihito, do you wanna have a beach volleyball showdown? Or should we go with capture the flag?"

"I wonder if the health resort has a beach… We were just at one, but it would probably feel a lot more like a resort without monsters," added Igarashi.

After I discussed with the party the honorary title Kozelka offered us, we'd decided to accept. Since that title also granted us the rights to use the Guild's health resort, we didn't even have to think about where we'd go on our break. The idea alone of a resort seemed to put everyone in high spirits. All the sports Misaki was proposing were sure to leave us with sore muscles the next day, though maybe Louisa could help out with a shiatsu massage. But I guess she was taking a day off, too, so I shouldn't ask too much of her.

Now it was time for the main issue at hand: the monster resources. The sharp blades on the counter had been removed so cleanly I had a hard time believing they were once part of the praying mantis.

"*Sickle Blades can be used to strengthen weapons or added to gauntlets to give them slicing attacks. They can also enhance or even double attacks on insects,*" explained Steiner. Even with their metal gauntlets on, they were carefully avoiding any contact with the blades' edges. Those blades had an almost ghostly air about them...but maybe that was an exaggeration.

"...*Master, your instincts are correct*," came Murakumo's voice.

I had removed Murakumo from its usual spot on my back and rested it on the weapons stand from where I alone could hear its voice coming clear as day. It appeared to be speaking directly to me.

By correct, *do you mean the Sickle Blades aren't normal materials?*

"*Power resides within those Sickle Blades. You called it a 'ghostly air,' but to me it is more of a 'swordly spirit.' I could obtain new abilities without need for forging if I were to absorb that power.*"

Murakumo was a Hidden God part, so it couldn't be strengthened through ordinary means. It was plenty strong already, but boosting that strength further might make it an even more powerful trump card, I thought. I debated whether to reveal Murakumo's secret to Ceres and Steiner and ultimately decided I could trust them with it.

"Ceres, Steiner, it looks like my sword might be able to absorb the power of these Sickle Blades."

"*What?*" said Steiner. "*...Does that mean yours is an ethereal weapon?*"

Ceres looked unsurprised, but this had clearly shaken Steiner. They asked my permission and then took the sheathed Murakumo into their hands.

"I had thought there was more to this sword than met the eye, but I had no idea it was an ethereal weapon...that it housed a spiritual being. Arihito, did that being tell you about this directly?" asked Ceres.

"Y-yes. But, Ceres, what does *ethereal* mean...?

"In this country, we call any item that is a vehicle for an invisible power *ethereal*," she explained. "They are extraordinarily rare artifacts—some say they are remnants of the gods' divine intervention in the world."

I could only barely grasp the general gist of what Ceres was saying. Igarashi and Suzuna were listening very intently as well, though the others may as well have had question marks hanging over their heads. Elitia looked over to the Scarlet Emperor she'd also left on the stand.

"...Do ethereal weapons have minds of their own?" she asked.

"This is my first time seeing one... I only realized that's what it was because Mr. Atobe said so. It can be impossible to tell just by looking at it," said Steiner.

"I see... Thank you, Steiner. I'm sorry I interrupted... Arihito, are you going to give the Sickle Blades to Murakumo?"

"Yeah, apparently it only needs one to obtain the Sickle Blades' powers. Steiner, what do you think we could use the other one for?"

"You could make a dagger out of it or use it to strengthen your existing weapons. You could even simply add a handle and use it as a sickle," they replied.

I figured I should decide what to do with this Sickle Blade first, though it was hard to picture how it could strengthen the armaments we had at the moment. Even if it did make them more effective against insect-type monsters, there was no guarantee we'd come across something like that. It was probably better to stick with something that would increase overall attack power.

"While you mull that over, why don't we have a look at what else you've got for us?" said Ceres.

"Of course. These are the Translucent Wings... Ah...!"

The key to the storage container in her hand, Madoka was trying to pull out the next items with her Unpack Goods, though it seemed like that was using up a lot of magic. I looked at my license and saw her blue magic indicator bar had decreased by about a third. She must have gotten dizzy after using so much in one go.

"Madoka, you've used a lot of magic. We'd better restore some of it," I said.

"R-right... But I'm just fine, really. I shouldn't get so tired this quickly..."

"I can help you with my Recovery Support, so don't push yourself too hard. It's best to have a bit of a cushion." I got up from my seat, walked behind Madoka, placed my hand on her back, and activated Charge Assist.

◆Current Status◆
> Arihito activated Charge Assist ⟶ Madoka recovered magic

"Oh my... I've seen people with such support skills before, but I didn't realize you had them, too, Arihito," marveled Ceres.

"*Ms. Madoka's maximum magic level is still relatively low, so this does not appear to task Mr. Atobe too harshly.*"

Steiner was right; my magic bar was still nearly full. My maximum magical potential had increased ever since I'd eaten the Apple of Wit. Usually, you'd find the total by multiplying my level 6 by ten, but the apple had put me around seventy or eighty magic points. It was also possible my job allowed for a greater increase in magic potential per level than most.

"Now that you mention it, I've heard a Silk Spider Hat is supposed to increase your maximum magic potential..."

"Oh! That's right, Arihito, I have a message for you from Mr. William at the Monster Ranch," said Madoka. "He told me the Arachnomage had been making a few spiders' nests, and when William warned it to not overdo it, the creature cleaned them up into something like a ball of string."

"That must be why we found those black net tights in the dropped loot when we ran into the arachnophilia," Elitia said, looking at her license. All the party members were really good about checking our results and things after battles. Misaki and Melissa looked like they'd just realized something.

"Oh... Arihito, haven't you been waiting, like, forever for something to fix those black spider tights with...?"

"I thought you might say that... I'm just curious what would happen with a complete set of armor of one property. It'd be nice if it was useful," I responded.

"I wonder if wearing the silk hat and tights would give some kind of added benefit...?" asked Kyouka. "It should be worth trying anyway."

"I think those tights would look suuuper good on you, Kyou-ka! It's like you're bursting at the seams with womanly charm. Black tights are sooo you!"

"...I—I don't wear fishnets...but I imagine they'd go really well with your dice and cards to complete your Gambler look, Misaki." The two pushed the tights on each other tit for tat, but Misaki looked like she might be more open to them than she let on.

"If you found part of that set around here, you might find the rest while you're in the seventh district. Otherwise, it could get more difficult to complete a set," explained Ceres.

"In that case, I'll use that silk to mend the tights. Believe it or not, I'm actually rather nimble with my hands."

"That would be great, Steiner. Thanks," I said.

With that settled, Madoka used Unpack Goods to pull out four large see-through, glass-like clumps; these turned out to be the Ocean Mantis's Translucent Wings, though they looked much less like wings than I'd imagined.

"This kind of glass material can't be used for weapons, can it?" I asked.

"Hmph, you'd think so. However, this is actually quite popular for battle gear," replied Ceres, motioning for Steiner to come over. Steiner pushed against one of the thick, roughly six-feet-tall wings, which bent with surprising elasticity at their touch.

"It may look like glass, but this material can withstand strong impacts and remain intact. It should be able to deflect a Cotton

Ball attack without a scratch. After all, it came from a level-six monster, so whatever defensive items you use it on will have equally substantial strength."

"Amazing... It looks just like crystal, but it's so flexible... How mysterious...," marveled Suzuna as she admired the four wings set leaning against the wall.

"Ocean Mantises are sea creatures, so their wings also possess water attributes. For your own purposes, you could say they're waterproof," continued Ceres.

"Is that something you can add to any armament?" asked Elitia in a show of interest. Any chance to strengthen armor must be vital to someone at such a high level.

"...I don't really like see-through things," said Melissa.

"What? ...D-does it have to be see-through?" asked Misaki. "I know the glass itself is, but..."

"Rest assured, we can use different materials where it counts or simply tack something on the back. Of course, I may tweak the design with my own aesthetic tastes in mind." Ceres seemed to be enjoying this. I decided I'd have them use these Translucent Wings on whatever they could for the time being.

◆Materials Acquired from Ocean Mantis◆
> Apply Sickle Blades to Arihito's Murakumo ⟶ Murakumo will gain a new skill.
> Apply Sickle Blades to Cion's ★Beast Claw +1 ⟶ ★Beast Claw +1 will gain Anti-Insect Attribute and Added Reinforced Slice 1, +3 strength

> Apply TRANSLUCENT WINGS to SUZUNA'S SILK SHAMAN'S
CLOTHES +3 ⟶ SILK SHAMAN'S CLOTHES +3 will gain
WATER-RESISTANT ATTRIBUTE 1 and IMPACT REDUCTION 1, +5
strength
> Apply TRANSLUCENT WINGS to THERESIA'S ★HIDE AND SEEK
+3 ⟶ ★HIDE AND SEEK +3 will gain WATER-RESISTANT
ATTRIBUTE 1 and IMPACT REDUCTION 1, +5 strength
> Apply TRANSLUCENT WINGS to repair KYOUKA'S VARIABLE
ARMOR +4 ⟶ VARIABLE ARMOR +4 will gain WATER-
RESISTANT ATTRIBUTE 1 and IMPACT REDUCTION 1, +6
strength
> Apply TRANSLUCENT WINGS to ELITIA'S HIGH MITHRIL
KNIGHTMAIL +5 ⟶ HIGH MITHRIL KNIGHTMAIL +5 will gain
WATER-RESISTANT ATTRIBUTE 1 and IMPACT REDUCTION 1, +7
strength

"Hmm, here's what we'll do... The Translucent Wings are quite large as you can see, so two of them should do the trick. Are you sure you don't want to use what's left for anything else?" asked Ceres.

"Right... Well, I think I'd like to start with this for now. In any case, Misaki and Melissa don't seem to want to use anything see-through," I responded.

"You make it sound like Suzu loves that kind of thing... Oh, you're sooo easy to read, Suzu! Your face is suuuper red, like a boiled lobster...!"

"...U-um... I think ceremonial attire can be a little see-through, if it needs to be..." Suzuna could be pretty practical about this kind of thing. Besides, I doubted Ceres would come up with anything too revealing.

"Heh-heh... This material is rather nice... Steiner, my dear, this is what I have in mind for the design."

"Master, I sometimes find it difficult to follow your train of thought when you come up with such bold plans... Maybe it's to do with your advanced age, however much your looks may belie it."

"I think I heard something, but I am choosing to ignore it. I am nothing if not tolerant," Ceres replied sharply, making Steiner flinch. At one hundred and fifteen years old, Ceres referred to herself as a *young lady*, but she looked like she could be about the same age as Madoka. Either way, it seemed asking a woman's age really was a sensitive matter.

"Now, about these magic stones," Ceres continued. "This blade edge stone can give weapons magic-powered slicing attacks, which could possibly inflict damage on enemies that might otherwise be impervious to physical attacks."

"I see... That's tricky, since we don't have too many weapons we can add stones to."

"We could enhance your slingshot to increase the number of magic stones it can carry. Another option would be to add it to Melissa's butcher's knife," suggested Ceres.

"You also have this manipulation stone, which will let you control anything you hit, living or inanimate, for a very short amount of time," added Steiner. *"Many monsters are immune to its effects, but if all else fails, it can also slightly boost your attack."*

In that case, maybe I should replace that for the confusion stone on my slingshot and see which is more useful. Both allow special attacks that impede your enemy's movements, so it might not be a bad idea. I should probably add the blade edge stone to Melissa's weapon and focus on trying to have the widest range of special attacks possible. The only problem is we won't be able to remove it once it's combined with Melissa's knife... This is a hard choice.

"The last thing we need to do is appraise your treasure. You must be very cautious when handling the equipment," warned Steiner.

Cursed items could sometimes possess you just by touching them during appraisal. Best practice was to avoid direct contact with anything whether you used a scroll or an Appraise skill.

◆Magical Stone Transfer◆
> Affixed Blade Edge Stone to Melissa's Steel Knife
> Swapped Confusion Stone on Arihito's Black Magical
  Slingshot +3 for Manipulation Stone
> Affixed Confusion Stone to Cion's Hound Leather Vest +3

I decided to give Cion the confusion stone. I wanted to do all I could to protect her from being Confused since she was our first line of defense. After that, Madoka carefully took out the items that needed appraisal with Unpack Goods. She neatly lined up the full-body warrior armor made from the Merciless Mourner's empty husk, which still looked like it could come alive at any second, and the items the sand crabs had dropped on a sheet spread out on the floor.

"...J-just...what kind of monster did you take down to get all this...?" stammered Ceres.

"*I feel a certain sense of affinity for these items... Oh, not because I'm cursed or anything,*" said Steiner.

Seeing the equipment left behind by the strongest Named Monster we'd faced yet sent a chill down my spine. They definitely looked cursed. However, we had no choice but to appraise all of it if we wanted to get to the parts we could use. I decided I'd ask Madoka to try her Appraise on them first. If that didn't work, I'd just borrow a Mid-grade Appraisal Scroll and try it myself.

Part II: Sand Crabs and Grains of Sterling Silver

We started with the "Bracelet-like Item" one of the Sand Scissors had dropped. Madoka had no trouble identifying it with her Appraise 1 skill.

◆Desert Rose◆
> Adorned with DESERT ROSE GEM.
> Especially effective against sandy terrain monsters. Increases damage against said monsters and reduces received damage.
> Enables sand-related attacks when equipped.
> Slightly increases defense against physical attacks.
> Slightly increases defense against magical attacks.
> Slightly increases agility.

Now, this was the kind of powerful accessory you didn't see every day. If only we'd had it back when we fought in the Beach of the Setting Sun…but you can't have everything. I couldn't see any downsides to keeping it since we'd probably find ourselves in some kind of desert again eventually.

"Wooow! If you take a closer look, the gem's kinda like a rose. At first I thought it was just a clump of sand, but if you brush off the dust, it reeeally sparkles," said Misaki.

"Since it's called a Desert Rose, I wonder if it's something that occurs naturally in a desert? If so, that's really incredible… Maybe someone who can only wear light armor should take this?" suggested Igarashi.

This was a tough call, since anyone could benefit from this item. I was starting to think maybe I could have someone in the vanguard wear it to help reduce damage they take, even if by a little, when—

"……"

"Hmm? What is it, Theresia?" I asked.

"Maybe she wants to touch it? She might have thought of something," offered Elitia. It felt that way to me also, so I handed the bracelet to Theresia. Just then—

"…T-Theresia's changing…!"

—Theresia's Hide and Seek and chameleon boots reacted to the bracelet and changed to a sandy color. Some kind of camouflage, maybe?

"So touching the Desert Rose turns her gear to the color of sand…?" asked Elitia.

"Maybe her equipment is meant to react that way. Or maybe it reacted to Theresia herself… I wonder which it is," said Suzuna.

Elitia and Suzuna quizzically watched this sudden turn of events unfold. I was reminded of how Theresia blended into her surroundings when using Active Stealth, so it was possible Theresia herself had some inherent camouflage skills. After a little while, Theresia reverted to her normal colors.

"If she has indeed reacted to the gem, it may have affected her in other ways as well. Arihito, why don't you take a gander at Theresia's skills?" suggested Ceres.

"S-sure. Let's see…"

I pulled up Theresia's page on my license and saw the following:

```
◆Subordinate Skills Display — Theresia◆
S-Mode Transformation: Sand Clad
Reaps benefits from the power of sand. Consumes
    magic during activation. Can be activated
    with special equipment.
```

"S-Mode…Transformation?"

"Hmm… Is that true? S-rated skills are especially rare, even among those that are activated in response to equipment," explained Ceres. "You could search for years and never find one like that."

If S stood for *Special*, then "Mode Transformation: Sand Clad" must be a kind of skill. It sounded a little abstract, though, so I guessed we'd have to actually use it in battle to find out what it was capable of. It definitely seemed worth trying.

"In that case, Theresia ought to take it," said Igarashi.

"Agreed," I replied. "I'd like her to test it out." Everyone else was on the same page as well, so we decided to have Theresia use the Desert Rose. She slid it onto her left wrist as if she knew that's where it was meant to go.

"……"

"Hey, it looks good on you. Let's try it out next time we're in battle," I told her. Theresia stared at me intently, then looked over at the other members. She seemed to be hesitating out of consideration for them.

"Kyouka's gonna get the samurai armor, so dooon't you worry about it!" said Misaki.

"…W-well, my armor did break, but I can still use it as long as it can be fixed," said Igarashi.

No matter how strong the armor might be, it would be useless to us if cursed. Seeing firsthand the Scarlet Emperor's great power and the risks that came with it made that much glaringly obvious. Still, we wouldn't have managed to fight our way here if it hadn't been for the Cursed Blade skills. Maybe even this deeply disquieting suit of armor could prove useful in some way. That said, just looking at it lying motionless there sent chills down my spine and made me break out in a cold sweat.

"Now then…the time has finally come. Arihito, be very careful," warned Ceres.

Madoka couldn't even get close to the armor the Merciless Mourner had left behind; she froze from Fear, which I had Igarashi dispel with her Mist of Bravery. I wouldn't have been able to keep my cool as I approached, either, if it hadn't been for Igarashi's help. I took the Mid-grade Appraisal Scroll and held it up over the armor, careful not to touch it, then looked down at my license to see the appraisal results.

◆★Demon Crab Suit of Armor◆
> Inflicts FEAR status on any ally or foe that approaches.
> Bears some type of curse.
> Possesses hidden powers.

Just as I'd expected, we wouldn't be able to see any detailed information unless someone equipped the armor. But it was far too powerful to leave lying around.

"This could prove more useful than a mangy guard dog...if you were able to lift the curse on it, that is," said Ceres.

"You're right... Do you think the rest of the armor is similarly cursed?" I asked.

"We have no way of knowing until you appraise them. Monsters are mysterious creatures, you see. Though I suppose I should say it's incredibly rare for a Dissector to determine a monster's whole body can be used as equipment in the first place." I continued appraising the other items as Ceres suggested, which turned out to be:

◆★Deva Kings' Helmet◆
> Cranial Protection: Protects against status ailments that affect the head.
> Bears some type of curse.
> Possesses hidden powers.

◆★Kottos's Gauntlets◆
> Special characteristic: Slicing attribute. Increases damage against enemies vulnerable to slice-type attacks.
> Increases equipment weight limit.
> Slightly increases defense against physical attacks.
> Special Effect: Double Down. Adds extra damage when an attack succeeds in partially destroying an enemy.
> Confers FIGHTING SPIRIT status when user depletes a fixed amount of stamina.

◆★Hannya's Greaves◆
> Especially effective against humanoids: Increases damage inflicted against enemy humanoids.
> Increases speed.
> Slightly increases defense against magical attacks.
> Slightly increases defense against indirect attacks.
> Allows user to activate YOSHITSUNE'S LEAP.

> Slightly increases effectiveness of skills
  that strengthen allies.

Before I appraised the helmet, I thought all of the equipment would be cursed, but my license didn't say anything about the arm and leg armor bearing curses.

"Who could have dreamed the Merciless Mourner was covered in starred armor...? No wonder it was so powerful," Elitia said in awe. If the armor was really behind its strength, we'd have to pay more attention going forward not just to humanoid monsters' levels but also their equipment.

Hannya's Greaves strengthen support skills, but they seem like they could really make anyone stronger. It's gonna be a tough choice.

I already had my boots that did the same thing, so maybe I could have someone with less leg armor use them—or so I thought.

"The gauntlets are appropriate for warrior types and for Melissa. The greaves can only be worn by Elitia, Kyouka, or Arihito," explained Madoka.

"Then we should probably have Arihito wear them. They look like they were designed for men anyway," said Elitia. I thought it more prudent to value function over fashion, but the latter seemed to be important to the ladies. Not that I minded, of course.

"All my upper-body armor is more valkyrie-esque, so it'd clash with a pair of greaves a samurai like Minamoto no Yoshitsune could've worn in the Warring States period. I'd generally prefer to have everything match," said Igarashi.

"I see... I think I might be testing new waters wearing greaves with a suit, but I guess I don't have any other choice if I want to get stronger in battle," I replied.

"I believe you have something called 'shin guards' in your world to protect yourself in fierce hand-to-hand combat. We could adapt the greaves into something like those, too. That way, they could also complement the boots you already have," suggested Ceres.

"*If you have more than one piece of armor with the same effects, you can sometimes amplify those effects if you combine them,*" explained Steiner. "*However, there is a limit; otherwise everyone would just use that trick to make themselves invincible. For example, if you have two pieces that increase the damage you can inflict, the weaker one would slightly add to the stronger piece of armor's effects.*"

That meant there were limits on the possible combinations we could make; you couldn't put absolutely anything and everything together. Steiner's level had fallen since their peak as an active Seeker, but because you can choose which skills you give up when you level down, they had chosen to keep the Synthesize Equipment 2 skill they acquired at level 5.

"Then would you please combine these greaves and my boots?" I asked.

"*Oh, that's right. We're out of the metal we'd need for that, so I need to stock up...but it's rather hard to come by,*" replied Steiner.

"There's no guarantee, but it's possible you could find some if you melt down those rusted metal ingots. Arihito, would you mind if I tried my hand at it? I don't imagine you have any other use for these," said Ceres.

"Yes, that would be great."

Inside the rented workshop was a small kiln-like oven that Steiner had apparently brought with them. It looked like a magical tool, which meant they probably wouldn't need to spend too much time preparing to purify the ingots. We all watched, transfixed.

"All right, here we go. O mighty forge set aflame by the gods of the labyrinth, I, Ceres Mistral, beseech thee to hear my prayer..." Ceres chanted as if calling out to the kiln as she added the ingots to its flames. Her brow broke out in sweat from the effort; this must have required quite a lot of magic. Steiner wiped her perspiration away and stood watch faithfully by her side, ready to assist.

Ceres added one ingot to the kiln and then another, and still the desired metal did not appear. Elmina iron probably had its uses, but it wasn't what we were looking for at the moment.

"Argh... This isn't turning out the way I wanted, is it...? Steiner, hand me the last one..."

"Yes, Master. Let's all join her in prayer, that even one piece comes out..."

Ceres added the last ingot to the flame and chanted over it. The rest of my party had joined her in prayer, so I closed my eyes, too, and hoped we would draw a winner. Just then—

◆Extracted Metals◆
> 4 pieces of ELMINA IRON
> 1 piece of GLOWING GOLD
> 1 GRAIN of STERLING SILVER SAND

*　　*　　*

"Phew… I had half a mind to sign myself up for a magic cleansing ritual if not even one of those six had panned out," said Ceres.

"Ceres, is this grain of sterling silver what you'll use to combine equipment?" I asked.

"Well, it is called a *grain*, but in reality, it's a cluster of infinitesimally fine particles. It helps create an attraction between the powers within each piece of equipment when applied to the combining process," she replied.

We'd acquired these rusted metal ingots from the Sand Scissors using Theresia's Triple Steal, and I wondered what our chances of obtaining them would have been without that skill. Considerations like that made me want to make sure we used Theresia's Morale Discharge whenever we defeated such a powerful enemy.

"You can use this glowing gold to enhance equipment with Light Attack 1 or Light Resistance 1, or you can use it to mend Kyouka's circlet should it break. It might not be a bad idea to hold on to it for the time being," continued Ceres.

"That's a good point… I'd like to think about how to use it after we see if there's anything we can apply to our equipment in the resources we harvested from the giant crabs. If this grain of sterling silver is as rare as you say, I get the feeling it might be a waste to use it now…"

"I understand your point, but I don't think leaving Hannya's Greaves in your storage is a wise option," said Ceres. "They're perfect for you, given you already have skills to strengthen your allies' powers. Personally, I'd suggest you leave them in my hands."

"Atobe, I don't know exactly what this Yoshitsune's Leap can do, but it would be great if it helped you move more nimbly. What do you all think?" asked Igarashi, hoping to hear how the others felt. They all agreed. Misaki raised her hand a little shyly.

"We get stronger whenever Arihito stands behind us, right? If this thing will boost that effect, then, um…doesn't that mean we'll get even more, like, excited every time…?"

"…Th-that's…that's probably because he gives us strength, which makes our Trust Levels go up more easily, no?"

"Among party members, it's easiest for Trust Levels to increase for people like healers and those in the vanguard who stop enemies' blows. They are the ones using their skills to protect their friends in the most direct way, after all," explained Ceres. "It's quite likely that your Trust Levels increase even more easily, since it looks like Arihito both directs *and* supports you all."

"……"

Theresia looked at me as if in agreement with Ceres. As a rearguard, I would be completely powerless without my friends. I thought our Trust Levels went up easily for that reason, but maybe our situation was unique even when compared to others with similar support-type jobs.

"Trust Levels measure, in a word, affection," Ceres continued. "I mean no offense in pointing this out, but obviously the greater affection you have for someone, the more you can trust them. It's precisely this trust that can help you scrape through some sticky situations, so I would say it's best to deepen your trust in one another as much as possible."

"Oh, I didn't think you'd take it so seriously," said Misaki. "That makes it sound like I'm the only one with my head in the gutter, y'knooow. The feeling you get when Arihito stands behind you is reeeally amazing! Even when I'm sleeping, once I start to think about him, I instantly wake up."

"...M-Misaki, if you're having such trouble staying asleep, shall I keep you company? Sleep deprivation is your skin's worst enemy, you know," offered Igarashi.

"...Arihito, I'm sorry, it sounds like we're all keeping a big secret from you...," said Suzuna. "But we all want you to keep getting a good sleep so you can recover from all the work you do..."

"Th-thanks, but I've been sleeping fine. What's wrong, everyone? Your faces are all red." Ceres had lit a fire to purify the metal, but it hadn't heated up the room *that* much. Theresia wasn't as flushed, though she couldn't hold my gaze for long and would quickly look away.

Have my skills started activating again while I'm sleeping...? No, I'm pretty sure nothing's happened recently. Maybe I'm just sleeping too deeply... Wait, don't tell me...

Even Melissa and Madoka avoided my glances, so I couldn't help but be curious about what was going on. Ceres smirked as she watched the lot of us and then turned to Steiner, something occurring to her.

"Before we return to District Eight, we might do well to book some accommodation. The cot I have in the workshop is hard on these old bones, so I'm well ready to rest my head on something a little softer."

"*Excellent point, Master. Would that be all right with you? We'll do our best to ensure we don't cause any trouble for you,*" asked Steiner.

"Of course, that's no problem. All right, everyone, what do you say we have some free time?"

""""Okay!""""

"Okaaay!"

"......"

Everyone answered in their own way and stood up to leave. Theresia looked like she wanted to come along with me at first. But she walked off with the others toward the apartment in the end. She must have gotten self-conscious about spending so much time apart from everyone.

"...She sure is admirable, that Theresia. And you, you could do with loosening up a little and simply letting her stay by your side, don't you think?" asked Ceres.

"We go everywhere together, all day, every day, you know. I think it's important for her to also have her own time every once in a while."

"There may be some truth to that, but don't you think that young lady feels most at ease when she's with you?"

"*I believe she's holding back, much like the others. I can just picture them all fighting over you on your days off.*"

I didn't think it was that bad, but Melissa and Madoka both waved at me as I left the workshop, and I realized I couldn't say anything for sure.

"This party's future rests on your integrity, Arihito. But I guess it'd be kinda mean of me to pick on you too much about that, huh? All right, Steiner, shall we get to it?"

"*Yes, Master.*"

...Is it just me, or did Ceres sound a little different for a second there...? Is this all an act? Does she only speak that way to sound more dignified?

Steiner also seemed like they were trying to build up this reputation as a mysterious suit of armor. If my suspicions were correct, those two really were a match made in heaven. I said good-bye and left the workshop to venture off on my own for the first time in a while. I decided I'd try to get my errands in without wandering about too much.

Part III: The Clothing Shop and the Dressing Room / White Subterfuge

I left the workshop and headed for Boutique Corleone, which looked as bustling as usual. There were two members of staff in the store: a young man who stood behind the cash register and a young lady who looked like she had just finished helping a customer.

"Excuse me, I'm here to see the owner, Luca. Is he available?" I asked.

"Oh! We've been expecting you. You must be Mr. Atobe, here

for your order-made suit, correct? Mr. Corleone has been spending every spare moment making the suit at a workshop nearby, but I could take a message if you'd like?"

In that case, it could be difficult to entice him to come out and see me—though maybe he'd reconsider if I asked him to join us for dinner.

"My, what a lucky coincidence, Arihito deary. I just popped by to check in on the store, and here you are!"

"Oh, Luca...perfect timing. I'm sorry to have sent you straight to the workshop after leaving the labyrinth."

"Don't worry your pretty little head about it; it's a labor of love. Raulo, the customer over there appears to be looking for something. Lend him a hand, would you?"

"Yes, sir!"

I took a closer look at the young man and saw he shared many facial features with Luca, who now held his cheek in his hand and looked slightly embarrassed. "That's my little brother, see. He'll be my spitting image when he gets older, the poor thing. Time truly is a cruel mistress."

"I wouldn't say that. I can tell he admires you just by looking at him."

"You think? Well, it is a blessing he's healthy and growing at all, especially when you think of the state he was in when we first reincarnated here... But look at me, skipping down memory lane so early in the day."

How long ago did they come here, and what could have caused

them both to reincarnate together? I wondered if I'd ever get the chance to ask.

"Suzanna, so sorry to leave everything to you, hon. Are the new arrivals selling well?" asked Luca.

"Yes, the tunics flew right off the shelves. I'd like to make a few more once I finish up here…," said Suzanna.

"All in good time my dear, or you'll work yourself to death. It's precisely when we're doing our best work that we need to make sure we sleep well."

"Thank you, Mr. Bernardi."

Raulo came back over while they were speaking and let Luca know the customer had decided to make a purchase. Luca went to thank the customer and asked Suzanna to ring him up. Raulo followed to shadow her, looking dead serious, as if determined to learn all he could.

"So anyhoo, Arihito. It'll still be a little while until your suit is ready, but is that all you came by for? If you meant to say thanks for earlier, please think nothing of it. I had an absolute ball."

"I was hoping to ask if you'd like to come to dinner with us this evening. But of course, I wouldn't want to cause any rifts by stealing you from a family dinner," I said.

"Luca, we'll be fine. We'll take care of everything, so go and have fun," said Raulo. Apparently, Luca lived not just with his younger brother but all the other staff members as well. Picturing a happy Corleone family made them seem even more like some Western film.

"Well, if you insist, maybe I will. What time are we meeting up?"

"Um, I was thinking around seven PM. Do you have a craving for any restaurant in particular?" I asked.

"Let's see... Knowing you, you'll probably invite a whole ragtag group of folks apart from your party members. There's a Belgian place nearby; have you been there?"

"No, I haven't gotten the chance yet."

"They have lots of dishes the ladies are sure to die for, so why don't we go there? I'm a bit of a habitué, so I'll pop in and make a rezzy for us all on my way back to the workshop. Would a room for twenty people be enough? That's the only space they have for groups bigger than ten."

"That would be great, thank you."

The residents of District Seven really did know their restaurants. I pulled up the district map on my license and saved the location Luca showed me. We agreed to make the reservation for seven on the dot, though some might arrive a bit before or after that, and I left the store.

Next, I headed into a back alley and paid a visit to Shichimuan. "Welcome... Oh, Mr. Atobe, how kind of you to stop by. I hope the others are well?" Shiori asked in greeting.

"Yes, they're doing fine... I wanted to thank you and Takuma for all your help in the Beach of the Setting Sun."

"I barely did anything at all, though I was pleased to see Takuma could be of some assistance. He's been his usual self ever since we got home, but... I'd never seen him express his own desires so clearly like that before." Had he sensed we were in danger? Maybe that was a special kind of intuition demi-humans had. I wasn't sure, but I did know Takuma had without a doubt been an enormous help in defeating the praying mantises.

"......"

"Takuma says welcome to you, too. You must remember Mr. Atobe brought you back your ring, don't you?"

"I'm just glad I could find it. It must have been destiny."

Shiori smiled behind her folding fan, then seemed to remember something and fished another fan out of her sleeve. "I know it's not much, but I wanted to prepare a gift for when you eventually move up to District Six. You have a Shrine Maiden in your party, don't you?"

"You must mean Suzuna."

"Yes. Shrine Maidens should be able to learn ceremonial dancing skills. When she does, she'll be able to enhance those moves with this fan. If you don't mind, would you take this for her?"

"Of course, I'll give it to her. Thank you very much, Shiori." She had remembered Suzuna's job and had clearly put a lot of thought into what might be a useful gift. Suzuna would surely be happy to hear it.

"When you run a pawn shop, you often get customers who want you to take whatever they've got as is. It's not every day we get items one might find in a Black Box, but I imagine we may come across a few that could prove useful to you."

"I would certainly like to see those... That's right, one of my party's members, Madoka, is a Merchant. If you're also part of the Merchants Guild, I believe we should be able to keep in touch through that."

"So you'd like me to let little Madoka know whenever I get something good? All right. We can also ship items to different districts if we go through the Merchants Guild... Otherwise, we'd have to sign a special contract to allow me to send you notice we've gotten new merchandise, and that could be a bit troublesome for you..."

"Oh... That's right, I'd forgotten about that option. If we could sign a special contract with your store as well, it'd be a great help," I said.

At this rate, we'd be signing special contracts with every store that helped us out—not that it'd pose any real problems. I had only a limited number of slots for these contracts on my license, so I could at some point theoretically run out of them and not be able to enter into a contract with a store even if I wanted to. But I'd cross that bridge when I got to it.

"...I thought you looked like a novice at first, but you're quite a player, aren't you?" commented Shiori.

"N-no... I just don't like the idea of cutting off ties with a store that's helped us because we've moved on to another district. I was really happy to find out the special contracts existed," I replied.

"Hee-hee... Sorry, I am pleased myself, but I just can't help teasing you. No wonder even my little brother worries about me ending up alone. He doesn't actually say anything of course, but I can tell."

"......"

Takuma stood as still as a statue. Shiori smiled wryly, re-adjusted the lapel of her kimono, and looked at me again.

"...Mr. Atobe, may I ask how old you are? I had thought perhaps I was older than you."

"I'm twenty-nine. I wouldn't blame Misaki and the girls around her age if they called me an old man."

"Hee-hee... I think you may still be a bit young for that."

Her saying so did bring some relief, but I still felt I was at an age where people expected you to start settling down in a lot of ways. Even if they didn't call me an old man, I'd like to be someone they'd call a stand-up adult.

"Still, who would've thought you were older than me... Ms. Falma was sure she had a few years on you... I'll have to break the news to her later." I knew Falma saw me as a younger brother to the point where she'd basically said she'd feel comfortable washing my back. Would her opinion of me change once she found out I was older than her? There was little chance Falma would actually come stay with us, but if the time ever came, I'd have to explain the situation. I didn't really know at that moment if that would be for better or for worse.

Shiori and Takuma agreed to join us for dinner later on, so I gave them the info on time and place and left the shop.

"Hey there. Arihito, was it? The hotshot leader of Ellie's party."

A voice called out to me as I left the alley and made my way for the main road. I turned to see a woman in a white cape leaning against the wall.

"You're... Shirone, right? What are you doing here?"

"Just checking in on Ellie. But it'd be such a bore to go straight home. Care to chat?"

Looking her over again now, she seemed a bit older than Misaki and Suzuna but not quite an adult. She was fixing me with a mischievous, childlike stare. Visible beneath the hood of her jacket were her long, white hair and golden eyes. Yet, buried within those same eyes, I glimpsed an abyss so unfathomable it unnerved me. It felt like she was trying to coerce me into something, no doubt thanks to the two small swords she wore around her waist. She realized what I was thinking, patted their sheaths, and grinned.

"Don't worry, I'm not here to threaten you. I'd hate for my karma to go up... Anyway, are you up to talking with me or not?"

"I wouldn't know what to talk about. And I don't have much time to waste."

"Are you still mad? I mean I get it, all that stuff I told you a little while back must've left a pretty bad taste in your mouth." Shirone belonged to the same White Night Brigade Elitia had once been a part of, and she was the one who'd abandoned Elitia's friend Rury within the labyrinth. She'd tried to explain away her actions by saying Rury had known what she'd signed up for, but I couldn't deny her story had left me unconvinced and with a fair amount of ill will toward her.

"But what else was I gonna do? I had to tell Ellie the truth. Her head is always in the clouds, and one day that's gonna get her killed. I wish I could stop her. I realize that's probably impossible, though," she continued. I'd thought maybe she'd try to apologize,

but her words were dripping with malice. She said it all with a smile, too, and I decided I really couldn't let Elitia see her so easily after all.

"...I understand your position. However, we will under no circumstances let Elitia die. Plus, we all share the same goals."

"Ellie's lightened up quite a bit, thanks to you. She never did really find her place in the Brigade, even with other members around our age. Then our leader handed her a sealed weapon, even though she was so low level, and of course she failed to master it. Doesn't help she's been called the Death Sword ever since."

"This leader of yours... Aren't they Elitia's family?"

"Yeah, her older brother. Her father's in the Brigade, too, but they decided to go by the merit system after getting reincarnated, so we follow her brother. That's just one way this country can screw with families after they come here, you know, if they go and reincarnate all at once." She said *screw* with such deeply felt delight; it was clear Elitia was not the only object of her disdain. Once I'd realized that, I felt reacting to her provocation would be rash. Shirone would probably just enjoy riling me up.

"Whenever we get to the same district as the Brigade, nothing will stop us from doing what we've set out to do. That's all I can say to you right now."

"Tee-hee! ...You're trying so hard not to lose your temper, aren't you? I love guys with that kinda pride. I think our leader's the same."

"...You think you can just read people's minds? Not exactly the most wholesome idea of fun."

"My bad, my bad. I'd kind of decided to give up on you if I couldn't get anything out of you there. But you passed, Arihito."

Passed what? ...Is she trying to get me to join the White Night Brigade?

"Guys like you don't jump ship from other parties too quick, you know. But we've gotten a few to make the leap. We were thirty strong at our peak, but now that Ellie and two others have run off, we're at twenty-seven. That's why we really want three people, you see... Two vanguards, one rearguard. I'm not saying I know who the other two would be this minute, but I'm sure you'd be a starter right away..."

"Sorry, but I'm not going to leave my party. Go ask someone else."

Shirone laughed so heavily her shoulders shook, as if she'd predicted exactly what I'd say. And then—

"I'll give you until the next time we meet to think it over. If you have a change of heart, come find me anytime."

—she came right up to me and whispered in my ear the instant she passed me by. She hadn't given up at all. I had to wonder why she was so fixated on me. I'd only met her twice, but I could tell from the look in her eyes that she was very blatantly trying to tempt me. Not that I would take any of it seriously, of course. I turned around, but she had already disappeared. I realized then I was holding on to a scrap of paper she must have slipped to me at some point.

When did she...? What did she just do...?

She'd written what looked like her hotel's address and building name on it. I had no idea when she'd slipped it to me; I checked my license but found no traces she'd used a skill. What if she'd use some kind of Conceal skill like Gray had? Or maybe the difference in our levels was so great I couldn't even register what she'd done.

"Oh... Arihito! Look, Ryouko, it's Arihito!" shouted Kaede.

"Teacher...! I didn't know you were here. We thought we'd come check Shichimuan out, too, after what you'd said in the labyrinth," added Ibuki.

The two walked my way from the same direction Shirone had headed, Ryouko and Anna coming up behind them.

"Hey, guys, what a coincidence... Thanks for your help earlier."

"Maaan, we got there after you'd taken care of all the good stuff. Talk about a letdown," said Kaede.

"They caught Gray, right? That's such a relief... Guys that hung around him were always calling out to us whenever we'd walk around town. It was kind of a problem," explained Ibuki. "Ryouko's a bit of a pushover, so I couldn't take my eyes off her for a second without worrying."

"Th-that's not true... I *am* an adult, you know. I wouldn't just go off with anyone who tries to order me around," protested Ryouko.

"...Arihito, are you all right? You look like you're feeling a little unwell...," Anna said as she peered up at me. She placed her cool hand on my forehead to check my temperature.

"Y-yeah, I'm fine... By the way, did you happen to pass a young lady in a white cape?"

"Yep, just back there... She a friend of yours? Looked like she was smilin' or something. Maybe I shoulda said hello," said Kaede.

"No, you're all right. I don't really know her... To be totally honest, we're not exactly on good terms," I replied. I could've warned them not to get close to Shirone, but she hadn't even done anything yet, and I didn't want to worry them for nothing.

Still, I got the feeling saying nothing would put them at greater risk. I changed my mind and decided to pick my words very carefully.

"That woman you saw used to be in the same seeking group with Elitia. But they had a falling out... Personally, I don't really want her getting close to Elitia now," I explained. The first thing Shirone had done after reuniting with Elitia was provoke her and rub salt in her wounds.

Elitia must be furious with her, to say the least. At the same time, if we just kept avoiding her because she was dangerous, we'd only kick this can farther down the road. I knew we'd have to find a way to resolve this issue at some point, but we needed to think carefully about how.

"If you say so, Arihito. We'll keep an eye out for her," said Kaede.

"It could be pretty difficult to make up right away if they got in a fight...," said Ibuki.

"...Is there no way they might be able to repair their relationship?" asked Anna. "Of course, it's perfectly reasonable to choose not to spend time with someone with whom you don't see eye to eye."

I still knew very little about Elitia's relationship with the

Brigade. I figured I shouldn't pry and instead wait until she brought it up on her own. But we couldn't just wait around like sitting ducks when it came to Shirone. Her attitude made it very clear she had something up her sleeve—there must be a reason she was still sticking around in this district.

"I'm sorry, I didn't mean to worry you... On another note—Ryouko, do you have any plans this evening?"

"...P-plans? I'd thought I'd pick up some groceries with these three and do a bit of cooking at home, but if you have something else in mind..."

"Ryouko, you're not getting it. If anythin', I think he's tryin' to ask us all out," piped in Kaede.

"G-good point. What a relief, I thought Ryouko was gonna go on a date without us," said Ibuki.

"...Arihito, Ryouko doesn't have much experience with such matters, so I'd appreciate if you could keep that in mind," added Anna.

"W-wait, that's not what I meant...," I stammered, then managed to explain how I'd asked Ceres and the others to join us for dinner. With that set straight, I extended the invitation to the four ladies as well, and they eagerly accepted.

Part IV: A Lively Banquet

When I returned to our suite, I found some members had retired to their rooms to rest. I myself took a short nap and a dip in the bath, got changed, and prepared to go out. Night had fallen, and lights illuminated the streets by the time we left the apartment. We made it to the Belgian restaurant, A Taste of Leuven, and saw a line of people waiting to get in that spilled out into the streets. It seemed most people in the Labyrinth Country preferred to eat out and nearly filled the restaurants to capacity every day.

Our large group included our party, the Four Seasons ladies, and our support team of Ceres, Steiner, Luca, Shiori, Takuma, and Louisa: nineteen people in total. The room had three tables with eight seats each. We picked seats randomly to start, knowing we'd probably get up and move around at some point. Theresia had been standing behind me so I had her sit next to me. Luca sat down on my other side and winked at me for some reason, but I decided to take it as just one of his jokes.

"Ahem... You may be wondering why I'm giving the toast, but as the eldest person in the room, I'll take the lead this time. Without further ado, cheers!" said Ceres.

""""Cheers!""""

"Ruff!"

Cion had been allowed to join us this time, so we ordered her some dishes specially made for guard dogs. The first to come out was a bone covered with meat and was already set down in front of her. Igarashi had commanded Cion to wait, but the toast lifted that order, and she dug in.

"Cheers, Arihito deary. I'm honestly thrilled we could have this little get-together and share a few drinks," said Luca.

"Me too, Luca. You've really helped us out so much," I replied.

The beer filling our glasses had a rich, dark color; apparently in the Labyrinth Country, the darker the beer, the higher the alcohol content. Since it was my first drink and came with Luca's recommendation, I ordered one to try. Even Shiori, who didn't normally drink beer, was sipping a dark amber-brown ale across the table from me. We'd heard this ale was popular with the ladies, so a few others had ordered it as well.

"*Gulp...* Hah! I don't often like beer, but I must say, this is rather good," commented Ceres.

"*That's because you're always drinking the medicinal liqueurs, Master. She says she can't feel anything if it's not strong,*" added Steiner.

"And you can't even drink anything aside from tea or juice, Steiner. I've been waiting for the day we could share a drink, but I'll let it slide since you whippersnappers invited us out." Shiori, who was sitting next to Ceres, refilled her glass. Ceres's cheeks started to flush, making her look the picture of satisfaction. Seeing such a young-looking lady get drunk made my law-abiding spirit ring half-hearted alarm bells, but she was undoubtedly a grown woman, and I had a feeling she'd give me an earful if I said anything.

"Atobe, great work as usual. This place has a really nice atmosphere, and the food looks delicious," said Kyouka. We'd ordered meat pâté hors d'oeuvres that burst with flavor when spread on the crisply toasted rye bread and paired well with the beer, too. We'd also gotten some crunchy, beautifully textured fries that were a far cry from those that had garnished our meals in other restaurants.

I couldn't wait for the Belgian-style croquettes we'd ordered to come out.

"Kyouka, you aaalways run off to Arihito's side straight off the bat. You promised you'd play the French fry game with us, remember?" protested Misaki.

"Th-they're pretty hot still, so it's probably best to hold off, don't you think? Plus, I've never even heard of the French fry game," replied Kyouka.

"We could make it the sausage game if you want? Oh, I know it kinda sounds like I'm drunk, but I'm toootally sober, so don't worry!"

"R-right... Misaki, try not to get too rowdy," I said.

Even though the Labyrinth Country didn't have a legal drinking age, Suzuna and Misaki seemed a bit timid about trying alcohol, so they'd ordered juice instead. Melissa, who was born in the Labyrinth Country, was having a beer like the rest of us; Madoka sat next to her drinking apple juice.

"......"

Strong alcohol would send Theresia's body temperature soaring, so she'd ordered a white beer like Melissa. Even so, she was already starting to blush red, so maybe she just didn't have a high tolerance for alcohol. I made a mental note to keep an eye her.

"Mr. Atobe, may I fill your cup?" asked Shiori.

"Please, thank you... You can really hold your drink, can't you, Shiori?"

"I don't normally have this much, but this is a special occasion... Takuma can't really drink anymore, but he still likes to have a little, too." Takuma had his beetle mask on, but unlike Theresia's lizard mask, it went down past his mouth. His would open whenever he drank to reveal his human mouth beneath. I marveled at the variety in the way each demi-human manifested their unique characteristics.

Just as beetles generally feed on tree sap, Takuma ate a sugary honey for most of his meals. It might not seem like much, but given his brawny frame, it appeared to be giving him all the nutrition he needed. "I'm so happy they serve sweet drinks here. My brother looks really pleased," said Shiori.

"I'm glad to hear that. Oh, but it looks like the alcohol might've already gone to his head a bit," I replied.

"...He seems to be having more fun than usual. Or maybe I'm just seeing what I want to, as his sister." Theresia was our first priority, but there might also be a chance Takuma could regain his human form again as well. If so, I wanted to share any information we got about what would need to be done with Shiori once we found out ourselves. We'd probably be able to help in some way, too.

"Well, aren't you Mr. Popular? Chitchat with you comes at a premium," Kaede cut in.

"Y-yeah...maybe we should let Ryouko talk with him first; I think she's been waiting a long time," said Ibuki.

"Don't you worry yourselves over me, girls. Just do what feels right to you," reassured Ryouko.

"Exactly. I've personally reached a stage where I feel at ease just being able to watch Mr. Atobe," concurred Louisa. She and

Ryouko grinned in agreement as if to say, *Right?* I wished they'd just talk to me like normal. No sooner had the thought crossed my mind than this time Anna came over, checked I didn't need my cup refilled yet, then skewered a French fry with her fork and offered it to me.

"...It appears you have enough to drink, so might I offer you this instead?"

"O-okay. Thanks."

I felt it'd be rude to turn her down, but Anna gazed at me so intensely I started to feel a little embarrassed. Anna noticed Madoka watching and looked over as if to say, *Go ahead.* I wondered how long this wave after wave of attacks, this chain of new drinks and force-feeding would last.

"A-Arihito... Would it be okay if I gave you something, too?" asked Madoka, bashful.

"Arihito, our main course with the beer-infused meat has arrived. Why don't we play a fun little game and guess what kind of meat it is? Every time he gets it wrong, Arihito has to take a sip of absinthe," said Luca, handing the dish the server had brought over to Madoka so she could feed it to me. It was called *beer-infused*, but it looked just like stew in color, and I imagined the alcohol content had probably burned off while it cooked. The meat was so tender it gave way to the gentlest prodding with a fork.

"Arihito, say... Aaaah."

"A-aaah..." I did as Madoka told me, and she placed a piece in my mouth. I knew this flavor. I had tasted it several times and come to recognize the beefy taste.

"Is this Marsh Ox meat?" I asked.

"What a clever boy you are!" said Luca. "You're exactly on point, love. All the beef you can get in District Seven and below is from Marsh Ox. Some more adventurous types go for Minotaur meat in the higher districts, but I just can't bring myself to eat a monster that walks around on two legs. It gives me the creeps."

"Luca, since Arihito guessed it on the first try, shouldn't you be drinking in his place?" asked Ceres.

"Oops, busted... I can't get anything past you, Ceres darling. Watch closely, Arihito. This is how I do things." Luca took the small, golden cup filled with alcohol—probably very strong alcohol—steadied his breath, and then threw it back in one gulp.

"Oooh... I feel like I'm about to burst into flames. The absinthe they serve here is actually a liqueur made with the same medicinal herbs they use to make potions, you know. It can increase your max vitality for a hot minute if you have some when you're already pretty high in vitality. Of course, it's bitter and spicy and has got an absolutely fierce kick to it, so it's basically only used for drinking games."

"Maximum vitality... When you put it that way, I am a little curious to try."

"Have you not already recovered all the vitality you lost before raiding the labyrinth, Arihito? And you, Luca, don't try to take more people down with you," chided Ceres.

"Now, now, Arihito himself said he'd like to try. Anyone else care to join in another game? This isn't something you'd drink willingly," suggested Luca, pouring himself some water from a pitcher and bringing it to his lips. The absinthe must be very bitter—probably best not to approach it too lightly or it'd come back to bite me.

"Heh-heh-heh... It seems my time has come! Arihito, don't even think you can beat me in a gamble. I challenge you to a game of dice!"

"Misaki, if you lose, you'll have to drink some really strong alcohol... Are you okay with that?" asked Suzuna, worried.

"Aargh! Suzu, you're already taking his side!" cried Misaki. "This is the only thing I'm good at, and you won't even back me up. You really love him more than you love your dearest friend, don't you?!"

"Th-that's not what I mean... Just, if you get drunk, it's going to cause a lot of trouble."

"We finally have a day off tomorrow, so don't go wasting it with a hangover," warned Elitia. Misaki checked the drink in Elitia's hands only to find that it wasn't alcohol but a simple juice.

"Wh-what...? I—I don't like alcohol enough to go out of my way and order it, you know...," Elitia stammered.

"Why don't you join us, Ellie? Don't worry, I'm not gonna cheat or anything. We're just gonna roll two dice and guess if the total will be even or odd," explained Misaki.

"Are those old-fashioned gambling games what the little ones are into these days...?" asked Luca.

"I—I mean...we use this in some other games, and the rules are simple enough. But even if I win, you don't have to force yourself to drink anything all right, Misaki?"

"Hee-hee, don't you worry about me. I do have a certain amount of pride, you know. If I lose, I'll get down on my knees and bow to you naked or something. I live my life by the roll of the dice!" Had Misaki always been the type to get fired up over games of chance, as you might expect from someone who chose to be a Gambler? Or was she just extra excited because of the party? Best not to overthink things. It was probably a bit of both.

"...G-get down on your knees naked? ...Are you into that kinda punishment, Arihito...?" asked Kaede timidly.

"U-um, Teacher, could you at least let me leave my spandex shorts on if I do something wrong...?"

"I suppose I could live with spandex shorts... Actually, I can avoid the issue simply by refraining from any mischief. Please disregard what I said," added Anna.

"I can't imagine Mr. Atobe would do anything so extreme... B-but then again, that must be an important part of bringing your party closer together. All right, I'll play as well," said Ryouko.

"I—I would never. Misaki made that up on the spot. Just ignore it," I cut in.

"...Good. I thought you were doing that before I joined the party," said Melissa.

"H-how could he...? Arihito would never do that. I believe in him!" added Madoka.

That prospect seemed to have Melissa and Madoka a little worried, but I was relieved to hear they trusted I wouldn't do that to them. I wanted to win at all costs so I could remind Misaki to show some self-restraint, especially since she was prone to such slips of the tongue. But sadly enough, I didn't have the slightest shred of hope that I'd beat the Gambler at her own game.

◆Current Status◆
> Arihito used Life-Giving Absinthe ⟶ Arihito's maximum vitality was temporarily increased
Arihito is Intoxicated
> Luca used Life-Giving Absinthe ⟶ Luca's maximum vitality was temporarily increased
Luca is Intoxicated
> Misaki used Life-Giving Absinthe ⟶ Misaki's maximum vitality was temporarily increased
Misaki is Intoxicated
> Ryouko used Life-Giving Absinthe ⟶ Ryouko's maximum vitality was temporarily increased
Ryouko is Intoxicated
> Ceres used Life-Giving Absinthe ⟶ All Ceres's powers were enhanced
Ceres is Intoxicated
Bind has been loosened

"A-Arihito... Thanks for everything, love... I had a fabulous evening," said Luca. "Let's do this again...but maybe next time, we'll go a little easier on the drinks..."

"Y-yeah... I had fun, too. Hey, Raulo, take care of Luca for me, okay?"

"Of course, I'll make sure he gets home safely. Oh! Not that way; our home is the other way," said Raulo, guiding Luca home with the other shop staff members who had also come to pick him up.

Misaki and Ryouko weren't the only ones who joined in on the dice game; a few others like Shiori and Ceres had gone head-to-head. Ceres lost, but since she regularly drank this kind of liqueur, she lapped up everything in the albeit small cup with a fervor. Misaki, on the other hand, could barely swallow a sip.

"Master, you really do have an affinity for alcohol. Mr. Atobe is going to start calling you a tank if you're not careful," teased Steiner.

"I think they call it 'drinking like a fish' in his country. I'm quite sure I heard someone say that before. Heh-heh... My, it really has been an age since I've been this boozed up. I feel amazing... Whoa!"

"—Careful. Are you all right, Ceres?" I caught her as she lost her footing. She felt incredibly light. Ceres held her arms up in defense, not to protect her body but her tricorn hat.

"...My apologies. I seem to have lost my composure... Can't set a good example as your elder like that. Steiner, would you be so kind as to carry me home?"

"I had thought you might say that. Oh, it looks like Cion is carrying Ms. Ryouko."

"...I'm so sorry... I... I always, always make such a fool of myself when I drink...," moaned Ryouko, swaying unsteadily on Cion's back. As for me, I was doing what I could to carry Misaki but would probably need to ask someone to take over at some point since I was also drunk. All I wanted was to get us home safely.

"I feel such sympathy for Ms. Natsume... I'm sure I would have ended up in precisely the same state if I had played the game as well," said Louisa, who had held back and only ordered the one drink all dinner so she could enjoy the upcoming day off, just like Elitia.

"I was hoping Seraphina could join us today, but it's too bad she couldn't make it. What should we do about tomorrow, Atobe? Do you want to try asking her if she can come before we head out for the health resort?" asked Igarashi.

"Yes, let's try that. Now then, shall we head back?"

"My house is in the opposite direction, so I'll leave you here. Thank you so much, everyone. This was a lot of fun," said Shiori.

"Let's do this again sometime. Please be careful on your way home."

"Definitely. Good night." Shiori bowed low and started off for Shichimuan with Takuma. Steiner had already started walking down the road with Ceres in tow, so the rest of them followed. Theresia walked directly behind me, pushing up Misaki's body-weight in an attempt to help me with my burden.

"Eep! ...S-stop pushing my butt...," protested Misaki.

"......"

"Uughh, Theresia only ever listens to what you say, Arihito. Can you tell her, *My butt is a big no-no?*"

"I guess you underestimated how good Shiori is at gambling. You wouldn't be in this situation if you hadn't picked a fight."

"Aww, but you were drinking so I wanted to try some, too, you know?"

"...Me too..."

"Seeee? Even Suzu thought the same thing. I wasn't the only one."

"…I—I was just…thinking you're so lucky Arihito's carrying you…"

"It looks like Suzuna's a little tipsy, too… I guess it's all right, as long as you didn't get drunk on purpose, Misaki," chided Elitia. Misaki gulped—Elitia must have hit the bull's-eye.

"Ha-ha-ha-ha… Why would I ever do thaaat? Right, Arihito…? Ack! Please stop pushing me up, it tickles…!"

"I totally see why Theresia'd want to get even. Misaki, you're so sneaky!" said Kaede.

"Still, Arihito would never do this for her otherwise… Oh! *I'd* never drink too much on purpose, though," added Ibuki.

"…You all had so much on your minds. Here I just thought it was a chance to have some delicious food and drinks, but I guess I should have been trying to catch Arihito's eye," said Anna.

"Catch his eye… Anna, how would you go about that?" asked Ibuki.

"…I—I haven't considered it yet. I imagine he only sees me as a child, so it would rather sting if he thought I was trying too hard to look mature."

A thought hit me as I watched the four ladies chatting congenially: Would the Four Seasons members also be interested in going to the health resort? Louisa had said other parties could get in as well as long as they went as guests. I asked them if they'd like to come, and they happily agreed.

A momentary respite from seeking. If we get to spend the whole day relaxing tomorrow, it'll feel like a long vacation. But I want to make sure we're all fully rested and recharged. We have a lot of work ahead of us.

The first thing I wanted to tackle was the trap cube we'd found in the Black Box we picked up when we defeated Silvanus the Enchanter's Messenger, the one that we could use to set up a teleportation link to a treasure labyrinth. I'd put this on the back burner, but we probably had enough firepower to conquer it if it was equivalent to a three-star labyrinth.

"Sheesh... You're so easy to read. Atobe, I know this is kind of rich coming from me, but please try to focus on relaxing on your days off, okay?" said Igarashi, interrupting my train of thought.

"R-right... Sorry, was it that obvious?"

"You always look so deep in thought when you have the labyrinths on your mind...," explained Elitia. "I've slowly but surely gotten better at telling what your different expressions mean, too. I wish you'd talk with us about it, though."

I explained to Igarashi and Elitia what I'd been thinking about. Recovery Support activated as I did, and the members in front of me started to sober up. I made a point to use Outside Assist so that Ryouko could also recover from her Intoxicated status.

Part V: Bargains

Everyone went their own ways after we got home. Some were still in party mode and continued chatting in their rooms while those who were tired took a moment to rest.

"Sorry for kinda crashin' your place. A-are you sure it's okay...?" said Kaede. The members of Four Seasons had been reluctant to go home straight away and had dropped by our apartment.

"Ngh... No, don't bite that... Mr. Atobe, that's a kickboard...," murmured Ryouko, apparently in the middle of a rather strange dream. Besides, I wasn't a kid at a swimming school, and I wouldn't go biting that kind of thing.

"I'm sorry, Teacher, to intrude on you like this..."

"Ryouko was worried we wouldn't have the chance to see you again before you moved up to District Six, so she was positively thrilled you extended us the invitation this evening," explained Anna.

"She talks all high and mighty, but Anna's pretty darn happy herself, even if she doesn't show it. That goes for me, too, of course," said Kaede.

"I had a great time, too. I feel for Ryouko... I also had some of that strong drink, so I feel a little light-headed," I replied. I knew I tended to get a bit of liquid courage when I drank, so I wanted to make sure I didn't cross any lines. That said, I was pretty sure almost everyone got that way when they drank.

"Kaede, why don't you guys let Ryouko sleep in one of our beds? We're not gonna sleep yet, so they're aaall open for the taking!" suggested Misaki.

"Are you sure that's all right? We don't want to overstay our welcome...," said Ibuki.

"It's gonna be a pain in the ass to carry her all the way up to the second floor...and Arihito just gave Misaki a piggyback ride all the way home," complained Kaede.

"Ha-ha-ha... Yeah, but I'm nearly sober. I'm sure she'll rest better on a bed than on the sofa, so if you don't think she'd mind, I can carry her up," I offered. It looked like Recovery Assist could help heal Intoxicated status with a little time, so I hoped Ryouko was well on the way to sobering up. I was getting a bit tired from using Outside Assist so much but figured I'd be all right after a good night's sleep.

We had until the end of the day to decide whether to buy the items available through Bargain. The ladies had all washed up before dinner, but some decided they wanted to take another dip and headed off for the baths. Madoka, however, remembered the deadline and came to discuss it with me before she joined them.

"Thank you for everything today, Arihito. Um, about the items I mentioned...," she started.

"Yeah, I was just gonna ask you about that. Could you show me what's available?"

"Yes. Um, it looks like the items we've requested aren't in stock yet, but... Oh!"

"What's wrong? Did someone beat us to the punch? I mean, with a name like Bargain, I could see that happening."

"N-no... But they just got one of the items I'd asked for. I wanted to give it to you as a present...," she said, hesitantly showing me her license. She looked embarrassed about something. I figured out exactly why when I saw the item she was showing me.

◆Bargain Inventory List◆
> Silk Necktie +1
> Light Leather Leotard +3
> Silent Bracelet +1
> ★Scholar's Ankh

"This necktie... Is this what you were picking out for me?" I asked. Madoka pulled down her turban to try to hide her face... unsuccessfully, of course. Even her ears had flushed bright red.

"...I shouldn't be shopping for things without asking, should I?"

"N-no... To be honest, I'm really happy you did that for me. A necktie, huh... I would love to wear one if it could help with something when equipped."

"O-of course. Do you think the fact they have one in stock means there are other people who wear suits, too?" she asked. I wasn't sure how it had come to be on sale, but this Silk Necktie was better suited for seeking than the one I was using since it could increase defense. It also looked easy enough to wear from the attached photo.

"...Oh! It appears Mr. Luca is the one who put it up for sale. Do you think he did that after dinner?"

"I guess he saw right through me... He really is a first-rate professional when it comes to clothes." He could've easily sold it to me personally, but I suspected he intentionally chose this method out of consideration for Madoka. Either way, the price was right at fifteen gold, so I decided to buy it on the spot. Looking at the product lineup, it seemed it really was pretty rare to find items of a similar caliber to what we could get from a Black Box. Still, there was one starred item; maybe it had some kind of catch?

"How about we go through them one by one? ...A leotard? What's that again?"

◆Light Leather Leotard +3◆
> Slightly increases defenses against physical attacks.
> Slightly increases defenses against magical attacks.
> Slightly increases agility.
> All effects enhanced with complete set.

"Uh... Th-this is a pretty risqué design..." Ceres had said it would be difficult to find items to complete a set started in District Seven once we moved up, but maybe this was part of the Magician's Armor Set.

"U-um... I'm sorry, I just remembered you talking about armor sets that added extra effects when completed, so I put out a request because I thought it might be nice if we were able to find the other pieces. It looks like this one came from a thrift shop in District Seven, but the design *is* pretty bold, so it never found a buyer."

A silk hat, leotard, and black tights—no wonder Igarashi isn't jumping at the chance to wear these. This kind of combination leaves you at a loss for words.

"Misaki's cape is a part of the set, too, which means she'd have four matching items. Apparently, the set effects start working after you have at least four items of one set," Madoka explained.

"In that case, maybe we should have Misaki test it out… But no, I think this could be hard to wear, no matter how useful it may be."

"Arihitooo? Madokaaa?"

"! …M-Misaki, you scared me…!" squealed Madoka as Misaki popped her head out from behind the sofa. We had been pretty deeply engrossed in the Bargain list, but I was still impressed by how Misaki had managed to sneak up behind us so easily.

"You're gonna make me nervous, gossiping about me while I'm in the baaath… Ooh, are these the Bargain items? Even the name kinda gets you excited, don't you think? …Hmm. Hmm?" Misaki spotted the leotard on the license and cleared her throat a bit.

"…Isn't this one of those tummy-tucking suits?" she asked.

"W-well, I don't think they call them that here. That's probably not a thing in the Labyrinth Country," I replied.

"That's not the poooint! If I wear th-this kind of thing around town, everyone's gonna think I'm suuuper into myself! Ugh, I'm sooo mad! I'm gonna steal Kyouka's change of clothes and switch it out with this!" huffed Misaki.

"C-calm down, Misaki. This is part of a set of armor. I'm not gonna force you to do anything, but I think it might be a good idea for someone to wear it if it's useful."

"I think you would look really nice in this, Misaki," offered Madoka. "You already have the cape from this set, and it looks amazing on you…"

"Look who's talking… Haaah, I can't get mad at you, Madoka. All right, fine; if you insist, Arihito, I'll try it on once, just for you."

"Not if you don't want to. But I may ask you to put it on if it looks like we might need you to, depending on the situation."

"I—I mean, if you care that much about it, I won't totally rule it out, all right?" While Misaki was doing her best to sound all high and mighty, Elitia and Suzuna walked toward us, fresh out of the bath.

"What are you up to, Misaki? …Can't you see you're making Arihito uncomfortable?" said Elitia.

"…Misaki, what were you looking at? …Oh…" The leotard seemed to be a bit too much for Suzuna also, who quickly turned red and pulled back. "…I think the important thing is to try to overcome your embarrassment and wear it when you need to."

"Of course, I'll wear it if I need to; don't think I won't! But you better watch what you say, or they're gonna use sooo much of that transparent stuff on your Shrine Maiden armor, and it'll be suuuper see-through."

"…I'm sure Ceres and Steiner would be more considerate than that… They would, wouldn't they…?

"Y-yeah, I think so… I don't think you need to worry too much about that." Knowing those two, I figured they could probably give us a run for our money, but they wouldn't actually go so far as to design something impossible to wear. We could definitely put our full trust in them with these matters. "So we'll test out the complete set effects after this arrives. What's next…this Silent Bracelet?"

◆Silent Bracelet +1◆
> Dampens sounds produced when moving and makes
  the user more difficult to detect.
> Any skills activated while undetected by
  enemy will be strengthened.

"I feel like this would work well with either Theresia's or Melissa's skills... Theresia already has a bracelet, so maybe we should have Melissa take it since she can already use Ambush... Wh-what's up?" It looked like the phrase *Silent Bracelet* had both shocked and flustered the four others in the room as soon as I'd mentioned it.

"Y-yes...you should give it to whoever you think would use it most effectively," said Elitia.

"Y-yeah, truuue, it's not like we want it or anything, you know?" added Misaki.

"Ellie, Misaki, if you look at it like that, you're going to make Arihito think..." Suzuna trailed off.

"Is there something wrong with this bracelet?" I asked them.

"Uh, nope, not really, just an inside thing... W-well, good niiight, Arihito!" Misaki said, then went upstairs with Elitia and Suzuna. I glanced at Madoka and saw she was rather flustered, too, but I still had one last item to check out.

◆★Scholar's Ankh◆
> If the user helps another person recover
  vitality or magic, he or she will recover a
  small amount of their own magic.

> Consumes vitality instead of magic when the user lacks sufficient magic to activate a skill.
> Small chance of withstanding a lethal attack and retaining a minuscule amount of vitality.
> Adds extra experience points when affected by MORIBUND status.

It appeared an ankh was a supplementary piece of armor similar to a protective charm in that you could activate its powers just by carrying it with you.

"...Looks like it could be useful," I said. "I wonder why it was put up for sale?"

"Apparently its previous owner met with failure in a labyrinth and needed money to get back on their feet. As a starred item, it's pretty valuable, but it's within our budget and available for us to purchase." I had asked Madoka to set our maximum budget at two thousand gold, thinking that might give us a greater range of options, regardless of whether we actually bought anything. This ankh cost one thousand five hundred gold—not all that expensive, if you considered what it could do.

If I equip this, I'll be able to recover magic every time I use Recovery Support. That way, I'll almost never run on empty magic...

We couldn't place too much stock in it as it was, since the ability to withstand a lethal attack depended on chance. However, we could guarantee it'd activate if we used Fortune Roll beforehand.

"Okay, let's go with this one, too. How long will it take to get here after we order?"

"The shop is also in District Seven, so it should be ready by tomorrow. Bargain is set up so that different items appear on the market for each district, and an equal number of Bargain Tickets are distributed among Bargain users. Of course, only Merchants or shop owners can use Bargain, so a limited number of people can actually purchase those items."

In that case, it looked like we were free to purchase everything we saw on the list if we wanted without a problem. The Merchants Guild had clearly put a lot of thought into this system to prevent inequality and support Seekers. I felt a renewed sense of appreciation for their efforts.

In total, we spent 2,915 gold. We had about 28,000 gold left in the bank, which started to feel like it might not be too much of a safety net in certain situations. We needed to plan out our income methodically, not just work on the assumption we'd find a lot of money in Black Boxes. I pondered this as I looked over the account ledger Madoka handed me. Fortunately, our meals were relatively inexpensive compared to our income, and since the Guild took care of paying for utilities, we didn't have to be too frugal with our daily expenses.

"......"

"U-uhhh... I guess you're right, I shouldn't just go to bed without washing up." Theresia had looked over at me as if to ask, *Are you going to go to sleep like* that? I did tend to get a bit heated after drinking, so a nice, refreshing bath would hit the spot.

I headed to the bath with Theresia hot on my trail, determined not to let me get away; I guess she'd noticed I'd been trying to avoid bathing with her. I took off my clothes with my back to her as usual, then made sure she'd gone in first before following her into the bath area. I stepped in and—

"...Hmm?"

—the room was steamier than usual, and some kind of letters were floating up from the floor through the mist. I almost screamed when I noticed a suit of armor sitting on its knees off in the corner, too large to miss even amid all the steam in the big room.

"Master, you're risking actually angering Mr. Atobe one of these days if you insist on doing things like this, you know...?" Steiner's voice floated over from the far side of the steam. It sounded different, as if it hadn't echoed through their armor like normal.

"If he takes baths with Theresia as often as they say, I don't see the issue. It really had been an age since I activated my powers in the labyrinth... Looks like my bind is coming a little loose."

"Uh...C-Ceres, I'm sorry, I didn't think anyone was in here... Theresia, I'm gonna step out for a bit...!" As I tried to head for the door, I heard a whoosh of water fall from across the steam, and a silhouette I didn't recognize got up from the bath. It should have been Ceres standing there, but this person was much taller. Her voice also sounded deeper, more mature, and not because it was echoing off the walls or anything like that.

"You have nothing to apologize for. This is the power of the runes... But no matter what, do not turn around. Theresia, what do you normally do when you take a bath with Arihito?"

"......"

She'd spoken so bluntly I couldn't guess the truth with any confidence, but it seemed Ceres had used one of her Runemaker skills to thicken the steam and carefully shown herself in so as not to tip me off.

"...Kyouka and Louisa started to get on edge about something as soon it came around to bath time, so I asked them what was wrong. You're quite a plucky young man, aren't you? I never would have pinned you as the type who'd be on such intimate terms with one of your party members."

"I-I'm not... We're not doing anything 'intimate'...," I stammered in protest.

"And that is why we are here. Steiner had to wash their armor you see. I can prevent it from rusting with a rune, though it gets tricky if they wash it while wearing it."

"P-please don't say such things, Master... I refuse to move an inch from this bathtub."

"Well, well, look who's getting cold feet now. And you're the one always blathering on about bravery. Say, Arihito. Wouldn't you say you'd be better off with a partner who takes the lead?"

"I—I suppose that's true..." Ceres spoke to me as she washed my back. I could tell she was definitely taller than usual, if perhaps not as tall as an average adult.

"Pay no heed to my appearance; you're still far too young

for it to matter. Of course, you're free to look if young ladies of this age are what strike your fancy... It won't cost me anything."

I was probably just a very young man at best from Ceres's point of view; a twenty-nine-year-old could easily look like a child to a one-hundred-and-fifteen-year-old. Still, I wanted to be seen as a proper adult, meaning it would be wrong to turn around to look at her. I shouldn't even look directly at her reflection in the mirror.

"...How gallant of you. I can see why those ladies in your party hold you in such esteem. Do you understand what a woman thinks when she sees a man carry himself like you do?" It wasn't my place to answer that, or even let my imagination wander down that road. I felt it would be breaking the rules.

"Of course, I did ask Kyouka and Louisa for permission. Nobody should much mind if I get to wash your back if they say it's all right. You did great work out there, Arihito."

So those two knew she would be here... Maybe they trusted nothing untoward would happen since Theresia would be with us, too.

"......"

"I wonder if steam is good for a lizardman's skin. Theresia's is positively glowing... Oh, youth is such thing of envy. Her skin is playing a lovely melody with the water."

"Master, if you take too much longer, Mr. Atobe will catch a cold."

"Hoh-hoh... Are you quite sure? Once I'm done here, Arihito is going to join you in that little tub."

"...Th-that's... Well, I have a Diving skill, so I'd be all right, but I'm going to end up like a prune if I'm in here much longer," said Steiner. They apparently subscribed to the *prevention is better than cure* line of thought and had some kind of skill that would help in case they fell into water in full armor. In the end, the two left to dry off before me, and I caught neither a glimpse of Steiner's real body, even though we went in the bath together, nor a proper look at Ceres.

"……"

Once it was just me and Theresia in the bath, I started rinsing off Theresia's back, and the thought hit me: *I'm so glad they didn't see me wash Theresia's tail.*

CHAPTER 3

The Seekers' Siesta

Part I: The Islet of Illusion

A little over a week had passed since I'd been reincarnated into the Labyrinth Country, and this was going to be my first full day off. Melissa woke up early to make breakfast as usual, and I got her to let me help.

The Four Seasons ladies were first shocked and then thankful to see breakfast served. They looked relieved my efforts in the kitchen hadn't sent any of the dishes awry. Apparently, if someone with a skill like Cooking directs an assistant on how to help, the resulting meal turns out just as good as if the assistant possessed the skill themselves. However, as soon as the other party members came down, they ordered me to sit still and get out of the kitchen since my turn to help only came around once a week. But I didn't feel right doing nothing.

After a brief post-breakfast rest, Four Seasons headed back to their apartments for a bit. We agreed to get ready and then meet up again at Green Hall.

Later, as we waited at our rendezvous point, Seraphina and Adeline came in through the back entrance to the building and walked toward us.

"Good morning, Mr. Atobe... I beg your pardon for addressing you on your day of rest."

"Seraphina, he really is just like Third-Class Dragon Captain Kozelka described him. If you'll excuse me, I'll take my leave..."

"Did you not insist a moment ago you would find a way to come even if I left you behind? There is no place for embarrassment here."

"Yes, ma'am! ...You're far too kind. Lieutenant Seraphina and Private Adeline, reporting to accompany you on a day of leave!"

"I was about to ask if you'd like to join us. I'm glad we ran into you here," I told the two Guild Saviors.

"Did you two perhaps know that we were going to the health resort?" asked Suzuna.

"Yes, Third-Class Dragon Captain Kozelka informed us. She granted us permission to accompany you as long as we did not have any other duties planned for the day..." It was hard to imagine the generally stern Kozelka instructing Seraphina and Adeline to take a day of leave, but I knew I shouldn't judge based on first impressions.

"I'm so sorry to keep you all waiting... Oh, Ms. Seraphina and Ms. Adeline, you've joined us as well? This looks like it will indeed be a merry gathering!"

"Ms. Louisa, if may I ask one question... What kind of place is the health resort we are about to visit?" asked Seraphina.

"It's a small island-type labyrinth called the Islet of Illusion. It has wonderfully scenic vistas, a beach we can use for recreation, lovely paths to stroll along, and other amenities for us to enjoy."

"Seraphina, I have a bathing suit with me. Our suit for underwater drills should work, right?"

"H-hmm… That shouldn't be a problem. Pardon me—I meant, I do not expect it to pose any issues."

"Please do let us know if you need anything, all right? I hope we all have a great time today," Igarashi told Seraphina. Once she'd said her greetings, the others followed suit. Cion lay down on the floor and patiently waited until we finished our conversation and the Four Seasons members arrived.

We teleported to the Islet of Illusion from a teleportation site near Green Hall. Inside the small building, we found an array of teleportation doors whose settings you could apparently adjust to your desired destination. Louisa took care of the settings for us, after which we walked through the dark for a bit before seeing another door come into view. We opened this door to find the sun gently shining down over the beach spread out before our eyes.

We'd come to the Islet of Illusion, one of the health resorts managed by the Guild, who had labeled it a Designated Safe Place—a low-risk labyrinth where the monsters that inhabited it were tamed and bred in a few different locations throughout the islet. Professional contractors had built an overwater hotel to accommodate guests, which gave it the feel of a destination resort—one I never would have dreamed I'd get to visit in my previous life.

"Whoaaa... *Amaaaazing* is the only word I've got for this!" exclaimed Misaki in wonder.

"You've got that right...," agreed Igarashi. "When I heard *health resort*, I pictured a quiet little cottage town, but this is something else..."

I'd expected Misaki to really go wild, but it seemed she'd been stunned into silence. Igarashi also looked really happy from what I could tell. Though in all fairness, there wasn't a single dissatisfied face in our group.

"I-is it really all right...for us to have such a beautiful place all to ourselves...?" I asked.

"Yes, since only a limited number of people can use the resort at a time," explained Louisa. "The hotel has two four-person, four three-person, and a couple of two-person rooms. The building you can see over there is for the maintenance staff. It's where the six Guild members who manage the facilities live."

"Louisa, you sound just like a tour guide, ya know?" said Kaede. "This is really startin' to feel like a vacation!"

"A one-night stay is more than good enough for me...," added Ibuki. "I can't wait to go for a run on the beach... I'll bet it feels really nice to run on this super-soft sand."

"It looks like there's a beach volleyball court set up... Might anyone be interested in playing?" suggested Anna.

"Some light exercise sounds like a great idea. If all we do is take it easy, we'll fall out of shape," said Ryouko, who'd already removed her boa coat, probably since it was so warm. I didn't mean to look, but I happened to see her adjust her swim pants and quickly averted my gaze to the safe harbors of the blue sky and the sea.

"I guess all men really are the same... But maybe that's going a bit too harsh on you, Atobe," said Igarashi.

"I am in total agreement. Mr. Atobe is the very picture of simplicity and fortitude; he is far removed from vulgar desires," concurred Seraphina. The two were hitting it off really well; I felt like I'd better learn to be a saint if I wanted to survive.

"Arihito, I see you came in your suit after all... Though I guess that's comforting, in a way," said Elitia.

"Hey, I brought a change of clothes, of course. It's too bad I couldn't get my hands on a swimsuit in time, but I should be fine as long as I don't go in the water... I'm surprised you could find one for everybody, Madoka." I found out just as we were leaving that Madoka had ordered bathing suits for those who hadn't gotten one yet. I didn't know what any of them looked like, but I figured maybe I'd see some soon enough.

"Mr. Atobe, how would you like to divide the room arrangements?" asked Louisa.

"I'd appreciate it if I could use one of the two-bed rooms for myself. Everyone else can choose their own rooms as they like..."

"......"

"...Theresia looks like she wants to ask, *Why would you sleep alone in a two-person room?*" Melissa translated, thrusting a figurative knife into my chest. It was true there shouldn't be a problem for the two of us to sleep there together...as long as nothing happened.

Theresia suddenly shook her head, making the ears on her lizard mask wave back and forth, then turned bright red and ran away across the beach.

"...Sorry. That was my fault."

"O oh, no, um... Theresia, don't run off too far!" I called after her. Theresia stopped short at the water's edge. It seemed lizard-men and salt water don't mix.

"Atobe, we'll talk it over and decide where Theresia should stay tonight. How about we all get changed and meet up on the beach?" suggested Igarashi.

"S-sure. Thank you, Igarashi. I'll need your help with Theresia."

I was far from the only adult with Igarashi, Louisa, Ryouko, and Seraphina around, so I knew they could take care of the room arrangements on their own. I decided to head to my room and drop off my things. I had brought my weapons just in case, but it didn't look like I'd be needing them. Then again, this was a labyrinth, after all. Better safe than sorry.

I ran into a member of the hotel staff in the middle of freshening up a room and asked if they had any swimsuits I could rent. It turned out they sold frogman swim trunks, so I picked up a pair for about five gold. That was how I learned the profits from the swimsuit sales were one way the Guild made money on the islet. I decided to keep my shirt on over the trunks in the end, since I felt it might be a bit insensitive to go out to meet the crew half-naked.

*　　*　　*

A few of the ladies rested on chaise lounge chairs that had been set up under a small grove of palm trees abutting the beach while some of us went at it in a game of beach volleyball.

"Here goes... Take that!"

Ryouko and I were facing off against the very athletic Elitia and Melissa in a mini game of beach volleyball. Ryouko dug Elitia's serve, and I set it up for her; surprisingly, the sand didn't hinder my movement too much.

"Ryouko...!"

"Nice set, Mr. Atobe!" cried Ryouko, not letting the sand get in the way of her speedy footwork as she skillfully turned my pass into a spike. Melissa, holding down the back line on the other side of the net, spun through the air to dig the ball exactly as a cat would, sending a scream of delight through the onlookers. The ball lofted up through the air, and Elitia got in place to spike it back on a second-touch attack.

"Get it, Ellie! Cut through those two like a knife!"

"Wh-what are you saying...?! Ah...?!" Misaki's cheer made Elitia lose her footing, but she recovered and managed to return the ball over the net. I probably should've seen that coming. Ryouko jumped up to block it.

"—Ryouko, I'll support you!"

It had looked like her hands wouldn't reach, but the Defense Support 1 wall activated with a *crack* and bounced the ball back.

"Nice block!"

"Th-thanks...! Same to you, Mr. Atobe!"

"Amazing… He can use that in volleyball, too… How the heck does that even work?" wondered Kaede.

"Just having Arihito on your team must make you that much stronger," said Ibuki.

I'd thought this would for sure be against the rules, but it seemed all skills were on the table in Labyrinth Country volleyball provided they didn't hurt anyone. If I could use Defense Support 1 against the other team, I didn't see how we could lose. But it wasn't going to be easy to break through Melissa's impenetrable defense.

"It's gonna take more than that…!"

"—Game on, Arihito…!"

Melissa set the ball, and Elitia unleashed a quick attack, fast as lightning in the realest sense. But I'd activated my Hawk Eyes and saw through it and where the ball was headed.

"—Ryouko!"

"On it…!"

I activated Cooperation Support 1 starting with my serve to make Ryouko's spike the second stage of our counterattack.

"…?!"

The ball flew right by Elitia and fell in a spot not even Melissa could reach. Ryouko swung a bit too hard and fell flat on her butt.

"Eek…!"

"Are you all right, Ryouko…? Wh-what's wrong, you two…?" Melissa I could understand, but even Elitia looked put out. I gathered they were angry.

"…W-well, a win is a win, I guess. Arihito, you *will* play a game on my team later, won't you?"

"...I want to try, too. I'm frustrated he beat me."

"A-actually... I was just thinking I shouldn't use my skills anymore."

"It's fine—I used Sonic Raid, too. We probably shouldn't use too much magic, but as long as we can recover it all in one night, we should be fine."

"All right, all right, you two," cut in Kaede. "Can we get in there? Arihito's starting to look a bit wiped out."

"I guess so... Okay, you guys take over the other half of the court." Elitia was definitely on fire; I wouldn't be surprised if she liked all sports.

"Elitia, just watch out your suit doesn't slip. You're really movin' out there," warned Kaede.

"R-right... Thanks, I'll be more careful."

Elitia had a red, white, and blue–striped bikini on under a light sweater she probably wore since the suit itself was rather revealing. The strings holding her bottom piece together had in fact loosened a bit from the fierce hustle, but Melissa noticed and retied them for her.

"...I should've gotten a swimsuit like yours, Melissa. It's great for defense...and covers a lot more."

"That's not true. Swimsuits are all the same... I just burn easily."

Melissa had gone with a tech suit swimsuit and was also wearing a light button-up shirt over it. I'd thought cats didn't like water, but that didn't seem to hold true for Melissa. Looking over the suits the ladies had chosen, I realized there probably hadn't been a great selection of suits available, so they'd gone with what they could get instead of what they might have actually wanted.

"Still… I wonder why Kyouka insists on hiding?" asked Elitia, puzzled. "She's definitely got the body for her suit. She should be more confident."

"…I don't have the guts to wear that in front of other people. Louisa's, either," said Melissa.

"Those two are… Well, never mind. Let's go check on them after we've finished playing. I'd like to go for a walk in the woods, also," suggested Ryouko.

"True that. You gotta enjoy one thing at a time, right?" agreed Kaede.

"Ummm, would it be all right if I practiced with you? I haven't played volleyball since gym class," asked Ibuki, timidly.

"Wow, Ibuki can do a jump serve… How marvelous."

The next game had already started. I watched as Melissa expertly dug Ibuki's serve and sent it up to Elitia for an attack.

"—Elitia, nice spike!" I called out.

"…Th-thanks… But it's not like I'm doing all this just so you can tell me how good I am, you know…"

"Ellie, you're sooo not honest about your feeeelings!"

"We're not doing anything but watching…," murmured Suzuna. "And yet after Arihito spoke, my chest got so…" I'd activated Morale Support 1 when I called out, not because I'd seen any real need to raise their morale, but since I figured it couldn't hurt.

I didn't have my Light Steel Chain Gloves or my Elluminate
Mountaineering Boots on, so the ladies' morale went up less than
usual. But I kept at it throughout the game and in the end wound
up raising their morale to about twenty.

Afterward, I walked over to the cottage set aside for the Guild
employees who managed the facilities to say hello and saw that
part of it had been fenced off.

"Coral Peigo Ranch…huh." This was most likely one of the
areas dedicated to breeding the monsters on the islet. *Coral* I took
to mean like coral reefs, but I'd never heard of *Peigo* before.

Igarashi had brought Cion with her to the fence as well and
was staring over the border, Adeline at her side.

"Oh, Mr. Atobe… Ms. Kyouka, I've found him."

"Give me a sec; I'm looking at something…"

Adeline bowed to me slightly in greeting, and I returned the
gesture. I walked over to Igarashi's side and peered over the fence.
Inside, fluffy little birdlike creatures were toddling about on two legs.

"Wow…they look just like stuffed animals. I guess a Peigo is
kind of like a penguin, huh?" I said.

"They're adorable… I wonder if we could keep a few at the
Monster Ranch…"

"I don't know about that, but it says 'Petting Allowed,' here, so
maybe they'd let you touch them if you asked."

"What? ...R-really? Then I'm going to ask one of the Guild members..." Igarashi trailed off and turned in my direction for the first time. I hadn't really thought too much about it when I'd glanced at her out of the corner of my eye, but now that she was facing me head-on, I really couldn't find a place to look.

"Oh! ...A-Atobe, I'm sorry, I was so caught up looking at these little guys..."

"N-no, I'm sorry..."

"Mr. Atobe, you're just like a bumblebee drawn to a flower. You simply can't help it. I even caught myself staring at first, and I've got my own pair. Our captain's got a great figure, too, but our swimsuits are made more with defense in mind. It's really such a shame," said Adeline, who'd gotten much chattier than usual.

Maybe she felt free to relax on her day off, or maybe it was easier since Seraphina wasn't around. And maybe in the Labyrinth Country, people cared more about how much defense a swimsuit provided rather than how revealing it might be—or so I forced myself to think as I frantically tried to take my mind off of Igarashi.

Back at the company, people would say she was trying to accentuate her chest whenever Igarashi would wear her ribbed knit sweater in the winter; they said she knew where her assets lay and was using them as a weapon. Looking at her now, I could see that was all way off base.

"I must say, though, I was surprised you'd pick something so bold, Ms. Kyouka... Was it because you knew Mr. Atobe would be there to appreciate it...?"

"O-of course not. I wanted to swap with Louisa, but I had no other choice... I couldn't turn down the suit Madoka had gone out of her way to get for me just because it might make me embarrassed, could I?"

"...I—I understand; I promise I won't joke about it anymore. Y-you're getting really close, Ms. Kyouka." I decided to learn from Adeline's mistake and choose my words with great care. I figured there was no way Igarashi would draw closer to me, but to think she could make contact at that distance—her chest was truly out of control.

"W-well, I think perhaps I'll go see Seraphina... Enjoy yourselves," said Adeline, and she slowly backed away. Igarashi readjusted the skirt wrap she had tied around her waist, finally seemed to regain her composure, and looked straight at me.

"...Very on brand of you to wear a button-up shirt at a resort."

"I'm in good company. I've heard plenty of insurance auditors wear suits in sandy deserts."

"Hee-hee... Is that something you got from a movie? Or maybe a manga?"

Movies, manga, they both took me back. Then again, realizing I didn't need that kind of entertainment to survive was in itself a happy discovery. A friend once told me he'd die without the Internet. I wanted to tell him just how wrong he was. Though to be fair, the licenses we got in the Labyrinth Country did operate on some kind of network, which made things a little more convenient. We definitely would have had to slow down for communication without the feature that let us get in touch with people over long distances. I could imagine our seeking would be much less efficient, too.

"I really do feel comfortable around you, you know..."

"Huh...?"

"Oh, nothing. Cion's being so careful not to scare the little ones. Let's go ask if we can get a closer look."

The others said Igarashi had been hiding from me ever since she'd changed, so I wondered if I should take that to mean she'd gotten used to her swimsuit. Either way, I had to be careful not to look directly at her. I didn't want my karma spiking.

Part II: At the Edge of Forest and Water

The woman working for the Guild as a caretaker opened the gate and let us in. Then while she got to feeding the Coral Peigoes, she told us a bit about them.

"These Coral Peigoes as a species are basically just like penguins. We have this fence go all the way out into the ocean so they can swim without getting lost," she said. Only a fellow reincarnate would think to explain it in such rough terms, but that was all the confirmation I needed. "They love fish like sword trout, but they'll also eat shrimp, crab, and other shellfish. They're also known for eating coral and other hard things, which is how they got their name."

Igarashi threw a small sword trout toward the ocean, and one of the Coral Peigoes swimming in the water jumped up deftly to catch it.

"I'd heard penguins sometimes eat rocks, too. Do you know why they do that?" I asked.

"There are various theories, but we do know why the Coral Peigoes do. They cultivate magic stones within their bodies and sometimes lay them as eggs."

"That's amazing... Do they produce a specific kind of magic stone?"

"The type of stone they lay varies depending on their diet; here, they mostly lay tide stones. We have them on sale as souvenirs. Would you care to take one home?"

"All right, could I get one, please?"

◆Tide Stone◆
> Magic stone with the power to produce salt
  water.

I bought one tide stone for ten gold. They apparently weren't extremely common since the Coral Peigoes only laid about one magic stone per week. The caretaker had said they could lay other types of stones depending on what they ate, and I found it hard to suppress my excitement at such a tantalizing thought.

"Is it possible for regular Seekers to keep Coral Peigoes?" I asked.

"We get that question a lot, but Seekers need to fulfill a major requirement before they can tame a Coral Peigo. More specifically, they must encounter a Named Monster of the species. But as I'm sure you're aware, that's no easy feat..."

"I see, thank you. In that case, I think we'll just look forward to visiting them again here."

"Of course. Please feel free to stay here with your friend as long as you'd like," the caretaker said, then headed back to the administration office. At that moment, Igarashi finished feeding the Coral Peigoes and walked toward me. White-plumed Coral Peigoes that stood about knee height followed her every step like a clutch of chicks.

"I think they're probably fully grown, but their *cheep-cheep*s are so cute," she cooed. "I know they're monsters, but I don't think I could ever bring myself to fight them."

"We have run across monsters like the Cotton Balls that looked more powerful up close...but watching these little guys just puts me at ease." They had started to climb all over Cion, who was sprawled out on the beach. The peaceful scene pulled straight out of a folk song warmed my heart.

It'd be nice to settle down here whenever I finally retire from the seeking life. I know that might be jumping the gun a bit, but this island is the closest thing to paradise that I've found so far.

"Thank you for asking about whether we could keep one. I feel like I'm always talking to you about the kind of pets I want to have..."

"When I heard they were basically penguins that lay eggs and magic stones, I thought they might be a good fit for the ranch. But it seems we can't really keep them unless we run into a Named Monster of their kind."

"Does that mean they've seen one on this island before? If someone defeated it, isn't it possible it could appear again?" asked Igarashi.

"I kind of doubt we'll run into it while we're here, but I suppose it's possible." The more we chatted about it, the more I came to think that might just happen, considering our track record.

I hadn't imagined the health resort would be in a labyrinth; while it was relaxing here, I also felt the thrill of adventure. But why was it called the Islet of Illusion? I wanted to meet up with the ladies on their walk and take a look around, though I was pretty sure other Seekers had already discovered all there was to explore by now.

"Igarashi, do you want to hang out with these guys here a bit longer?"

"I do… But the longer we stay, the harder it'll be to leave. Don't worry, little ones, I'll be back to see you again whenever I get some time off," she reassured the Coral Peigoes gathered around her legs, patting each one on the head, before she and I turned around and started walking away from the ranch. The Coral Peigoes chirped like little chicks after us, causing Igarashi to wince in pain as if someone was pulling her hair from behind. I couldn't blame her; they were very cute.

A walking path wound through the forest covering the majority of the islet. Water apparently sprang up from deep within the forest and flowed through it, not quite deeply enough to be called a small river, but more like a shallow brook that trickled over a pebbled path. Cion looked thirsty, so I pulled out a Mid-grade Appraisal Scroll from my pouch and examined the stream. It turned out to be good, safe drinking water with a low mineral content, and we took a break to let Cion quench her thirst.

"There are so many huge trees here; it feels almost mystical. I can't see hardly any animals, and it's so quiet...," said Igarashi.

"I guess it's no surprise this place is called the Islet of Illusion. You can see some traces of where they started cutting trees for lumber, but it looks like they gave up on that pretty quickly... Do you think that's because the Guild decided to use it as a health resort?"

"Maybe that's it. They do have a map, so I suppose they did explore the entire island, but..." We'd been able to bring up a map of the island on our licenses as soon as we first arrived. Apparently, all labyrinths under the Guild's management shared this feature.

"Oh! Arihito, great job in the game," said Madoka in greeting.

"Mr. Atobe, you have impeccable timing. I was with Ms. Theresia until just a moment ago. We found a small spring farther back in the woods. She's waiting there for you now," said Seraphina.

"Atobe, since we're all here, want me to see who else might want to join us on a little seeking?"

"...You're curious, too, aren't you, Igarashi?" I asked her with a laugh. She smiled shyly; I could tell she wanted to see if we could find the Coral Peigo Named Monster.

"I won't go too far looking for it, of course. And if we don't find it, I promise I'll switch gears and focus only on relaxing."

"This sounds intriguing. May I be of service in some way?" asked Seraphina.

"If you're looking for something, I'll use the Merchant's Glass Arihito gave me and do my best to help, too!" added Madoka. She and Seraphina seemed up for an adventure. I explained the gist of what we'd heard and how we wanted to look for a Named Monster on the islet, even though we knew we didn't have much chance of finding one just by looking for it. The group had agreed earlier to have recreational time between lunch and dinner, so we decided whoever felt up to it could join us.

Louisa appreciated how easy it was to avoid getting a sunburn on this islet and had been resting on a chaise lounge chair while the rest of us played volleyball. It seemed Melissa also loved basking in the sun. She'd taken a little rest after playing and gotten sleepy, so she stayed behind relaxing with Louisa.

The weather was perfect, neither hot nor cold, and we saw only a few animals every once in a while. But above all else, I was grateful there were no insects. We'd all embarked on our walks in our swimsuits, so we lucked out in not having to worry about bug bites.

"...Wow, I've gone pretty far in," I muttered to myself. I'd split with Igarashi and the others and started on my way to meet up with Theresia but couldn't seem to find her. Seraphina I could understand, but surprisingly not even Madoka had seemed tired, even though they had both gone all the way to the spring and back. I also felt it was odd how little the exercise was getting to me. Maybe it was difficult to feel tired unless I lost vitality?

The trickle winding through the forest grew deep enough to

call a proper stream, which I thought might mean I was getting closer to the spring. At one point the path cut off, so I started making my own way through the trees. Just then—

Splash!

—I heard what sounded like water up ahead. I carefully pushed aside the leafy branches blocking my way and approached the source of the noise. I came upon a clearing where I found a crystalline spring about the size of a swimming pool. That's when I saw Theresia's chameleon boots next to the spring.

"—Theresia?!"

There's no way she took those off herself. Something must have happened, I thought, and I couldn't restrain myself from calling out for her. In an instant, a wave began to ripple over the spring—I heard a loud splash, and something came flying out from the water.

"……"

"…There…sia?"

No doubt about it, the person standing in front of me was Theresia all right. I gathered she'd taken off her boots so she could swim in the spring. Water drip-dropped from the wet black hair peeking out from underneath her lizard hood. I'd seen her in her swimsuit in the bath, but she looked totally different now; the scenic wooded spring gave her a certain mystique.

"…!"

Theresia shook herself from side to side, though of course that wasn't enough to get all the water off. Some of it landed on me, but

I didn't mind too much. It felt relatively warm—a perfect temperature for swimming.

"......"

"O-oh, it's okay if I get a little wet... Theresia, you sure you
don't want to dry off?" I asked and handed her the towel I'd
brought just in case I decided to go for a swim. She tucked the
towel under her hood and patted her hair dry a bit but didn't seem
to care for much more and handed it back to me.

"......"

"Wh-what's wrong? It looks like you're hesitating to suggest
something..."

We went everywhere together, so a little time apart every
once in a while could do us some good... At least, that's what I'd
thought, and it looked like she'd read my mind.

"The water's so clear... I definitely get why you'd want to take
a dip."

"......"

Theresia looked back at the water, slowly lifted her right hand
up, and pointed toward the deeper part of the spring. As clear as
the water was, we still couldn't see all the way to the bottom.

"Did you find something in there?"

She nodded, then started to head back in but stopped herself,
turned around, and reached her right hand out to me.

"...You want to show me what you found?"

She nodded once more. If that's what she wanted, it was time
for me to lose the shirt. I placed it on top of a nearby larger rock,

hoping I wouldn't scare the others when they came, the way I'd been scared when I found Theresia's boots.

"......"

"Ohhh, these? They had them on sale at the hotel. I'm glad I wore them just in case."

Theresia stared straight at me. I felt a little unnerved under such close inspection, but I thought I had a pretty normal body type. If anything, I'd say I'd somehow gained a little muscle since coming to the Labyrinth Country. I guess fighting monsters was a good workout, too.

"......"

"Let me warm up a bit before I jump in... If I get a cramp, I'll be a burden." Theresia shook her head in response, then started doing warm-ups with me. She looked like she was learning by imitation, stretching and bending her legs as I did.

"You were just swimming so you probably don't need this. But you didn't want to leave me alone, huh?"

"......"

She didn't answer but bent down to touch her toes like me—and made me realize these moves were a little dicey for someone in a swimsuit. A few gaps had opened up in different places and, depending on the angle, came close to revealing what lay underneath.

"I think we're good now. Shall we get in?"

I started getting the limbs farthest from my heart used to the water. It was cool to the touch but perfect for swimming. Theresia slid silently into the water. This time I imitated her and carefully tiptoed deeper into the spring—but slipped on the pebbles under my feet and lost my balance.

"Bwaah—!"

"...!"

I thought I'd be okay since it wasn't that deep, but Theresia jumped to my rescue as soon as I fell into the water.

"...Yeah, sorry, Theresia... That was a little careless of me."

"......"

She held me up, made sure I could properly stand, then slowly backed away. I looked into the water and saw Theresia kicking her legs to tread. Was she doing that instinctively? Or had she swum like that before?

"......"

"I'm okay; it's not like I can't swim. Can you take me to what you found?"

Theresia nodded in response, then swam the breaststroke deeper into the spring. I followed after her with a freestyle stroke, keeping my head above water. I knew it was risky to swim somewhere monsters could appear, but I didn't sense anything around me. Theresia had her Scout Range Extension 1, too, so she would most likely be able to notice right away should anything approach. She turned around to look at me once we made it to the deepest part of the spring.

"......"

"Is it below us? I guess we'll have to dive down..."

I kicked myself for not asking our resident swimming expert

Ryouko to come with me. She had said she was going to relax with Louisa after volleyball, though, and I'd have felt bad waking her up from a nap.

"…All right, let's see what's down there."

Theresia nodded, took a deep breath, and dived beneath the surface; I followed close behind. I couldn't open my eyes at first but then forced myself to try. Light streamed in through the pure water, making everything look vibrantly blue. Theresia took me by the hand and led me deeper through the crystal-clear water. I was shocked lizardmen were such deft swimmers but managed to keep up by kicking my legs behind me like fins.

…! This is—!

The spring was much deeper than I'd thought. It hadn't looked nearly this deep when I peered down from the water's edge. No one could have guessed without actually diving down to see. When we finally got to the bottom, I saw the sand had been disturbed in one area, most likely the spot Theresia had been investigating.

Something was down there. But I could only take a cursory look on this dive and started to run out of breath before I saw much of anything.

I—I can't let myself drown here… Can I make it back to the top…?!

"……!"

Theresia saw the danger I was in, took my hand, and pulled me up through the water. Just as we were about to reach the surface, I realized I'd made a grave mistake and felt my consciousness start to slip away.

Part III: Secrets in the Spring

I hear voices.

I knew those voices. That meant I was alive somehow, not in heaven or something. I breathed a huge sigh of relief.

"...Arihito!"

"Arihito, please wake up! If you leave us here, I swear I'll go right after youuu!"

"Arihito! Arihito... Please, open up your eyes... Oh—!"

I cracked open my eyes to find Suzuna sitting right by my side. She leaned over me and became all I could see.

"Thank goodness... Thank goodness, Arihito..."

"I'm sorry... I underestimated how deep the water was and ran out of breath before I made it back to the surface...," I managed to say. Everyone else looked relieved. Anything could have happened in the water. I guess swimming underwater took a bit of getting used to, and I'd gone down too deep on the first try.

"...I'm so glad you're okay... I was so worried..."

"Seriously... Arihito, don't scare us like that."

I heard Igarashi and then Elitia speak. Suzuna calmed down after a minute, then lifted her chin, wiped away tears from her reddened eyes, and smiled shyly.

"Ungh... Where's Theresia...?"

"Hmm? You were all alone when we found you," explained Misaki. "You were just laid out on the ground. We couldn't see any injuries, so it looked like you were sleeping. We were sooo worried..." In other words, I'd only lost consciousness, but I was breathing on my own.

"—Oh! Theresia... I'm glad you're okay," said Igarashi.

"Theresia, did you leave to call for help?" I asked.

"......"

It looked like Theresia had been nearby all along. She came out from behind the trees but immediately hid again as soon as she saw me.

"...? What's wrong with Theresia?" wondered Igarashi.

"Never mind that. Are you all right, Arihito? Do you remember our names?" asked Elitia.

"Yeah, I'm fine. Sorry to worry you..."

"We were really...all so very worried. Mr. Atobe, you need to be very careful and get yourself used to diving underwater in a labyrinth over time," said Ryouko, walking over with Louisa. I tried to get up, but for some reason, they both laid me back down to rest.

"U-ummm... Does that mean it's different from normal swimming?"

"Yes. So I wouldn't say you were careless exactly, but you do need a swimming instructor... You need my skills."

"Some people are more naturally suited for it, like Ms. Theresia appears to be. Unfortunately, our licenses cannot display our aptitude for this task. However, you can avoid drowning in most cases if you have the Diving skill," explained Louisa. She and Ryouko spoke down from either side of me, sounding just like teachers scolding a disobedient student. I couldn't help but feel a little abashed.

So basically, even if you have some breath left, you can still drown if you dive too deep? ...That was a close one. Good thing Theresia's such a natural in the water.

Everyone but Melissa, Cion, and Seraphina had gathered around me. They'd apparently split up to look for me since I had taken so long to return.

"Arihito, you were diving down there, right? Did you find anything?" asked Suzuna.

"Yeah, I was... There's something down at the bottom. Theresia found it and showed it to me. But I didn't have enough time to find out what from a single trip."

Even if there is something down there, we shouldn't be too quick to touch it in case it's dangerous. Still, whatever it is, it didn't set off Theresia's Trap Detection 1, so it's probably not a trap at least. Maybe we shouldn't get too involved... But it would be a shame to just leave it without figuring out what it is, since Theresia found it for us...

As I was thinking along those lines, I suddenly had an idea. Suzuna seemed to think of it at exactly the same moment.

"Arihito, if there really is something down there..."

"Yeah, exactly. We might be able to find out what it is if we use your Morale Discharge."

"Which means... Arihito, you're gonna need me, aren't you...?" Misaki cut in.

"He probably will, but you don't need to be so flirty about it," chided Elitia. Misaki stuck her tongue out at Elitia in protest.

On the third floor of the Field of Dawn, we'd connected

Misaki's Fortune Roll to Suzuna's Moon Reading and discovered the teleportation pad leading to the hidden floor.

Could that combination help us out here, too? Maybe whatever's down there has something to do with why Named Monsters haven't appeared yet... It's possible, at least.

I was pretty sure other Seekers with the Diving skill had come here before, but if the sand had covered anything below and they'd missed it...that could mean there were still secrets to uncover on this islet.

"Atobe, Melissa is making lunch with the Guild employees now. Why don't we touch base for a bit first?" suggested Igarashi.

"Good idea... All right, let's all head back for now."

Theresia kept herself hidden as we all walked back through the path in the woods. I poked my head around a tree she was using as cover, and she looked up at me fearfully. "I'm sorry I worried you, Theresia. I'll be all right as long as I get used to diving bit by bit."

"......"

"Look, I'm just fine... Theresia?"

At that moment, Theresia's lips moved as if to say something, but no sound came out. If I learned to read lips, would I be able to understand her, even if she couldn't speak? Then again, it would probably be difficult to interpret anything from little more than slightly trembling lips.

"......"

"Hmm? ...Wh-what's wrong? You're turning kinda red."

"...!"

Theresia ran off ahead. I was glad to see she had that much energy, but her odd behavior had me a little worried. I retrieved my shirt for the time being and headed back for the beach. As soon as I started walking, I realized something—my cheeks and chest were wet. It was almost as if someone had wiped me off, then touched me again with a wet hand, or dripped water over me.

Nothing beats a barbecue at the beach, and it seems that's just as true in the Labyrinth Country, too. We had a great time grilling fresh fish and meat using a magical grill. We must have gotten a late start on lunch because the sunset had begun to paint the sky by the time we finished cleaning up. I wondered if what I saw sinking into the horizon was the real sun, or a star from a different world that had the same function.

"You found something in the woods...? How very intriguing."

"Your party really is something special, isn't it, Mr. Atobe? Only you would discover something new in this resort the Guild has been using for so long."

I had explained the situation to Seraphina and Adeline and told them I was considering whether to further examine the spring in the woods.

"I'm afraid I would not be able to equip my shield in the water...," said Seraphina.

"I see, that makes sense... I'd thought anyone could swim if Ryouko used her Lecture skill, but I suppose it could be difficult with heavy armor."

"In that case, I'll keep watch here with Seraphina," said Adeline. "If I went by myself while she couldn't go, it'd look like I was being sneaky."

"I—I wouldn't say I share that view... Although, however low the possibility of battle may be, you should always prepare for the worst-case scenario. Mr. Atobe, please take great care in considering your party composition and the armaments you equip."

"Thank you, Seraphina."

She and Adeline left for their room. They would be staying in the two-person room next to mine.

I knew we were taking a risk diving down in nothing but swimwear, so I decided I'd bring at least my slingshot since it most likely would not rust in the water. Most of my party members' armor and equipment would be useless. Anything steel could rust, so Misaki, for example, could only bring her dice; the others faced similar limitations as well.

"Arihito, you really pumped us up during the barbecue... I'm suuuper set to go!"

"Thank you very much, Arihito. We're all ready."

Misaki and Suzuna weren't the only ones. I'd managed to max out everyone's morale, and we were all prepared to set out. I'd asked Madoka and Louisa to stay behind with Seraphina and Adeline, just in case we did end up facing a Named Monster.

```
◆Current Party◆
1: Arihito    ✕★○※      Level 6
2: Theresia   Rogue      Level 6
3: Kyouka     Valkyrie            Level 5
4: Elitia     Cursed Blade        Level 10
5: Misaki     Gambler             Level 5
```

```
6: Suzuna    Shrine Maiden    Level 5
7: Cion      Silver Hound     Level 5
8: Melissa   Dissector        Level 6


Standby Party Member 1: Madoka    Merchant
    Level 4
Standby Party Member 2: Louisa    Receptionist
    Level 4


◆Cooperating Party◆
Party Name: Four Seasons
1: Kaede    Kendo Master          Level 5
2: Ibuki    Karate Master         Level 5
3: Anna     Tennis Player         Level 5
4: Ryouko   Swimming Instructor   Level 5
```

The members of Four Seasons said they wanted to come along, so I added them to our group. We would all essentially have Diving 1 for a limited time after Ryouko used her Lecture skill, meaning we wouldn't run the risk of drowning.

"Hmm, it's getting darker...," I commented.

"It's still pretty light out even with the sun setting. I wonder if we'll be all right with just the light of the moon... Or do you think it'll be too dark in the forest?" asked Igarashi.

"On this islet, it never gets too dark, even after nightfall. One can roam around during the day and at night, which is one of the reasons it's so popular as a health resort," explained Louisa. She was exactly right; we could see well enough that we didn't have to worry about losing our footing. If anything, nightfall served to highlight the illusionary feel of the scenery. Here and there, the undergrowth in the forest shone with a pale luminescent light and swayed gently in the breeze like fireflies.

"Everyone, please do be very careful," said Madoka.

"We rested up all afternoon, so we'll keep each other company and wait for you to come back," added Louisa.

"We'll be back as quickly as we can. All right, see you two later," I said, and we all set out for the forest. It turned out to be bright under the trees as well, so we had no trouble finding the spring again.

However, it looked completely different than under the afternoon sky. Moonbeams shone upon the spring and reflected against the white sand deep below.

"It's stunning... Who could have guessed it'd look like this at night...," said Igarashi, captivated by its beauty. She had on a rather eclectic outfit composed of her swimsuit, sandals, and her spear. Still, we were all in a pretty similar state since nobody else had the luxury of choice, either.

"All right, now let's get ready to swim. You'll be able to hold your breath longer than usual, but please be careful not to go overboard," said Ryouko.

◆Current Status◆
> Ryouko activated Lecture: Diving 1 ⟶ Target: Arihito's Party, Four Seasons

```
> ARIHITO activated OUTSIDE ASSIST
> ARIHITO activated CHARGE ASSIST ──→ RYOUKO recovered
  magic
```

"Th-thank you very much… Mr. Atobe. This is amazing; I used so much magic, but you filled me up again so quickly."

"It's nothing—don't mention it. It's all thanks to you that we can even swim, you know."

The Scholar's Ankh I had hanging from a string around my neck activated after I used Outside Assist and helped me recover some of my magic. This was a huge help; it restored about one third of the magic I shared with Ryouko. I took a swig of a Mid-grade Mana Potion to bring my magic back up to max just in case. Then we all stepped into the water. The whole spring shone with light, making it easy for us to wade in without much hesitation.

"This is kind of cool, like a fun night activity," said Misaki. "And it's not even scary like a dare."

"A pure spirit flows through this spring. I don't believe a monster would be living in here…," added Suzuna. This could be a dead end in terms of finding that Named Monster if that were true, but I still wanted to try and uncover the secrets this spring held.

"We'll start diving around here. Don't push yourselves too much, all right?" I called out to everyone.

Ryouko and Theresia took the lead and I followed. The bottom had felt so far away the first time I'd dived down, but this time I made it to the spot we wanted to inspect without feeling out of breath thanks to Ryouko's Diving 1.

I looked over at Misaki, who made an *okay* circle with her pointer finger and thumb in response. Suzuna nodded as if to say, *I'm ready when you are,* and then—

◆Current Status◆
> Misaki activated Fortune Roll ⟶ Next action will succeed automatically
> Suzuna activated Moon Reading ⟶ Success

"...?!"

All the moonlight streaming in through the water seemed to gather around Suzuna and envelop her in a bluish-white light, transforming her into an angelic vision. She stretched out her hand toward the streambed where sand had once again buried and hidden our prior discovery. Then, as if responding to her call, five points began to shine in the ground. We split up and dug around those spots—and uncovered five round marble slabs that someone, or something, must have buried.

What do we do with these...? Nothing happens when we touch them. Do their positions mean anything? Or did we fail to meet some requirement? ...Hmm?

I felt a tap on my shoulder while I was thinking. It was Igarashi. She pointed toward Suzuna, who was swimming straight for the rocks on the floor, her hand outstretched.

Suzuna... Does she know what we have to do? Does Moon Reading reveal that much to her...?

A beam of light shone forth from Suzuna's hand and pierced

through the water. She aimed it at one marble slab, then the next, drawing some sort of figure in light. The moment she finished, we realized what it was: a pentagram. Traces of light floated up from the circle, enclosing the star shape within.

"You are all about to be forcibly teleported. Dear devotee, you must try not to separate from your party members."

...! Everyone, grab the hand of the person next to you!

I had no way of knowing if they got my message through the water, but I followed Ariadne's advice and grabbed hold of someone's hand so we wouldn't get split up.

A bright light covered everything before my eyes, and I felt like I was floating. The next second, I realized I'd been whisked away to a forest somewhere.

"...A-Arihito, what the hell just happened to us...?"

"I'm terribly sorry, Arihito... I instinctively took your hand..."

"Ruff!"

It was just Kaede, Anna, Cion, and me. Cion had been swimming after us and must have been close by. I tried checking where the other members were on my license, but all it said was Currently on the Islet of Illusion: First Floor. I pulled up the map and couldn't believe my eyes—we'd landed in an unexplored area far away from the Islet of Illusion.

"...What you saw was a teleportation mechanism. And we are now standing on a totally different island," I explained.

"A different island... W-was that even on the map?" asked Kaede.

"So in other words...this labyrinth is actually a vast ocean studded with islands? It was probably originally explored by ship, so unless you teleport, you wouldn't be able to make it here..."

I agreed with Anna's theory. Luckily, the landscape was very similar to the first island, so we could still see well enough around us, even though we were in the middle of the woods.

"In that case, ya think that means the others got blown away to some other place on this island, too? Maybe we can yell for them... No, I guess that'd be risky if there were monsters around," said Kaede.

"True. Let's take a careful look around this area. If it doesn't seem like we'll find anybody, we'll... Actually, no, I have a feeling they're close."

"Seriously? Arihito, you got a sixth sense or something? I don't feel a thing."

"Cion just came out of the water, so her sense of smell looks like it isn't working yet, but she should recover soon." Cion seemed to understand she shouldn't make any loud noises. She didn't bark at all but shook her body to dry off, sending water everywhere. Kaede removed the wooden katana she had hung on a string from her back and wiped it to remove the moisture. Anna's racket appeared to be water-resistant, so she was able to use it without any issue. I was pretty sure my sling would also be all right, but I wiped it off too just in case.

"Arihito, d'ya think it might be a good idea to redo our formation in case we run into a monster?" asked Kaede.

"Not a bad idea... Could you all try to stay in front of me? I'd appreciate it if you could keep that in mind."

"Understood, I'll make sure to keep ahead of you," said Anna.

"Guess me and Cion'll be up in front, then."

With Cion and Kaede taking up the vanguard, Anna the mid-guard, and me bringing up the rear, we began to make our way through the forest. I could vaguely sense the rest of the group off in two different directions, both of which took us deeper into the woods.

"Think we could get our bearings by looking at the stars? ...Probably not, huh?" wondered Kaede.

"We don't even know if the sun rises in the east... In any case, we can't tell which direction we're heading since we teleported here," said Anna.

"Actually, if my license is correct, we're headed northwest."

"Oh yeah, I'd forgotten it could do that. Good thing we don't need a compass."

"Our licenses so often impress me. The Guild must have gathered its members' skill sets to make them, don't you—?" Cion had been leading the way and cut Anna off by picking up speed and turning back to look at us. It looked like she'd found something. When we caught up to her, we saw a huge impression in the ground: an enormous groove that divided into three branches.

"Is this...? Could it be a footprint?"

"I-it's friggin' huge... Think it's fresh?"

"This looks like Coral Peigo tracks but exponentially bigger...," said Anna. "If this is any indication of how large the monster is..."

The Named Monster was somewhere on this island. I decided to take a look at our surroundings with the Owl Scope I'd brought along with my weapon.

"...There's a clearing up ahead. Looks like there's some water there, too."

"So, like...a watering hole that monsters use?"

"Let's proceed very carefully," cautioned Anna. "We have no choice but to continue exploring this island if we are ever to return to the Islet of Illusion."

"We still have the Return Scroll as a last resort if we need it, so let's not do anything too drastic," I said. The scroll still worked, even when wet. Older models were apparently useless if submerged in water, but the new ones had been upgraded to avoid that kind of problem.

"Arihito, you're a regular Mary Poppins. All I got is my wooden sword..."

"I believe we may have been a little lax in our preparations..."

"'Better safe than sorry' is my motto...but even I wasn't prepared for this much adventure."

We could've enjoyed a simple day of rest and said good-bye to this labyrinth, but the fact that we didn't all but proves we're workaholics. I guess Seekers just can't let loose, even on days off.

I walked up next to Cion and took a look through the Owl Scope. I was still checking if it was water-resistant, but so far, I could use it without issue.

"...Hmm?" I felt like I saw something dash across my line of sight. I moved the scope around to check, but nothing popped up.

"Arihito, see anythin'...?"

"Yeah... There's definitely something up there."

"...We're about to encounter a strange monster while seeking in a mysterious land... It's a bit scary yet, at the same time, rather exciting... Do you think that's a touch reckless of me?" Anna asked. She always spoke with restraint beyond her years, but I guess she also had a curious nature more appropriate for her age.

"Not at all. I think you're much better off just enjoying it instead of worrying about that... Of course, we don't often have that kind of mental space when we're fighting for our lives."

"Heh-heh...true that," said Kaede. "I gotta say I'm pretty glad I followed you here, too. Beach volleyball is great and all, but getting flown off to new places and seeking together is fun, too, ya know?"

"...This will serve as a fond memory someday, if we make it back safely. But now I must brace myself." Anna gripped her racket tightly. She'd removed the tennis ball that'd been tied to it in case she needed to use it.

"Do you only need the one ball?" I asked.

"Yes, I can activate my skills and use it several times without breaking it."

"Anna's ball always returns to her hand, so she's good with just one. She's playing tennis, but it's like she's using magic."

I had seen it once for myself already and was yet again counting on Anna's skills to be an asset in battle. We'd ideally be able to hold off on fighting until we met up with the others, but we'd have to make it through the clearing up ahead first.

"Cion, if we run into an enemy, make sure you hang back and get a feel for it first. It's too dangerous to rush in," I warned. She wagged her tail in response and led us onward. It was tough going walking around the footprint; one false step could send us tumbling.

Finally, we made it out of the forest into a meadow next to a river. We would have no trouble finding our friends if they came here.

"What the—? It looks like we just stepped into some sorta hunting game... Everything 'bout this looks mad suspicious."

"I think the others are probably somewhere down that trail over there... We've got no choice but to cut through here."

"Ufff!" Cion tried to respond without barking and instead let out something more like a sneeze. I was so impressed at how smart she was, I couldn't help but smile. Still, Anna was exactly right; we needed to be on guard now more than ever. We cautiously stepped out into the meadow. Then, as we were making our way forward—

"...Th-the heck's over there? ...A shadow or somethin'?"

"Hmm...?"

A faint shadow now loomed over the meadow. I was sure it hadn't been there a moment ago. A chill ran down my spine.

"—KRAAAAH!!!"

Something came crashing down from the sky and emitted an earsplitting birdlike cry. Whatever this something was, it had been using a skill to conceal its shadow as it flew over us. Now that it had locked onto us as prey, it revealed itself and dived down.

"Cion, get back—!"

"Grrrr...!"

""Eeeeek...!!""

The giant monster landed with a loud thud. The earth shook, and Kaede and Anna screamed.

◆Monster Encountered◆
★Jeweled Wings Dancing over Frozen Wasteland
Level 7
Hostile
Dropped Loot: ???

"...Did that thing...make those footprints...?"

All the Named Monsters we'd fought so far had looked evil, even the Cotton Ball one. But the nine-foot-tall monster that stood before us now, huge as it was, looked just as cute as the Coral Peigoes.

Part IV: Blizzard

"KRAH! KRAH!"

"I-is it just me, or is that thing tryin' to say something?"

The huge penguin covered in fluffy white feathers screeched at us. It looked like a stuffed animal, but as a level-7 Named Monster, we couldn't afford to let our guard slip for even a second.

"I believe it's saying, *I'm surprised you made it this far, O brave humans and dog.*"

"Y-you think…?"

Anna stood there unnerved, closely observing the monster. If that's what she thought it was saying, strange as it might sound, she could be right.

"Bow! Bow!"

"She's saying, *O ruler of this island, if you cross my master, you will pay for it dearly.*"

"Th-that sounds accurate, but isn't that thing gonna think Cion's pickin' a fight…?"

A huge penguin and large dog: I doubted their conversation would actually be that theatrical if translated, but it did feel like Anna had gotten the gist right. As if to prove the point, Cion and the penguin, or Jeweled Wings, as it showed up on my license, both looked ready to pounce at any moment. I guess we weren't getting out of this without a fight.

"—Get ready; it's coming!"

"KRAAAH—!!"

◆Current Status◆
> ★Jeweled Wings Dancing over Frozen Wasteland activated Silver Wonderland ⟶ The landscape was changed to Frozen Soil

The giant penguin, or Jeweled Wings Dancing over Frozen Wasteland, as it was apparently called, hopped up and down and vigorously flapped its wings.

"A-Arihito—! The ground is freezing around its legs…!" cried Kaede.

I would've thought a monster like this would prefer a warm climate given its natural environment, but I was totally off. The white feathers coating this Coral Peigo Named Monster were perfectly adapted for the environment it created by activating its skills.

"Bow! Bow!"

Cion looked strong as ever even in the cold, but the freezing air the penguin spewed drastically dropped the temperature around us so much we could see our breath. At this rate, the cold would quickly drain our body heat and slow us down.

"Looks like we'll have to put an end to this quickly…," said Anna.

"Or hold it off until the others get here. It's a higher level than us, and a Named Monster to boot… A single blow could take us out," I countered.

"Its beak looks real sharp, too. We're gonna have to stay on our toes and make sure it doesn't get a good shot at us… Arihito, I don't care who I'm up against, I can *always* land the first strike—just say the word." I had a fairly good grip on Kaede's and Anna's fighting styles, but with the ground frozen, we ran the risk of losing our footing if we rushed in.

"KRAH! KRAH!" Jeweled Wings cried in a lower voice, as if to say, *Now that I've frozen it, this field is mine.*

"—Grrrr…!"

◆Current Status◆
> CION activated HEAT CLAW

Cion decided on her own to activate the fire garnet on her Insect-Repelling Anklet. At that, the frozen soil around her paws began to thaw, and steam rose up from the ground.

Go for it, Cion…!

I winked at Cion, and she knew exactly what I wanted her to do: strike while our enemy still thought it had the upper hand. If this battle proved too difficult, we could always consider retreating, but I wanted to do whatever we could first.

"—Kaede, get on Cion's back!"

"…O-okay! —Whoaaa!"

Cion set off running, showing no signs of slipping on the ice. She scooped up Kaede and charged at Jeweled Wings. Her speed caught the monster off guard and stalled its reaction, giving Kaede enough time to prepare her stance and get a firm grip on her wooden sword. I took my sling and got ready to try the new stone I'd just added to it: the manipulation stone.

"—Hyaaa! Eat this!"

"Cooperation Support…vanguards!"

◆Current Status◆
> CION activated BATTLE HOWL and HOUND GALLOP ⟶
  Vanguards' attack power increased
CION's speed increased

> KAEDE activated KAKEGOE ⟶ Intimidated ★JEWELED
  WINGS DANCING OVER FROZEN WASTELAND
> ARIHITO activated COOPERATION SUPPORT 1 and ATTACK
  SUPPORT 2 ⟶ Support Type: FORCE SHOT (DOLL)
> CION activated HEAT CLAW ⟶ Hit ★JEWELED WINGS
  DANCING OVER FROZEN WASTELAND
Combined attack stage 1
> KAEDE activated SHITSURAITOU ⟶ ★JEWELED WINGS DANCING
  OVER FROZEN WASTELAND was STUNNED
Combined attack stage 2
> ATTACK SUPPORT 2 activated 2 times ⟶ Accrued
  manipulation points over ★JEWELED WINGS DANCING
  OVER FROZEN WASTELAND
> Cooperation Attack: RED HOT THUNDER STRIKE ⟶ Hit
  ★JEWELED WINGS DANCING OVER FROZEN WASTELAND
★JEWELED WINGS DANCING OVER FROZEN WASTELAND was BURNED
STUN time extended

"KRAAAAH—!!"

Our first combination attack went off perfectly. Cion ran at
Jeweled Wings and scratched up the monster, while Kaede rode on
her back and fired off strike after strike with her wooden sword.
She was so quick I could barely see her. The manipulation stone, it
turned out, wasn't a one-and-done deal, but would only work after
several hits. It looked like each successive hit would help Force
Shot deal a stronger blow, though with less additional power than
when I used Attack Support 1. The slingshot really couldn't compare to Murakumo in terms of decisive force.

"—Anna, time for us to bust in!"

"Okay! ...Here I go!" She tossed the tennis ball in the air and swung the racket we'd used lumber from Thunder Head to make. I didn't know if she'd activated a special skill, but for a second, it looked like the racket flashed a bolt of lightning as she struck.

"Cooperation Support...rearguards!"

◆Current Status◆
> Arihito activated Cooperation Support 1 and Attack
  Support 2 —→ Support Type: Force Shot (Stun)
> Arihito activated Force Shot (Stun) —→ Hit ★Jeweled
  Wings Dancing over Frozen Wasteland
Stun time increased
Combined attack stage 1
> Anna activated Thunder Shot —→ Hit ★Jeweled Wings
  Dancing over Frozen Wasteland
Weak spot attack
Caused Electrocution
Stun time increased
Combined attack stage 2
> Combined attack: Force, Thunder —→ Hit ★Jeweled
  Wings Dancing over Frozen Wasteland
Electrocution time increased

"KRAAAH—!!"

"—We did it...!" Anna yelled after seeing the damage we'd inflicted. Her special racket attack didn't just deal a lightning-type strike. It also added on an electric shock, an extremely useful means to safely take down an enemy.

"Arihito! I'm goin' in for one more...!"

"—Wait, Kaede! Back up now!"

"...!"

Some of the feathers covering Jeweled Wings's body stood up and turned blue. We'd driven it into a corner so quickly it'd realized we could not be taken lightly. White spots started appearing on the blue feathers; the moisture in the air froze and shrouded the monster's entire body like a suit of armor.

"Arihito...!"

"—KRAAAH!"

At the first sight of danger, there was only ever one choice to make—the safest one.

Please, let me make it in time...!

◆Current Status◆

> ★Jeweled Wings Dancing over Frozen Wasteland activated Blanket Of Snow ⟶ Transformed to Frosted status
> ★Jeweled Wings Dancing over Frozen Wasteland's status ailments were removed
> Cion activated Step Back
> Arihito activated Rear Stance ⟶ Target: Cion
> ★Jeweled Wings Dancing over Frozen Wasteland activated Frozen Pain ⟶ Ice Thorns sprouted from Frozen Soil

Jeweled Wings let out a piercing cry, and it felt as though the air around me froze. Instantly, icy spikes started shooting out of the frozen ground one after the other.

"...Arihito, are you all right?!"

"Yeah, I'm fine...! It's using the soil to attack... We'll be at a disadvantage if we fight on frozen ground...!"

I immediately picked up Anna and used Rear Stance, then transported us behind Cion, who had escaped the enemy's range of attack. Just a split second later and we would've been hit with those thorns that shot out from the ground. They probably wouldn't have skewered us, but if we'd caught one in our leg, it would've definitely taken us out of the battle.

"A-Arihito... I'm fine now, if you'll put me down..."

"All right, everyone, stay out of its range of attack and give me a second! I'm going to check it out!"

"—No, don't! It's too dangerous to split up...!" cried Kaede.

"If I need to, I can dodge in an instant like you just saw... With the ground like this, we've got no choice but to shoot at it long-distance!" I started running, avoiding the frozen areas and making my way around to the other side of the ice thorns to Jeweled Wings.

Maybe we should give up this fight and run... No, I can feel the others getting closer. I need to find out what this thing's got up its sleeve before they get here...!

"KRAAAH...!"

◆Current Status◆
> ARIHITO loaded MAGIC GUN with DARK BULLET STONE
> ARIHITO fired DARKNESS BULLET
> ★JEWELED WINGS DANCING OVER FROZEN WASTELAND activated
  WINGED PARRY

> Arihito's attack hit ★Jeweled Wings Dancing over Frozen
  Wasteland
Weak spot attack
Caused Electrocution

"KRAAAAH...!!"

Jeweled Wings flapped its wings ferociously, but the bullets the magic gun shot out inflicted a magical attack, not a physical one. Maybe that was why it failed to neutralize the black lightning that Electrocuted and slowed down the creature. It looked like we would be able to maintain the upper hand as long as Anna and I alternated attacks and kept delivering electric shocks to the enemy. And once Igarashi joined us, she could also hit its weak spot with her Lightning Rage.

Actually...it looks a little shaken since it misread that attack... No, this isn't the time for wishful thinking...! It's gotta have some way to attack us, even with all those spikes on the ground. There's ice covering its stomach, so maybe it can slide over the ground like a sled. Then again, that's the trouble with monsters in the Labyrinth Country—they never do what you'd expect.

"VRROO... VRROORROO..."

It sounded like the massive penguin monster was blowing a whistle whenever breath leaked out through its beak, possibly due to the electric shock. But it never let its guard down or became any less hostile toward us. Then it let out a loud, clear cry that echoed through the meadow.

◆Current Status◆
> ★Jeweled Wings Dancing over Frozen Wasteland activated
  Snow Powder ⟶ Ice Thorns were destroyed
A Blizzard broke out
> ★Jeweled Wings Dancing over Frozen Wasteland activated
  Snow White

"KRAAAAH...!!"

".......!!"

The ice thorns exploded into powdered snow that blocked everything from view. A glittering white blizzard instantly filled the sky and shrouded Jeweled Wings from our sight.

"—Arihito, on your right!"

Even Hawk Eyes couldn't detect it. I suddenly sensed a murderous spirit on my right and reacted as quickly as I could, cocking my gun loaded with dark bullet stones. But I never pulled the trigger, because what I saw when I turned to the right looked like a hazy ghost in the shape of a Coral Peigo.

"Arihito...!"

"Arihitooo...!!"

I sensed that murderous spirit now coming from my left. I'd seen nothing but empty space there a second earlier, but now Jeweled Wings was right there and just about to open its beak.

"Woof!"

◆Current Status◆
> Cion activated Covering ⟶ Target: Arihito

> Arihito activated Defense Support 1 ⟶ Target: Cion
> ★Jeweled Wings Dancing over Frozen Wasteland activated
  White Breath ⟶ Hit Cion
> Cion was Frozen

"Yiiip...!"

"—Cion!"

Cion let Kaede off her back and jumped in between me and Jeweled Wings. White Breath blew over the right half of her body, instantly freezing it. Yet Jeweled Wings showed no mercy and raised its wings to follow up with yet another blow.

"—Hyaaaa!"

"I won't let you...!"

◆Current Status◆
> Kaede activated Kakegoe ⟶ Intimidated ★Jeweled
  Wings Dancing over Frozen Wasteland
> Kaede activated Enhi ⟶ Hit ★Jeweled Wings Dancing
  over Frozen Wasteland
> Anna activated Thunder Shot ⟶ Hit ★Jeweled Wings
  Dancing over Frozen Wasteland
Weak spot attack
Caused Electrocution
★Jeweled Wings Dancing over Frozen Wasteland's attack was
  canceled

"KRAAAAH...!!"

"—Grrrrr!!"

◆Current Status◆
> Cɪᴏɴ activated Hᴇᴀᴛ Cʟᴀᴡ ⟶ Cɪᴏɴ's Fʀᴏᴢᴇɴ status
  was removed
> Cɪᴏɴ activated Wᴏʟғ Sʟᴀsʜ ⟶ ★Jᴇᴡᴇʟᴇᴅ Wɪɴɢs Dᴀɴᴄɪɴɢ
  ᴏᴠᴇʀ Fʀᴏᴢᴇɴ Wᴀsᴛᴇʟᴀɴᴅ evaded

Its attack disrupted, Jeweled Wings leaned backward. In that brief pause, Cion activated her fire garnet and used the heat to melt away her Frozen status. She immediately lunged at the retreating enemy, but Jeweled Wings had already faded into the blizzard.

"Everyone, get back into position! It's using some kind of illusion to get your attention, then attack your blind spot! Don't get distracted!"

"—KRAAAH!!"

"......!!"

◆Current Status◆
> ★Jᴇᴡᴇʟᴇᴅ Wɪɴɢs Dᴀɴᴄɪɴɢ ᴏᴠᴇʀ Fʀᴏᴢᴇɴ Wᴀsᴛᴇʟᴀɴᴅ attacked
  ⟶ Kᴀᴇᴅᴇ evaded

"I dodged it...somehow...!"

Kaede's quick reflexes allowed her to evade Jeweled Wings even after she noticed its presence. However, it disappeared into the driving snow the next second and denied her the chance for a counterattack. I recovered the damage Cion had taken as best I could with Recovery Support 1, but she still wasn't back to full health.

I knew our friends would reach us if we could hold on just a little longer. I thought we might be able to kill time if we focused only on evading Jeweled Wings's attacks, but the freezing climate it had created was definitely slowing us down.

...What's going on? It's not attacking... What's it doing...?

I'd thought Jeweled Wings was using the blizzard for both defense and offense, blocking our line of sight and having the phantom enemies disturb our concentration. But we could now see several of those phantom bodies playfully dancing amid the snow and howling winds. Jeweled Wings's eyes glinted sharply over the scene, warning us not to invade its playground.

"KRAAAH!"

◆Current Status◆
> ★Jeweled Wings Dancing over Frozen Wasteland activated
  Blizzard Blossom Isle ⟶ ★Jeweled Wings Dancing over
  Frozen Wasteland's attack and defense power and
  agility increased
Acquired Dancing Shadows status

"Wh-what the hell are those...?!"

Jeweled Wings's forehead began to emit a red light from the other side of the blizzard curtain. Then, the feathers on its head stood up, and the monster that had looked like a baby chick at once transformed into a fully grown southern rockhopper penguin.

"...KRAH... KRAAHH...!!"

Its White Breath added to the already freezing winds crackling the air as they whipped around its body. They looked cold enough to freeze you with a single touch. Snow White, it appeared, was nothing more than a first step needed to prepare for this move. Faint, white, shadowy Coral Peigoes danced around the monster as if frolicking in the snow.

"...Is it playing...with the shadows it made...?"

Anna saw the same thing I did. This was no trick of the imagination, nor were we overthinking things. Even though it was still engaging us in battle, it looked like Jeweled Wings was enjoying the ghostly figures it'd summoned in the likeness of its own species.

I wouldn't be surprised if it had Coral Peigoes following it since it's a Named Monster version. But it's the only one here...and I don't see any other Coral Peigoes coming out, either.

What did this mean? I knew I shouldn't be trying to walk a mile in my enemy's shoes as I fought it, but I couldn't stop the thought from crossing my mind.

"D'ya think...it's lonely? So lonely it'd make its own friends, even though they're just dumb shadows...?"

"...It's possible. But first things first, we need to find a way to survive this."

"True... Plus, I think we're kinda trapped...!"

The warm woods we'd been walking through that night now opened up by the riverbed into a massive snowscape. At some point in the chaos, we'd lost sight of anything past the sheets of falling snow. I had no idea what the scene looked like from the outside, but it seemed we wouldn't be able to escape this arena Jeweled Wings had cordoned off so easily.

"...Bow!"

Cion's determination never wavered despite our dire situation. She really was built for snow country, silver fur and all. But I couldn't have her draw the enemy's attack; it was too dangerous. At the same time, we had to find a way out of this. The shadowy figures dancing around Jeweled Wings could still throw us off, and we had no idea what other powers they might have. No matter how many there were, we had to make it through the first strike. Everything else counted on it.

"—Anna, let's start with a long-range attack!"

"...Here I go...!"

◆Current Status◆
> Arihito activated Attack Support 2 ⟶ Support
   Type: Force Shot (Doll)
> Anna activated Thunder Shot ⟶ ★Jeweled Wings Dancing
   over Frozen Wasteland evaded
> ★Jeweled Wings Dancing over Frozen Wasteland's Dancing
   Shadows status was strengthened

"—I missed...?!"

The ball Anna shot directly at Jeweled Wings cut through one of its ghostly dancers instead. The real Jeweled Wings danced in the field and cast a swaying shadow over the battlefield, just as its name foretold.

"—Wooof!"

"Cion, wait!"

Cion charged over the snow to fulfill her role as vanguard. She slashed with her claws mid-jump yet had no better luck and hit nothing but the illusions.

"Grrr...!!"

"Dodge it, Cion!"

◆Current Status◆
> ★Jeweled wings Dancing over Frozen Wasteland activated Ice Scraper ⟶ Dancing Shadows activated 2 additional attacks

Jeweled Wings raised its bright white beak and plunged it downward. The white dancing ghosts gathered together to form two giants as big as Jeweled Wings itself and proceeded to surround Cion.

"—Ariadne, I request your help!" I shouted.

◆Current Status◆
> Arihito activated Defense Support 1 ⟶ Target: Cion
> Arihito requested temporary support from Ariadne ⟶ Target: Cion
> Ariadne activated Guard Arm
> Ice Scraper attacked Guard Arm
2 stages hit
> Ice Scraper hit Cion
Damage reduced by half
> Cion was Frozen

"Yiiip…!!"

Ariadne's Guard Arm managed to block only two of the blows—one of the giant clones jabbed Cion with its sharp beak and sent her flying.

"—Cion!"

"—Kaede, Anna, please! We can't let this chance Cion gave us go to waste!"

"…Hyaaaaa!!"

◆Current Status◆
> ARIHITO activated COOPERATION SUPPORT 1 and ATTACK
   SUPPORT 2 ⟶ Support Type: FORCE SHOT (DOLL)
> KAEDE activated NIDAN–TSUKI ⟶ 2 stages hit
   ★JEWELED WINGS DANCING OVER FROZEN WASTELAND
Combined attack stage 1
> ANNA activated THUNDER SHOT ⟶ Hit ★JEWELED WINGS
   DANCING OVER FROZEN WASTELAND
Caused ELECTROCUTION
Combined attack stage 2
> Combined attack: TWIN, THUNDER ⟶ Hit ★JEWELED
   WINGS DANCING OVER FROZEN WASTELAND
Weak spot attack
ELECTROCUTION time extended
> ATTACK SUPPORT 2 activated 3 times ⟶ Hit ★JEWELED
   WINGS DANCING OVER FROZEN WASTELAND
Manipulation points accrued

"KRAAAAAH…AHH…"

Jeweled Wings stumbled under the onslaught of attacks. The

electric-type strikes had an immediate effect—they split open the feathers forming a sort of crest on its head with a loud crackle. Kaede went in with a multiple-stage attack, which also increased the number of support attacks. I could feel something building up in the magical bullets powered by the manipulation stone.

"KRA...KRAAAH..."

"H-hey, looks like it's gettin' tired... Think we can push it over the edge...?"

"—KRAAAH!" cried Jeweled Wings, as if to deny what Kaede had said. Just then, the dancing shadows gathered around it and formed an orderly formation.

◆Current Status◆
> ★Jeweled Wings Dancing over Frozen Wasteland activated Battle Formation: Deadly Wing ⟶ All attack power increased and defense decreased

"—Oh no...! It's...!"

◆Current Status◆
> Anna activated Assess Battle ⟶ Predicted ★Jeweled Wings Dancing over Frozen Wasteland's next move: Attack will be extremely dangerous

I felt it just as Anna called out to warn us: Jeweled Wings had abandoned its defenses in order to build up and deal some kind of blow that would wipe us all out. Its cute appearance and somewhat human mannerisms aside, this was still a monster. And monsters were driven to take out Seekers by any means necessary.

But still...what is this feeling I'm getting...?

I didn't know if we should kill it. Sure, this thing hurt Cion and was building up another attack right before my eyes, yet doubts still crept into my mind. All those Coral Peigoes at the ranch...and this Named Monster no one had seen for ages, stranded on this island. It'd been alone for so long that it had summoned snowy replacements for its lost brethren.

By all rights, shouldn't it be with its own kind? What if something had torn them apart, leaving the Named Monster here all alone on this island?

"—Are you stuck here without your family?! We could take you to them!"

"...KRAH..."

Jeweled Wings cried in a low voice as if it'd already made its decision. Then it covered itself and its clones in ice and started to transform into an enormous bird.

"Arihito, stop! If it comes at us like that, we're all done for...!" Kaede yelled out. I knew it wasn't particularly wise for the rearguard to rush in, but this was the only way I could stop the monster. I had to use Rear Stance to send myself behind Jeweled Wings. But if I failed to cancel its attack, I'd let a vast-ranging assault engulf us all.

A rearguard really is only strong when he's surrounded by fighters. That much is painfully clear. If only we could hold this thing off a little longer...but there's no time left to come up with Plan B.

Part V: Warm Rain

"—Atobe!"

"......!!"

In the split second before I activated Rear Stance, I was sure I heard it—her voice.

◆Current Status◆
> Kyouka activated Thunderbolt ⟶ Hit ★Jeweled Wings
   Dancing over Frozen Wasteland
Weak spot attack
Caused Electrocution
> Theresia activated Accel Dash

Igarashi and Theresia jumped out from the forest behind us. Igarashi's Thunderbolt ripped through the air and rained down upon Jeweled Wings mid-transformation. The Electrocution slowed its progress for just one second, but the brief pause gave Theresia enough time to land the next strike.

"So that's the Coral Peigo Named Monster... You want us to stop it, right...?!"

I didn't even need to explain the situation for Igarashi to figure it out. The moisture in the air around us had begun to freeze over again, and the enormous bird-shaped mass of ice grew larger and larger.

"—Mr. Atobe! Everyone!"

"Arihito!"

That's when Ryouko and Ibuki reached us. Theresia sneaked her way around, stealthily closing the gap between her and the monster. Ryouko had showed up close to the river, meaning she could use *that* skill.

"—Ryouko, shoot an Aqua Dolphin over its head!" I yelled.

"A-all right…!"

"……!"

Theresia read my mind and knew exactly what I wanted her to do—I could feel it. She unleashed her Morale Discharge just before setting up a team attack.

"Cooperation Support…Magic Crossing!"

◆Current Status◆

> THERESIA activated TRIPLE STEAL —→ All party members received TRIPLE STEAL effects

> ARIHITO activated OUTSIDE ASSIST

> ARIHITO activated COOPERATION SUPPORT 1, ATTACK SUPPORT 2 —→ Support Type: FORCE SHOT (DOLL)

> RYOUKO activated AQUA DOLPHIN —→ Hit ★JEWELED WINGS DANCING OVER FROZEN WASTELAND

Combined attack stage 1

> THERESIA activated ACCEL SLASH —→ Hit ★JEWELED WINGS DANCING OVER FROZEN WASTELAND

Weak point attack

Knockback effects nullified

Combined attack stage 2

```
> Combined attack: Azure, Dolphin → Generated Warm
  Rain
Outer layer of ★Jeweled Wings Dancing over Frozen
  Wasteland's Ice Armor destroyed
Dropped materials
> Attack Support 2 activated 2 times →
  Accumulated manipulation points over ★Jeweled
  Wings Dancing over Frozen Wasteland
Manipulation Stone may now be used
> Theresia and Arihito recovered vitality and magic
Successfully stole loot
```

"KRAAAH...?!"

After the dolphin Ryouko made from river water hit Jeweled Wings, Theresia activated the blue flame stone and set her sword aglow with a pale blue light. She sliced through the dolphin, instantly turning it into a warm rain shower with the heat from her blade. At that moment, Ibuki jumped in and pummeled her fists into the remaining ice armor covering Jeweled Wings's body.

"—Haaaah!"

```
◆Current Status◆
> Ibuki activated Rock Crush → Hit ★Jeweled Wings
  Dancing over Frozen Wasteland
Partial damage inflicted
Ice Armor completely destroyed
Dancing Shadows status was removed
```

All of the ice protecting its body splintered and fell away. Jeweled Wings stumbled back one step, then another, then fell flat on its bottom and stopped moving.

"K-KRAH..."

The red light shining from its head disappeared, and the feathers standing up on its head reverted to their former positions. The monster's eyes still flickered with the last remnants of its will to fight, but it could move no longer. Then, as if to signal it'd accepted defeat, the penguin monster hung its head and grew still.

"Haaah, aaah... A-Arihito...I...," panted Ibuki.

"Yeah... Good job making it here, all of you... But please, could you not finish it off just yet?"

The air was still full of steam from Theresia and Ryouko's combined attack, leaving us all soaking wet. But we didn't have time to worry about that.

"Whoaaa! ...I-it's a huuuge penguin...!"

"Thank goodness... I'm glad you're all safe. I'm so sorry we got here late."

"...It's a Named Monster, but I can't harvest it for resources. Too cute."

"Way to go, Arihito... You took complete command, even with new members."

Misaki, Suzuna, Melissa, and Elitia finally caught up with us, and at last we were all together again. I used my Recovery Support on Cion and further healed her wounds. I petted her head as she licked my hand, then stepped closer to Jeweled Wings.

"A-Atobe…are you sure it's okay to get so close?"

"I'm sure… I tested out the manipulation stone during that battle. I think you have to use it a few times first, and it won't necessarily work on everyone, but it looks like I can control…I mean, negotiate with this monster and get it to work with us."

"B-but you're not a Monster Tamer… Can you even do that…?" asked Kaede incredulously. In my understanding, Monster Tamers fought alongside monsters in battle, though it seemed not many reincarnates chose to go into that line of work. We already had experience capturing the Demi-Harpies and others and gotten them to join our team. I was willing to bet any party could get monsters to fight with them, as long as they met the right conditions.

"…Did you guys see any monsters on this island?" I asked the group.

"Now that you mention it…we didn't see anything at all until we got here," replied Igarashi.

"Us neither. We got blown suuuper far away, so it was really hard to get here…," explained Misaki.

"S-same for us," added Ibuki. "Teacher, did you guys run into any other monsters aside from this one?"

We'd been scattered across the island, but no one had seen a single monster. There was very likely nothing here except for Jeweled Wings.

"For some reason or another, this Named Monster was the only creature to appear on this island, and the rest of the Coral Peigoes only exist on the island with our hotel. I think that's why there haven't been Named Monster sightings on the islet," I explained.

"Assuming the Guild didn't know there'd be an island on the other side of the ocean...the theory holds up." Elitia also approached Jeweled Wings, who started to visibly tremble; perhaps it sensed the power in her blade.

"So...if possible, I'd like to spare this little guy and take him back with us. Maybe even reunite him with his friends..."

"Arihito, is that what you had on your mind during that fight? I was in total kill-or-be-killed mode...," said Kaede.

"Me too... I didn't have the composure to think clearly. I jumped at the chance to show you what I could do with my new racket..."

"Well, we had to fight first to use the manipulation stone... Plus, he'd decided we were enemies, too. No matter what brought him here, we only have this chance now because you all worked so hard."

I wanted to make it clear I didn't think it would be easy to capture and get this Named Monster to join us. It hadn't left us a lot of room to pull punches, and I'd chosen all the attacks I'd thought would affect it the most, leaving it heavily wounded as a result. We were betting against the house that this creature would hear us out. It wouldn't shock me if it refused to even listen.

"...Will you come with us? I'll do whatever I can to take you to your friends, but you're gonna have to listen to what we say, even after that."

Jeweled Wings watched me closely through its barely opened eyes. It shifted its wings slightly as if to beat them but, instead of struggling, parted its beak by a hair.

"...KRAH."

◆Current Status◆
> ★JEWELED WINGS DANCING OVER FROZEN WASTELAND is no
  longer hostile
Successfully entered into service

"...Did he just answer you...?"

"I—I think so..."

"Then we need to heal him! He's hurt real bad! And his feathers are all over the plaaace!"

"Some potions are dangerous for monsters, so we need to hurry and get him back to the Islet of Illusion to get him help..."

We had fought this monster practically to its death, and now we were trying to treat its wounds. But none of the members of Four Seasons complained or called it unfair. Kaede turned around to wipe her eyes, and tears welled up in the other three ladies' eyes, too. It was nice to also have this option and not simply defeat every monster we fought. I decided to use Outside Assist on the creature to try to restore its vitality.

"...Whoa... S-sorry, Theresia. I think I used too much magic."

"......"

"I wish we could give you loads of Apples of Wit... I saw a few growing back the way we came," said Igarashi.

"What? ...R-really?"

The others had also seen fruit-bearing trees, though in their rush to get to us, they hadn't had time to pick anything. They went off to bring back what they'd found while I stayed behind and healed Jeweled Wings.

I checked my license to see what we'd picked up when we destroyed Jeweled Wings's Ice Armor and stolen loot through Triple Steal. What I found surpassed my hopes for anything we'd find on this island.

◆Newest Acquisitions◆
> 1 Herculean Walnut
> 2 Apples of Wit
> 1 Nimble Grape
> 2 Frost Stones
> 1 Snow Quartz
> 1 Jeweled Wing Feather

I healed Jeweled Wings until he had a good amount of vitality. After a moment, he got up on his own two legs and started walking off somewhere. We followed after him and eventually came upon a teleportation pad set in the ground. Perhaps he hadn't been able to activate the pad on his own and thought maybe we could do something about it? He couldn't speak our language but had calmed down ever since I restored his vitality and would answer my friends with a "KRAH!" whenever they spoke to him.

Luckily, we didn't need to dive underwater or combine Fortune Roll and Moon Reading this time. We could've used the Return Scroll, but I wanted to find some other way back without relying on that.

The Guild staff members were still up awaiting our arrival when we finally returned to the islet. Their jaws dropped when they first saw Jeweled Wings, but they agreed to lead us to Coral Peigo Ranch once I explained what happened.

"As I mentioned when you visited us this afternoon, in order for the Coral Peigoes to obey your orders, you need to have a White Jeweled Feather. But I never expected you would be able to find one today…"

"KRAH!"

"On top of that, you tamed this Named Monster and brought him back with you. I know I speak for the entire staff when I say we almost fainted at the sight. You really are an incredible band of rookies…," said the Guild staff member in amazement. She looked about the same age as Louisa and exchanged greetings with her after Louisa ran over to us.

"So in regard to how this all played out…," I started, trying to explain what we knew about Jeweled Wings. I wanted to prepare the Guild employees in case another Named Monster showed up on this islet, too. But the woman held up a finger to stop me and smiled.

"That kind of information is as valuable as precious jewels for Seekers. We Guild members must not question you about such matters without offering anything in return. Your only duty in terms of sharing information with us is if it pertains to a stampede."

"…I see. It just feels like we're stealing some secrets and taking them back with us. Are you sure that's all right?"

"Of course, please do not concern yourself with that at all. As long as this Named Monster lives, no others will appear on this island. In other words, we have you to thank for securing our safety... Please allow me to express our appreciation again on behalf of all the members of our staff. I hope you'll consider seeking here once more should you ever have the chance to visit again... But perhaps I shouldn't suggest that, since this is a health resort, after all," she replied and opened the gate to the Coral Peigoes ranch.

"...KRAH!"

"It's okay, go ahead," I reassured Jeweled Wings. He timidly stepped forward and almost got stuck in the gate but managed somehow to pull himself through.

""""Cheeeep!!""""

We could hear the Coral Peigoes' cries coming from inside the ranch. I don't speak Coral Peigo, but even I knew those were shouts of surprise and joy.

"...KRAH..."

Jeweled Wings seemed at a loss as he watched the Coral Peigoes gather around and follow him. He looked just like a parent playing with his children, and the little ones looked like they'd reunited with a long-lost friend.

"...KRAAH!"

"Whoaaa... L-look, Arihito! Gems or something are dripping out of the big penguin's eyes...!" cried Misaki.

"Tears from a Jeweled Wings Dancing over Frozen Wasteland turn into gems called Snow Drops," said the Guild staff member. "I've heard it's extremely rare to see it in action..."

"...Good thing we brought him back. He gets to stay here and hang out with others like him."

"Yes... You're right. I'm sure he'll be happy here," agreed Igarashi, sounding a little disappointed. Still, she kept her distance from Jeweled Wings and the Coral Peigoes and turned her back on the ranch.

"I'm sorry if bringing such a big guy here all of a sudden causes you any trouble," I told the Guild employee. "We'd be happy to help if there's anything we can do."

"Thank you, but that's part of our job, so... Oh?" Jeweled Wings turned and walked toward me just as I was about to leave him in the Guild's care.

"KRAH! KRAH!"

"...Are you maybe saying you want to come with us?"

"KRAAH!"

I worried he'd be lonely again if he joined us after all he went through to be reunited with his flock. But it seemed his mind was made up.

"If he has accepted you as his master, it should be possible for you to keep him at the Monster Ranch you have a contract with, as long as it is all right with you," offered the Guild employee.

"But will he be all right, away from his family?"

"If that's your concern...now that you have a White Jeweled Feather, you have the option of keeping Coral Peigoes as well." Even if we did that, though, we'd be taking them away from the rest of the group—or so I thought.

"Cheep!"

"Cheep!"

Two Coral Peigoes came chirping after Jeweled Wings. They turned back to the group and raised their wings as if to wave good-bye.

"...These little ones really can surprise you. They really love each other, and they're so clever."

"That's...true. I suppose he wouldn't be lonely if he had some family with him at the ranch."

"KRAH!" cried Jeweled Wings, happily. The Coral Peigoes jumped onto his back and climbed up on top of his head.

"You're going to live together from now on, the three of you. There will be other friends for you to meet, so try your best not to fight with them," I told them.

"KRAH!"

Jeweled Wings had really cheered up and paid close attention to whatever I said. It looked like he'd do just fine at the Monster Ranch.

"Haaah, I'm suuuch a sucker for this kinda thing. I cry so much people are gonna think I've got allergies."

"A-are you okay...? The staff are gonna laugh at you if you sob like that, you know?"

It wasn't just Misaki—there wasn't a dry eye in the group. And to think, if we'd defeated Jeweled Wings, we never would have gotten to see such a moving scene.

Louisa and Seraphina came over after everyone calmed down a bit. Louisa looked completely refreshed except for her eyes, which had also turned a bit red. "Mr. Atobe, everyone, excellent work today. I'm sorry I couldn't be with you, but I hope I can make it up to you some other way…"

"Thank you very much. I'm sorry to have kept you waiting so long."

"We trusted you would be all right, Mr. Atobe. You've inspired me to find a shield I could take with me to any environment, so as to not burden anyone again in such a situation…"

"It took us a long time to find Arihito and the others, so we don't know the full story yet," said Elitia. "Arihito, could you tell us what happened?"

"Sure. Cion, Kaede, Anna, and I got blown away together. Right away we encountered Jeweled Wings and engaged him in battle…" I decided I'd tell the members who'd been waiting for us all about the battle with Jeweled Wings, the teleportation device at the bottom of the spring, and everything else.

We headed to the overwater restaurant that doubled as a cottage, which every large group of visitors to the resort could use once. Madoka and Adeline came out to greet us, the lights shining warmly in the cottage behind them.

CHAPTER 4

The Contractors

Part I: Naming

Our one-night stay and adventures in the Islet of Illusion came to a close, so we bade the Guild staff members farewell and left. Our first stop was the Monster Ranch—a few adjustments, and the teleportation door took us directly there from the islet.

We found the ranch manager, William, in the middle of harvesting black thread from the Arachnomage's spider nest. Since this thread could be collected periodically, I'd decided to sell any leftover on the market to cover the Monster Ranch maintenance costs.

"Why, Mr. Atobe! The newest additions to your monster crew here are doing splendidly. I see you've already called on them a few times... I do hope they can continue to play an active role in your seeking."

"Thank you for all your hard work, William. Actually, I have a few new monsters I'd like to leave in your care..."

"KRAH!"

Jeweled Wings stepped out in front. William stared in wide-eyed wonder at the creature who was easily twice my size. Arachnomage was fairly large as well, and I worried if leaving all these giant monsters would cause too much trouble for William and the ranch.

"Is this...a Named Monster of the Peigo species? I never would have dreamed the day would come when we'd look after one of these at our ranch..."

"Would it be possible to leave him here with you? He's from an island, so I'm concerned he may find it difficult to adapt to the environment here."

"We have an area dedicated to caring for aquatic species so that we can provide for monsters who need to live in or around water without causing them stress... However, if he requires a saltwater environment, we would have to ask you to rent a specialized pasture."

"We found him in the forests, so I don't think he absolutely needs salt water... But I'd appreciate it if you could let me know should that change."

"I also think he should be all right here, but I'll be sure to monitor him... Well now, it looks like you've got two regular Coral Peigoes with you as well. I hope they can get along with the Demi-Harpies, seeing as they're all avian monsters."

The Demi-Harpies watched us from their perch on a nearby tree, and Jeweled Wings returned their gaze. They seemed curious about one another, based on what I could tell from the Demi-Harpies' expressions, but we'd have to wait to see.

"In that case, I'll keep these fellows in the corral over there where there's a bit of water. Would it be okay with you if I got them started on the standard diet plan? I know this species lays different magic stones depending on the type of food they eat."

"Yes, please. I am indeed interested in the magic stones, but I didn't bring them here specifically to lay them."

"I see... Well, these guys *are* pretty popular with the ladies. You must really put a lot of thought into keeping your party members happy."

"Wooow! He's so fluffy! See ya, Mr. Big Penguin! I'll come back to visit again soon!"

"Misaki, you really are something... You don't hold back..."

"Seriously... I wish I could do that, too, but it gets a bit harder as an adult."

Misaki had thrown her arms around Jeweled Wings without abandon and buried herself in his plumage. Jeweled Wings looked a bit confused about how to react to the Coral Peigoes clamoring around him. Suzuna and Igarashi seemed like they wanted to hug him, too, but they didn't have it in them to be quite as bold as Misaki.

The caretaker Millith, who we'd met before, came over to us while we talked. She looked the picture of a young farm lass, hoe in hand and wearing a T-shirt, overalls, and straw hat.

"Welcome back, Mr. Atobe. I was just feeding Himiko and the others, but they flew right over as soon as they saw you..."

"Good to see you again, Millith. I've brought a few new monsters over today."

"KRAH!"

"Ooh…I can't believe we get to take care of Peigoes. These little ones won't listen to anyone unless the person who drops them off meets certain requirements, you knooow." Millith apparently had a tendency to drag out words whenever she saw something cute. I had something more important to ask her rather than dwell on that, though. But before I could even get the question out, she asked me something else instead.

"What would you like to do about their names? I'm sure your Arachnomage would appreciate one, too."

"Good point… Does anyone have any ideas?" I asked the group.

"Jeweled Wings Dancing over Frozen Wasteland… How about Snow?" suggested Igarashi.

"Ooh, I like that!" said Misaki. "Definitely better to go with a simple name than trying to get all fancy. He's white, too, so it's perfect for him."

"KRAH!"

Everyone agreed with Igarashi's idea, so Jeweled Wings officially became Snow. Next up was the Arachnomage, who turned out to be a little challenging since her name already had magical and spider elements to it. We went through various suggestions, but in the end decided a straightforward name would be best and chose the name Mage. One of the Coral Peigoes that had come along with Snow was male and the other female, so we went with Penta and Rupee. Misaki suggested Penta, and Madoka chose Rupee. She said it had a cute ring to it, but I thought it also sounded like a fitting choice for a Merchant.

"Millith, I wanted to ask you about the Vine Puppeteer seed I brought the other day. How is it doing?"

"Oh…I-I'm so sorry, it actually budded and started growing a vine. You've made a contract with it, so I don't believe it will be dangerous, but I completely forgot to send you our observation journal entries."

"It's fine, as long as it's not dangerous. Thank you for the update."

"Actually, I have one more thing to apologize for… As it was growing, the first tendril that came out was made of this incredibly strong fiber. I thought it might be useful for something, so I plucked and preserved it," she continued.

I thought tendrils got stronger the more they grew, but I guess this one was strong enough to turn that bit of common sense on its head… That does sound like it could be useful.

"I think I'll take that back with me and ask a specialist about how we might use it."

"Yes, of course. I'm so glad you asked me, or I never would have remembered," said Millith, breathing a sigh of relief and smiling. William stroked his beard and forced a grim smile, but I thought she'd done just fine with her report.

We made our way back to the teleportation center near Green Hall, and the members of Four Seasons started to head back to their own apartment. Everyone looked sad to see them go, but I was sure we'd meet again someday.

"Mr. Atobe, everyone, I truly enjoyed this trip. It was the most fun I've had since coming to the Labyrinth Country," said Ryouko.

"I'm so happy I got to hang out with you all. I was sure you'd leave for District Six right away...," added Ibuki.

"...It was such a pleasure to be able to show you all what I could do with the racket you helped create. And I shall never forget fighting by your side, Arihito."

We would be forced to part once we moved up to the next district no matter what. It seemed this fact weighed heavily on the minds of the Four Seasons ladies.

"...Listen up, guys, we're gonna do whatever we can do so one day we can see y'all again with our heads held high," said Kaede, but it looked like even she knew her voice lacked conviction. Her face flashed with the realization, and she shook her hands in denial. "Wh-what the hell, I sound hella sappy. Just wait, we're gonna catch up so quick, you won't even have time to miss us..."

"We know. We'll be waiting for you, too. You're the first group we've gotten this close to since we came here."

"Let's meet again soon. Even if we're in another district, we'll always..."

Suzuna spoke after Igarashi and stepped up to Kaede, who smiled easily and offered out her right hand; Suzuna met it with hers, and the two tightly shook hands.

"Thanks. I feel like you haven't exactly let your guard down enough to call me your friend, but..."

"That's why I promise you we'll meet again, just like this time... Right, everyone?" said Suzuna, turning to the group.

"Certainly. There are so many things I'd love to discuss with

Kyouka and Louisa…and Seraphina, things we can only talk about among adults."

"…I agree. Ms. Ryouko, I have every faith you four have what it takes to meet the requirements for progressing to the next district. However, even if you don't, it would be my pleasure to join you again the next time we meet," replied Seraphina.

We needed to move up as quickly as possible. But we'd risk wearing ourselves out mentally and physically if all we did was rush, and we couldn't afford that. We'd found a way to share precious time together, and that was going to help push us forward once more. That was as fast as we could go.

After we returned to the suite, we received a report from Rikerton on the dissection of the Merciless Guillotine. However, it would take him a few more days to update our equipment, so I decided to hold on to whatever materials we got for the time being. Ceres and Steiner had finished the work we'd requested them to do. They gave me a pair of what looked like shin guards made from Hannya's Greaves, and the other members tried on the equipment the two had upgraded with Translucent Wings and other materials. Parts of the resulting armor were indeed see-through, though much to the ladies' relief, not in a way that would make it uncomfortable to walk around town in them.

"You've really outdone yourself, Steiner… These are incredibly well made," I said.

"*Hearing you say that really is the best part. It makes me so glad I became a blacksmith.*"

"I know you lot took a day off, but knowing you, I'd have thought you'd bring back some new materials... Wait, you actually have some?" asked Ceres.

"I'm sorry, I do actually have a few things I'd like to ask you about... Would that be all right?"

"Certainly. There may be some things we can use right away, after all. If it looks like it'll take a few days, we might wind up delaying your move, though."

I took the materials out from my pouch one by one. I could almost see question marks hanging above both Ceres and Steiner as they looked at each item.

◆Materials Presented to Ceres◆
> 1 Living Young Vine
> 2 Frost Stones
> 1 Snow Quartz

We could apparently obtain another White Jeweled Feather from Snow once it grew back, but I decided to hold on to it for the time being since we only had the one.

"Wh-what in heaven's name is this vine...? Is it part of a monster?" asked Ceres incredulously. "It's dormant now, but this is without a doubt alive."

"The vine-type Named Monster we fought left a seed behind. We made a contract with it and are having the Monster Ranch raise it for us..."

"H-hmph… I see, quite. In monsters of the vine variety, there are materials you can only harvest in each stage of growth. Medicinal herbs are much the same; their vitality is most concentrated in young buds."

"*This vine looks amazingly strong. It's also got excellent elasticity when pulled… It's a bit too short for a bow, so perhaps we could use it on the slingshot you have, Mr. Atobe?*"

"You were meant to visit a place that required you to wear swimsuits, so how did you come by a snow quartz…? I do believe you'll need to regale us with your exploits."

"Well, what happened was…," I began, then summarized what we went through on the Islet of Illusion.

"What?! You solved a mystery in the Guild health resort? You truly are a roaming band of curiosity itself…"

"*I wish I could go there, too… I'd love to see the beautiful sandy beaches and natural forests…but I know, it's only there to reward hardworking Seekers.*"

"Oh, um…I think you could go, from what I saw."

"Wh-what?! You knew that and left us behind? Not that I would hold a grudge over that. I'm sure you'll take us one day."

"I-I'm sorry; I'll make sure not to submit any orders before we go next time."

"*No, no, it's okay. We've gotten to experience a lot of new things thanks to you.*"

Still, the two looked disappointed. Given our different roles, it would be difficult to schedule a shared day off for both Seekers and support staff, but since they'd agreed to work exclusively for us, I decided I should try to create an opportunity where we could all take a breather together.

"Heh-heh... You're a diligent one, but it's good to see that's not all there is to you. All work and no play can make leaders such a bore to eligible young ladies, you see."

"W-well...I'm really straitlaced, so I'm sure I can be pretty boring."

"She's saying you're good at balancing being both a serious and easygoing boss. Just like she is."

"Don't try to butter me up—you won't be getting a raise... Although we do essentially run this business together. Anyhow, what did you want to do with this magic stone? You can add magic stones to your boots now, so would you like to put one on? That won't take more than a minute."

"Actually...could you please replace the ricochet stone with the frost stone on my slingshot? The ricochet stone has proved useful, but I'd like to try out attacks with this new attribute."

"Snow quartz has many uses, but it does take some time to apply, so we'll keep it for now, if that's all right."

I'd already explained we planned to go to the treasure labyrinth that day, so I had them change the band on my slingshot after hearing it would be quick.

```
◆Black Magical Slingshot +4◆
> Attack power increases at critical moments
```

> Slightly increases hit rate
> Slightly increases attack range
> Enables Magical Bullet shots
> Enables Vine Bullet shots
> Fitted with Gaze Stone
> Fitted with Frost Stone
> Fitted with Manipulation Stone

◆Upgraded Hannya's Greaves +3◆
> Can nullify enemy attacks that inflict status
  ailments on rare occasions (upgrade)
> Slightly increased defense against physical
  attacks
> Extra effective against humanoids
> Increases damage inflicted against enemy
  humanoids
> Increases speed
> Slightly increases defense against magical
  attacks
> Slightly increases defense against indirect
  attacks
> Allows user to activate Yoshitsune's Leap
> Increases effectiveness of skills that
  strengthen allies (upgrade)

"Hmm, not too shabby, if I do say so myself. I can't say I know what the vine bullets are, but give it a try next time you have a chance. I doubt it'll hurt in any event," recommended Ceres.

"I will, thank you very much."

"I've never seen leg armor this strong before... But do you think everybody has something like this in the upper districts?"

"I have heard tell armor with special features can sell for mind-bogglingly high prices," said Ceres. "I couldn't even begin to guess how much these greaves with Yoshitsune's Leap could be worth." I'd gotten the chance to acquire an incredibly valuable set of equipment. Now I needed to make sure I put it to good use and did not simply take comfort in the safety it provided.

I'd just finished putting on the greaves when Misaki came out of the fitting room. She'd finally gotten a matching set of Magician's armor, but it seemed she hadn't been able to take the plunge and strutted out in her normal outfit. I didn't want to force her into anything; it would be better if she could make her up mind to wear it on her own.

"Ah! ...Please don't—don't look at me. You might be asking, *Why aren't you putting on the armor that'll make you stronger?*— but all I can say is, these are very delicate matters for a lady."

"It's a pretty eye-catching outfit, so I can understand it takes a bit of courage to wear it. But I think you'd be safer with it on," I told her.

"Ugh, I knew you'd say that. But I've never even worn black tights before, you knooow? They're only for more matuuure ladies like Kyouka."

"She's going to hear you if you keep talking about her... Oh! Hi, Igarashi."

"Eeeek...!"

Misaki jumped up in surprise. She hurriedly sat down and

pretended to drink tea with Ceres, but that only made her seem more suspicious, and Igarashi saw the whole thing.

Soon enough, all the others who had tried on their new items came out as well. Igarashi, Theresia, Suzuna, and Elitia all wore armor newly enhanced with Translucent Wings, which made it see-through in different areas. But the armor didn't expose more skin than usual or anything, so the ladies looked comfortable.

"...Misaki, what happened?" asked Igarashi.

"Oh, uh, I was just saying I need a bit more courage before I can wear my new armor."

"I mean, it does look a little mature...and it is kind of bold. But I think it'd look good on you, Misaki," Igarashi said, reassuring her.

"Ohhh, easy for you to say! Don't think for a second I'll hand it over, even if it ends up having superstrong powers. But I'm still not gonna wear it juuust yet," said Misaki with pouted lips. Igarashi smiled back awkwardly as if in a tough spot. Then she looked over at me again and studied me from head to toe. It put me on edge.

"Those greaves go with that suit better than I'd thought," she commented.

"You all look great, too. It's also a little curious to think those come with Shock Reduction 1," I replied.

"I think it's a really lovely material, though I can imagine we might exchange it for something even better at some point...and the design makes it easy to move in," added Elitia.

"You say that now, Ellie, but weren't you also complaining about how it'd be see-through?"

"I-I'll admit I was nervous before I saw it...but it looks fine, doesn't it?" replied Elitia, before twirling around to show us. I froze unintentionally when I caught a glimpse of her back.

"Very well made, I say. Your skills really shine through, Steiner," noted Ceres.

"*Ha-ha-ha... You designed it after all, Master. All I did was follow the pattern you made.*"

I was sure Elitia's armor used to cover her back like most do, but you could now see through to her skin in the area where the Translucent Wings material had been added. It definitely surprised me since I hadn't expected it at all, but many people wore that style of clothing, so it was probably fine. It was a little odd she hadn't noticed, but it looked like she'd been a little nervous when she tried it on.

"...My knife got sharper with the blade edge stone."

"G-great... Try it out next time it seems right."

A smile crept over Melissa's usually expressionless face as she appraised her knife and sent a slight chill down my spine. But maybe her love of blades was fine as long as she didn't use them in a dangerous way? That felt like a tricky question to me.

"All right, now that we've all changed, shall we head off?" I asked the group.

"Arihito, since Cion is off today, won't we be a bit short-handed in the vanguard?" asked Misaki.

"I asked Seraphina yesterday if she'd join us, so let's go meet up with her."

Cion had fully recovered from the injuries she got in the battle against Jeweled Wings, but I had her rest for a day just to be on the safe side. Madoka was also holding down the fort at the suite. I'd asked her to negotiate with the construction company to see if she could get a good price for the materials we couldn't use from the Merciless Guillotine and told her she could spend the rest of the day as she saw fit. I trusted her judgment and knew I could leave everything to her.

Seraphina had readily agreed to come along once I told her about our goals for the treasure labyrinth. We never knew if we'd come across something like Murakumo, so having her and her shield on our side would be an enormous help.

"In that case, maybe I'll pay you folks a visit for lunch," said Ceres.

"After that, we're going to head back to District Eight to check on our shop. If anything comes up, just call us, and we'll come right away."

I could imagine they were starting to get a little worried about their shop; some clients might have visited while they were gone, and above all else, that was their home. Even we were starting to want somewhere to settle down, something more permanent than a leased apartment. But until the right time came, we needed to focus on the seeking ahead of us.

Part II: The Treasure Labyrinth

Seraphina met us outside the rented workshop, still equipped with her Mirrored Shell Pavis. We'd returned her Shuddering Tower

Shield, which she'd apparently put away in storage. She told us the Guild recommended Seekers borrow one of their designated rooms whenever attempting to use a trap cube to teleport to a treasure labyrinth. We headed over to the teleportation center by the Green Hall to do so and on the way caught a glimpse of the members of Four Seasons. They were pretty far away, so we quickly lost sight of them, but it looked like they were also en route to a labyrinth.

"Seraphina, do you know what's over in that direction?" I asked.

"Yes, that road leads to the entrance of the Plateau of Primary Colors. The monsters that appear there are on the peculiar side for District Seven, although I believe the first floor of the labyrinth should be safe enough for hunting."

"I see... Then I don't suppose we need to worry about them."

"I don't think they'd do anything rash, but if you're worried, do you want to go with them?" asked Igarashi.

"Don't you think we'd put them in an awkward position if we changed our plans to go after them?" Misaki pointed out.

Both Igarashi and Misaki were exactly right. Plus, it would be rude to the ladies of Four Seasons to worry about them too much. They'd also proven themselves capable Seekers time and time again.

"They're doing their best... It's on us to do the same," said Elitia.

"Yeah, you're right. Let's keep our eyes peeled," I replied. At Elitia's words, we all started walking. I decided I'd ask Melissa about her skills on our way.

"Melissa, if it's all right with you, I'd like to look over your new skills while we have a moment…"

"…Okay. Feel free to ask me anytime." She pulled her license out of her apron pocket, toggled over to her skills page, and showed it to me.

```
◆Acquired Skills◆
Helm Splitter
Lop Off
Cat's Call
Ambush
Knife Artistry
Dissection Mastery 1
Cooking 1
Assess 1
Magic Item Creation 2
Repository
Preserve Freshness


◆Available Skills◆
Level 2 Skills
Awl: Overrides target's defense on attack. Can
    only be used when attacking with a weapon.
Moonsault: Unleashes attacks with increased
    chances of hitting flying enemies.
Scale Removal: Increases chance of reducing the
    target's defense on attack. (Prerequisite:
    Lop Off)
```

Hang and Cut: Hangs the target up and then
  attacks. Increases chances of Partial
  Destruction. (Prerequisite: Dissection
  Mastery 1)
Frenzied Scratch: A bare-handed attack
  consisting of up to 8 consecutive strikes.
  Inflicts Bleed status. (Prerequisite: Scratch)
Break Bones: Adds Bludgeoning damage to attack
  regardless of weapon type. Inflicts greater
  damage than a normal attack.
Loud Voice: Emits a threatening cry that causes
  target to faint and reduces their magic.
Dissection Mastery 2: Improves Dissection
  technique and increases range of materials
  that can be harvested. (Prerequisite:
  Dissection Mastery 1)

Level 1 Skills
Silent Mew: Reduces target's hostility toward
  user.
Thorn Removal: Destroys thorns that appear in
  the terrain.
Cat Whisperer: Allows user to understand speech
  of cats and feline monsters.
Scratch: A bare-handed attack consisting of 2
  consecutive strikes. Inflicts Bleed status.
Cat's Landing: User takes no damage even when
  falling from a significant height.
Groom: Nullifies systemic status ailments
  affecting the target's body.

Cat Walk: Allows user to pass through extremely
    narrow spaces.
Sharpen Nails: Increases damage of attacks
    inflicted with user's nails. Heals any
    psychological status ailments.

Remaining Skill Points: 5

Melissa had a wide range of skills available to her through her
job as a Dissector and her werecat lineage.

"We did talk about Groom earlier, so how about you take that
one first?"

"Okay. And I'm a Dissector, so I need Dissection Mastery 2."

She didn't have her eyes set on any others, meaning she had two
skill points left. Awl looked like it'd require a pointed weapon, so
she wouldn't even be able to use it now. Cat Whisperer could prove
enormously effective in certain situations; still, Moonsault, Silent
Mew, Thorn Removal, and the attack skills could also be useful.

◆Melissa's Newly Acquired Skills◆
☆Dissection Mastery 2
☆Groom

Remaining Skill Points: 2

"Let's take these two for now, and you can take any others
whenever you need to," I suggested. "It's so hard to tell which of
these battle-type skills could be better than the others."

"...I wish I could take them all, but it'd be a waste if I don't use them, so I think that's a good idea."

It can't be easy to pick up a skill at the eleventh hour, though it would give us some options in a pinch. Still, we could have an advantage if we got the skills ahead of time, so it's a tricky choice.

We finished going over her skills just as we reached the teleportation center. Seraphina set our destination on the door for us, and we stepped into a large, bright room without any lights, much like the rooms we'd used to open boxes.

I took out the trap cube, placed it on the floor, and had everyone stand in a circle around it. Then I activated it; all I had to do was wish for it to happen. The crystal balls embedded in the metal frame began to shine, and we were once again greeted by the familiar feeling of being whisked away, just like when teleporting.

...No, something's different... What is this feeling...?

Whenever we teleported, I got this feeling we were all being swept away in a single direction. But now, it felt oddly like we were floating aimlessly.

"—*Your destination is shifting. There has been some sort of causal interference... It is reacting to your contract with me for divine protection...*"

"*Master, this place you are heading is unlike most. When the time comes, do not hesitate to use me.*"

Ariadne and Murakumo called out to me, but no one else had noticed yet. They had no idea the trap cube had reacted to our contract with Ariadne and overwritten our destination, sending us not to a normal treasure labyrinth but to some entirely different place.

"…Is this the treasure labyrinth…?"

"Wait… Really? I mean, this place is…"

It looked just like the floor where we'd found Ariadne—not a natural labyrinth, but a place constructed by something definitely not human. The walls and floor were made of materials similar to what we'd seen there, though it was much brighter here. I looked up and saw there was no ceiling. Was that sheet of blue I saw the sky? Something about it felt fake.

"A-Arihito…there are some really rusty coins here, too, but look…," said Misaki.

A pile of completely bleached bones sat in one corner of the large room we now found ourselves in. How did they get there? Had they used a trap cube like us? We could see nothing in the way of their armor. Was it locked away in a box belonging to what you might call the master of this floor, like we'd seen before? The bones hinted at the decimation of not just a single person, but at least one whole party.

"This space… It looks like decomposition happens quicker here than outside," I said.

"Perhaps time flows more quickly here?" speculated Igarashi. "…Maybe the longer we stay here, the more time passes outside? Or…"

If time passed many times more quickly here than it did outside, we needed to find a way out fast. Even a few hours here could mean several days in the outside world. I prayed we were wrong, but we'd known for a while that time flows differently inside the labyrinths.

"In any case, if we don't get a move on, we'll never get out…"

"Yeah, that's true. Let's just be very careful," agreed Igarashi.

"……"

I wanted to believe Theresia would catch anything that awaited us with her Scout Range Extension 1 or Trap Detection 1. She brought up the midguard now, but her senses should be able to extend past Seraphina in the vanguard.

"Arihito, those things on the other side of the wall… Are they clouds?" asked Misaki. We were walking down a hallway with thin slits widely interspaced throughout the walls. They didn't seem to let any air in but did afford us a view of the outside scenery.

"They do…look like clouds. I think we're way past trying to use common sense to explain anything we see…but it looks like we're in an enormous, box-shaped maze floating in the air. That, or what we see outside is some kind of illusion…"

"But…it looks very much like the labyrinth where we found Ariadne. I can also feel wandering spirits, just like I did there…," said Suzuna.

"…I knew it, ghosts really do haunt their final resting place, don't they?" said Igarashi, trembling with fright. She could sometimes get easily spooked. It's not like it didn't get to me at all, but when I thought about the regrets those Seekers must still feel, I felt more moved to bring my hands together in prayer like Suzuna.

We eventually reached a room larger than the one we'd first

arrived in. Even after all the barren sights we'd just passed, this room was undeniably strange.

"Is that...ivy all over the place...?" asked Igarashi dubiously. She sounded so unsure because the vines that looked like ivy had completely dried out and turned as hard as stone. The sinuous ivy snaked out from the center of the room and wounds its way over the floor and up the walls. Up overhead where there should have been no ceiling, it entwined and wove itself into a kind of net through which a few streaks of light filtered into the room.

"...Are those...cogs...? No, a carriage...?" I wondered aloud.

"This ivy's suuuper tangled all over it and turned to stone..."

"If we want to keep moving, we'll need to do something about the ivy that's blocking the path. Looks like we'll have to borrow Arihito's strength and slice through them."

"Elitia, hold on a second. There's something off in this room..."

I called out to Elitia—just as she stepped on some dry ivy on the floor.

"......?!"

Instantly, a breathtaking light filled the room. It was a different color than the one we'd seen before, but this light was definitely—

Stellar Vehicle awakens; Self-Defense Mode activated.

A Hidden God part... So that's what it was...!
When Ariadne called out in warning before we teleported, she'd tried to tell us we were being sent to a different destination

because of our contract with her. This must be the kind of place devotees were drawn to when they used a trap cube. It was easy enough to imagine anything you'd find in such places would have something to do with those same Hidden Gods.

"Everyone, stay away from the vines on the floor! They're—!"

The dried ivy husks crumbled away to reveal dazzling green vines beneath. No mistake about it: The vines had not actually grown around and out from the wheels. Rather, the ivy and the wheels were one sentient being that moved of its own free will.

```
◆Monster Encountered◆
?Intelligent Vehicle
Level 8
In Combat
Impervious to lightning
Dropped Loot: ???
```

Sections of the ivy sprawled across the floor pulled up and gathered around the wheels in the center of the room. Then cracks spread over the surface of the vehicle and unveiled...a black chariot. The two-wheeled carriage had an area above the axle binding it together where a person could ride. A half-translucent feminine figure much like the manifestation of Murakumo's sentience appeared on the spot—a queen crowned with a thorny diadem at the helm of her chariot.

"We are the Stellar Vehicle that races across the heavens. All those who stand before us shall endure our trials."

"Mr. Atobe, it's coming—!" cried Seraphina.

```
◆Current Status◆
> ?Intelligent Vehicle activated Royal Thorns ⟶
  Acquired Tactile Absorb status
Can now absorb physical attacks
```

◆◇◆

Thorny vines wrapped around our enemy almost like a defensive wall. The ghostly apparition stood calmly behind it and looked over at us with what appeared to be a smirk on her face.

"—Everyone, don't even try to hit her with physical attacks! Only nonlightning magic attacks will get through!" I called out in warning.

"...But that means—!"

We could only either hit it with a bomb blast from Misaki's cards or Suzuna's violent winds. However, both combined physical and magical attacks, meaning our enemy could just absorb any direct hits.

The magic probably outweighs the physical power in those attacks, so we might be able to use them to chip away at its vitality. But I can't imagine it'll go down that easy... We've got to do something to take those vines out of the picture.

"All those who rebel against the crown of thorns shall writhe and dance in agony—wither and die."

"—Oh no you don't...!" I yelled.


```
◆Current Status◆
> ?Intelligent Vehicle activated Dancing Rose
```

```
> ARIHITO activated FORCE SHOT (FREEZE) —→ Hit
  ?INTELLIGENT WEAPON
Interrupted action
```

I aimed my strike at the enemy's core through the gaps in its thorny barrier. It was a good thing I'd used the frost stone; without it, the Force Shot would have been the driving force behind a purely magical attack that almost surely would not have packed enough punch.

"Don't, it's still—!"

But I'd failed to realize something pivotal—the enemy had seemed to recoil but had actually forced the attack I interrupted to resume.

"Everyone, dodge it!"

```
◆Current Status◆
> ?INTELLIGENT VEHICLE activated BRAZEN CORONATION trait
  —→ Blocked action cancellation
> ARIHITO activated DEFENSE SUPPORT 1 —→ Target: All
  party members
> ?INTELLIGENT VEHICLE activated DANCING ROSE
> KYOUKA activated MIRAGE STEP
> ELITIA activated SONIC RAID
> THERESIA activated ACCEL DASH
```

This time, the vines creeping along the floor and the walls, not those on the chariot's defensive barrier, sprang to life. They instantly ensnared all my party members without evasion skills by the legs.

"Agh—!!"

"Eeeek…!"

"D-don't, not my legs, not my legs—!"

"......!!"

◆Current Status◆

> Seraphina, Suzuna, Misaki, and Melissa's legs were
  Bound and Blood Drained

Support Defense 1 can't block this binding attack...!

It wasn't omnipotent; I'd known that all along, but I'd placed too much faith in my own skills. Our chances of winning would become infinitesimally small if I got caught here, too. I could hear Ariadne's and Murakumo's voices ringing in my ears—but I saw something else to do first.

"—Come on...!"

◆Current Status◆

> Arihito activated Yoshitsune's Leap

I leaped and dodged the vines flying toward me in attack, but they turned in midair and followed after me, determined not to let me escape. Under ordinary circumstances, I'd have been powerless to elude them, but with Hannya's Greaves, these were no ordinary circumstances. I suddenly got a strong sense I could fly and followed that instinct—

"—Whoaaa...!!"

The greaves activated, and I "jumped" again in midair. In an almost out-of-body experience, I found I could move around in the air at will.

Come after me... That'll at least buy us some time...!

"Arihito! Run! If you keep using that, you're going to run out of magic—!" shouted Elitia. She was exactly right; each jump through the air with Yoshitsune's Leap clearly drained my magic.

As long as the enemy could absorb physical attacks, we'd face the threat of Dancing Rose over and over again. Should I use the gaze stone to try to interfere? No, even if I did Stun it, the enemy would power through with that same trick and complete the attack. It was a plant and a chariot: a monster made of metal components. Did we even have anything that could hit both parts in their weak spot...?

Yes! That's right, we have that *stone...!*

I reached into my pocket and pulled out a little magic stone we'd picked up in the Islet of Illusion—the tide stone laid by the Coral Peigoes.

Part III: Weak Spot

I flew around the ghostly apparition at the helm of the chariot, loaded the tide stone in my magic gun, and aimed at its back.

"—!"

◆Current Status◆
> Arihito loaded Magic Gun with Tide Stone
> Arihito fired Tide Bullet ⟶ Hit ?Intelligent Vehicle

```
?INTELLIGENT VEHICLE was weakened
Inflicted RUST status
```

The gun recoiled as it shot out the bullets. Power drawn from the magic stone hit the apparition standing on the chariot's litter and immediately swelled into spheres of water that rose up overhead and burst open, raining down over the enemy.

"*This...this should not exist here... This salt water...,*" protested the chariot.

Normally, a little salt water wouldn't be enough to dry a plant out on the spot. But salt damage can harm many kinds of plants and eventually cause them to wither. And in this place where everything degraded rapidly, those effects should take hold more quickly than in the outside world.

"—Mr. Atobe!" Seraphina cried out.

"*All those...who defile the crown of thorns...shall be punished...*"

```
◆Current Status◆
> ?INTELLIGENT VEHICLE activated ROSE JAVELIN
> ARIHITO activated REAR STANCE —→ Target: SERAPHINA
Insufficient magic
> ★SCHOLAR'S ANKH activated —→ Converted vitality
  into magic
```

Its movements had been slowed, but the enemy shaped its thorns into a javelin and struck back. I caught a glimpse of Seraphina, realized I was in front of her, and teleported behind her to escape.

"—Gak—!"

"Mr. Atobe…you're meant to be the rearguard, and yet you put yourself in such danger…"

"Ow, ow! —*Pant*, it finally let go… That's not even a little bit funny, you know, going around sucking a young lady's blood…!"

"Arihito, thank you so much…!" cried Suzuna.

With my friends finally free, I once again checked my license.

◆Current Status◆
> SERAPHINA, SUZUNA, MISAKI, and MELISSA were freed
  from BIND and BLOOD DRAIN
> ?INTELLIGENT VEHICLE's RUST status intensified
Attack power and speed decreased
TACTILE ABSORB status was removed
Weak spot altered

"Arihito, now can we go after it…?!" asked Elitia.

"No, wait—!"

◆Current Status◆
> ?INTELLIGENT VEHICLE activated IRON MAIDEN ⟶
  Shape-shifted using products of BLOOD DRAIN
?INTELLIGENT VEHICLE's RUST status was removed

The thorny vines had trapped the four and drained their blood—blood that was now dyeing it red.

"*—Through this offering of maiden blood, the crown of thorns regains its glory.*"

The crimson thorns converted that blood into energy and began to power the chariot. Its wheels started turning and glowing with a pale light, and the rust that had formed peeled off and disappeared piece by piece. Normally, even if you remove the rust from a wheel, it will never be the same again. However, these looked completely restored.

If that chariot is a Hidden God part, then it's alive and sentient…which must mean it can heal…

"I-is that red…from us…?"

Elitia's expression clouded over at Misaki's words. If she struck the thorns now, she'd risk getting splashed with blood.

"…I'll never let myself…lose control from my friends' blood again… No matter what… I—!"

"Elitia…"

I remembered what Elitia said not long after she joined the party: "*I'm not a murderer!*" She still hadn't completely gotten over what had happened in the past.

"I just have to make sure I don't get any on me… But if I fail…"

"I will hold you back, Ellie. By any means necessary."

"…Suzuna…" Elitia and Suzuna shared a look. It was risky, but even so, we needed Elitia to assume her role and attack.

"And so the wheels begin to turn. All will thrash in pain as they race down the trials of the thorny road—and long for salvation."

"—Here it comes!"

```
◆Current Status◆
> ?INTELLIGENT VEHICLE activated AURA SPIKE ⟶
  Strengthened physical attack power and
  expanded attack range
```

Light engulfed the two wheels. It not only strengthened them but formed into needles imbued with physical power, which lifted the chariot and its litter into the air. I couldn't decide whether to evade or have Seraphina block the hit. But as soon as the wheels began to turn, I instinctively knew the latter was not an option.

"—Seraphina, please dodge this attack!"

"...?!"

```
◆Current Status◆
> ?INTELLIGENT VEHICLE activated UNHINGED DEVASTATION
```

It all happened in the blink of an eye—the thorns embedded in the wall behind us suddenly shot out and drew the chariot in the middle of the room toward them.

"Gah—!"

"Whoaaa—!"

Seraphina and I stood smack-dab in the path of the oncoming chariot. We flung ourselves out to the sides as it barreled toward us, narrowly dodging the attack. The chariot slid past us through the air and continued racing up the wall.

"The crown of thorns looks down on its subjects."

"—Misaki! Suzuna!"

◆Current Status◆
> ARIHITO activated DEFENSE SUPPORT 1 ⟶ Target:
  MISAKI and SUZUNA
> ?INTELLIGENT VEHICLE destroyed surrounding
  architecture
> DEBRIS DOWNPOUR hit MISAKI and SUZUNA ⟶ No damage

"Eeeek—!"

"Misaki! Suzuna!" cried Igarashi.

"...We're okay! But look—!"

The spikes of light emitting from the chariot had pierced the ceiling from where the apparition at the helm now stood looking down at us. Red thorns spun from the chariot and reached out to intertwine with the vines around the room.

They're not just making the wheels spin... Those thorns are what give it speed—!

"—Suzuna! Aim for those red thorns!"

"—Okay! Strike your target!"

We'd need Suzuna to activate her powerful Auto-Hit to shoot through those thorns with exact precision and anchor them to the ceiling. And with my Cooperation Support, we could make that the first link in a chain of blows.

"Fall to your death!"

◆Current Status◆
> ARIHITO activated COOPERATION SUPPORT 1 and ATTACK
  SUPPORT 1

```
> ELITIA activated SONIC RAID
> SUZUNA activated AUTO-HIT —→ Next two shots will
  automatically hit
> SUZUNA activated STORM ARROW —→ Hit ?INTELLIGENT
  VEHICLE
Decreased speed and impeded action
Combined attack stage 1
> ELITIA activated RISING BOLT —→ Hit ?INTELLIGENT
  VEHICLE
Combined attack stage 2
> ELITIA activated additional attack —→ Hit
  ?INTELLIGENT VEHICLE
```

Suzuna's arrows pierced through the red thorns, and the ensuing windstorm stopped the chariot in its tracks. Elitia leaped up to meet it there, unleashing strike after strike in midair.

"Me too—!"

But it wasn't over yet. Melissa took her butcher's knife and jumped into the fray, adding on to the combined attack. Normally, if you tried to hit an enemy hanging down from the ceiling just by jumping, you'd only ever get in a shallow hit. But one of Melissa's unclaimed available skills had the power to flip the power balance with an airborne enemy—Moonsault.

```
◆Current Status◆
> MELISSA activated MOONSAULT —→ Hit ?INTELLIGENT VEHICLE
Reduced defense
Combined attack stage 3
```

```
Combined attack: STORM, BOLT, MOON ⟶ 52 support
  damage
18 additional cooperation damage
Speed further reduced
```

I'd gone with Attack Support 1 to make sure our attacks got
through the metal chariot, like when we battled Murakumo, and
the gamble paid off far better than I could have imagined.

"External forces…and foreign winds…impede our chariot."

"Eeeek! I-it's coming dooown—!" cried Misaki.
"—Hyaaaaa!"

```
◆Current Status◆
> ARIHITO activated DEFENSE SUPPORT 1 ⟶ Target:
  SERAPHINA
> SERAPHINA activated DEFENSIVE STANCE
> SERAPHINA activated DEFENSE FORCE
> SERAPHINA activated SURGING WAVE ADVANCE ⟶
  Increased speed while on defense
```

Seraphina rushed madly ahead and hurled herself at the enemy
as it fell to save her friends from the crash, then pushed on and
cornered the chariot against the wall.

"—Seraphina, get back!" screamed Igarashi.
"…!"

"Igarashi, Theresia... Misaki, I'm counting on you!"

"Eeeek! Y-you got it! I can help, too, you know—!"

◆Current Status◆

> ARIHITO activated COOPERATION SUPPORT 1 and ATTACK
  SUPPORT 1

> KYOUKA activated LIGHTNING RAGE ⟶ Hit ?INTELLIGENT
  VEHICLE

Weak spot attack

Caused ELECTROCUTION

Combined attack stage 1

> LIGHTNING RAGE activated additional attack ⟶
  3 stages hit ?INTELLIGENT VEHICLE

> THERESIA activated AZURE SLASH ⟶ Hit ?INTELLIGENT
  VEHICLE

Slight knockback

Burned magic

Combined attack stage 2

> MISAKI activated BLAST CARD ⟶ Hit ?INTELLIGENT
  VEHICLE

Combined attack stage 3

> Combined attack: LIGHTNING, AZURE, BLAST ⟶ 39
  support damage

13 additional cooperation damage

ELECTROCUTION time extended

Attack Support 1 didn't cover the additional attack Lightning
Rage activated, but the three-part combination attacks landed one
right after the other and took a real toll on the enemy.

"D-did we get it...?!"

"—Don't let down your guard, Misaki!" Elitia cautioned. Hidden behind the explosive winds, our enemy had already turned itself back around to face us.

"...*The lightning disturbs our gears... And yet, it also...*"

Powers them. A flash of lightning enveloped the chariot as the apparition said those final words, then shot out into the mangled vines scattered about the room.

"Everyone, get behind me—!" screamed Seraphina.

◆Current Status◆
> ARIHITO activated DEFENSE SUPPORT 1 —→ Target:
   SERAPHINA
> SERAPHINA activated AURA SHIELD
> ★MIRRORED SHELL PAVIS activated special effects
   —→ SERAPHINA's magical defense greatly
   increased
> SERAPHINA activated DEFENSE FORCE
> ?INTELLIGENT VEHICLE activated THUNDEROUS BANQUET —→
   Target: SERAPHINA
Unleashed counterattack using accumulated
   lightning
Caused ELECTROCUTION
> ?INTELLIGENT VEHICLE recovered from reduced speed
Recoiled from lightning counterattack

"Seraphina—!"

"It's okay... I'm all right—!"

Seraphina gave us a close-up view of just how strong her shield could be against magical attacks: She completely intercepted the powerful electric shock the thorns shot out at her and protected all of us who'd jumped behind her.

"I'm sorry, Atobe... I thought it was a weak spot, so I went for it..."

"No, I was about to ask you to do the same... Plus, take a look. It looks like that counterattack also caused a recoil effect."

"...It's down to its last dregs of strength, too. We had to push it to this point or we'd never have a chance... Here it comes—!"

```
◆Current Status◆
> ?INTELLIGENT VEHICLE activated WHEEL OF FATE ─→
  ?INTELLIGENT VEHICLE released power
```

"The crown of thorns has fulfilled our duty. The chariots' wheels spin and wander across the stars."

```
◆Current Status◆
> ?INTELLIGENT VEHICLE activated ENDLESS LOOP ─→
  ?INTELLIGENT VEHICLE stopped consuming magic
> ?INTELLIGENT VEHICLE activated THORN RUT
> ?INTELLIGENT VEHICLE activated PERPETUAL DEVASTATION
  ─→ ?INTELLIGENT VEHICLE began attacking
  indiscriminately
```

I'd thought the thorns were weapons and fuel needed to accelerate the chariot's speed, but I was wrong. They were mere trifles the chariot used to determine whether we deserved to undertake the real "trials" ahead. And now, the chariot had decided we were worthy of witnessing its true power. However, that meant the attacks we'd borne so far would be nothing compared to those we were about to see.

We all fell silent. The thorns strewn about the room transformed into tracks on which the chariot could run; along the walls, the floor, the ceiling, in any direction all at breakneck speed.

"Oh no... We can't—!"

None of us could find our mark, not even Elitia at her top speed or Suzuna with her Auto-Hit. We had to find a way to stop it, or sooner or later, we'd all bear the brunt of its attacks.

"I-if it comes this way, we're doomed—!"

"—Catch me if you can—!"

"Igarashi—!"

◆Current Status◆
> KYOUKA activated FORCE TARGET ⟶ Target: KYOUKA
> KYOUKA activated EVASION STEP
> ?INTELLIGENT VEHICLE attacked ⟶ KYOUKA dodged
> KYOUKA's dodge rate increased

"I'm not done yet—!"

Igarashi used Force Target on herself and drew the enemy's attack toward her. She dodged, but it chased after and threw itself at her relentlessly.

◆Current Status◆
> ?INTELLIGENT VEHICLE attacked ⟶ KYOUKA dodged

```
> Kʏᴏᴜᴋᴀ's dodge rate increased
> ?Iɴᴛᴇʟʟɪɢᴇɴᴛ Vᴇʜɪᴄʟᴇ attacked ⟶ Kʏᴏᴜᴋᴀ dodged
> Kʏᴏᴜᴋᴀ's dodge rate increased
```

Igarashi... Every time she dodges, she's getting faster and faster... This must be the true power of Evasion Step—!

"—I won't let you lay a finger on them—!" Kyouka yelled.

```
◆Current Status◆
> ?Iɴᴛᴇʟʟɪɢᴇɴᴛ Vᴇʜɪᴄʟᴇ attacked ⟶ Kʏᴏᴜᴋᴀ dodged
> Kʏᴏᴜᴋᴀ's dodge rate increased
> ?Iɴᴛᴇʟʟɪɢᴇɴᴛ Vᴇʜɪᴄʟᴇ attacked ⟶ Kʏᴏᴜᴋᴀ dodged
> Kʏᴏᴜᴋᴀ's dodge rate increased
```

"Kyouka, stop! If you keep using that—!" shouted Elitia.

"It's okay... I can still—!"

Her dodge rate increased with every attack she avoided while activating Evasion Step. But even that did not provide any guarantees, and each evasion drained her magic. She wasn't going to have enough for the next one. In that case—

"—Use Mirage Step, Igarashi!"

"......!"

```
◆Current Status◆
> Kʏᴏᴜᴋᴀ's magic decreased
Eᴠᴀsɪᴏɴ Sᴛᴇᴘ effects were lifted
```

> ARIHITO activated CHARGE ASSIST ⟶ KYOUKA recovered
  magic
> ?INTELLIGENT VEHICLE attacked
> KYOUKA's activated MIRAGE STEP ⟶ Dodged attack

"Igarashi, use Mirage Step once more!"

"Arihito, wha—?!"

"—Everyone, the next time she dodges, aim for exactly where
I tell you!"

◆Current Status◆
> ARIHITO activated HAWK EYES ⟶ Increased ability
  to monitor the situation

*Focus... You've already seen it run through those tracks so many
times. Which track will it take to attack her next...?!*

*"Master, use my powers. This chariot has abandoned its defenses to
intensify its attacks. My slash attack should prove effective against it."*

I could hear Murakumo's voice. This would be my one and
only chance, and it'd be over in a split second. I gripped the sword
on my back and got ready to strike as hard as I possibly could.

"Please... Do it one more time—!"

◆Current Status◆
> ?INTELLIGENT VEHICLE attacked
> KYOUKA activated MIRAGE STEP ⟶ Dodged attack

"—There!"

"—Hit your mark!"

◆Current Status◆
> ARIHITO activated COMMAND SUPPORT 1 ⟶ Now capable
  of guiding party members' target
> ARIHITO activated COOPERATION SUPPORT 1 and ATTACK
  SUPPORT 2 ⟶ Support Type: BLADE OF HEAVEN AND EARTH
> SUZUNA activated STORM ARROW ⟶ Hit ?INTELLIGENT VEHICLE
Decreased speed
Combined attack stage 1

Suzuna fired the first two shots with Auto-Hit. The chariot ran past where Igarashi had been, up along the wall, and sped over the roof to attack once more—but Suzuna was waiting for it. The arrow she loosed shot toward what should have been an empty target and flawlessly met its mark.

Part IV: Northern Sky

"—Scatter like flower petals! *Blossom Blade!*"

◆Current Status◆
> ELITIA activated BLOSSOM BLADE ⟶ 12 stages hit
  ?INTELLIGENT VEHICLE

```
Combined attack stage 2
> ELITIA activated additional attack ─→ 8 stages
  hit ?INTELLIGENT VEHICLE
```

"It's my turn next—! Take that!"

"……!"

```
◆Current Status◆
> MISAKI activated BLAST CARD ─→ Hit ?INTELLIGENT VEHICLE
Combined attack stage 3
> THERESIA activated AZURE SLASH ─→ Hit ?INTELLIGENT
  VEHICLE
Slight knockback
Burned magic
Combined attack stage 4
```

"No one...can stop...the wheel...of fate..."

"Me too—!

Theresia's attacked unleashed powerful winds that pushed the enemy back to where Melissa lay in wait with her enormous butcher's knife.

```
◆Current Status◆
> MELISSA activated LOP OFF ─→ Activated AMBUSH
Hit ?INTELLIGENT VEHICLE
Critical hit
Combined attack stage 5
```

"......!"

Her blade failed to cut through the metal chariot and bounced back with a loud *clang*, but Melissa still stood in the enemy's blind spot. And her attack gave Murakumo just enough time to deliver her knockout blow.

"*—The same power our holy Mechanical God wields to protect her beloved devotee flows through me. And just as my master and his retinue garner new skills, so too do I grow in strength. One day, all will fall before my blade.*"

Murakumo began to materialize, powered not only by my magic but also by Ariadne's, which now coursed through me to unloose Murakumo's true strength.

"*Through the vehicle of my devotee's flesh, the Stellar Sword and I are joined as one. In accordance with our holy union, I hereby release the second stage of bonds on thy power—,*" Ariadne chanted.

◆Current Status◆
> Arihito activated Rear Stance ⟶ Target: Melissa
> Arihito activated Northern Cross Strike ⟶ 6 stages
  hit ?Intelligent Vehicle
Combined attack stage 6
> Attack Support 2 limit breaker
Blade of Heaven and Earth struck 28 times

I activated Rear Stance and teleported behind Melissa. The next instant, Murakumo in her corporeal form took the blade from my hands—and unleashed an attack I'd never seen before.

"—Your power, Master, is the key to my strength. My very own Blade of Heaven and Earth propels my attack."

◆Current Status◆
> Northern Cross Strike and Blade of Heaven and Earth resonated in 4 stages
> Combined attack: Azure Erosion Strike, Northern Cross, Heaven and Earth ⟶ Further decreased ?Intelligent Vehicle's speed
Slight knockback
Burned magic

"The forgotten…crown of the northern skies…oh, Hidden God…"

The chariot pressed on even after that powerful string of attacks as if to say, *I must keep going.*

"…Time to put an end to this. I *will* stop you—!" cried Seraphina.

◆Current Status◆
> Seraphina activated Provoke ⟶ ?Intelligent Vehicle's hostility toward Seraphina increased
> Arihito activated Defense Support 1 ⟶ Target: Seraphina
> Seraphina activated Wide Stance ⟶ Nullified knockbacks against Seraphina
> Seraphina activated Defensive Stance
> Seraphina activated Aura Shield

> ★Mɪʀʀᴏʀᴇᴅ Sʜᴇʟʟ Pᴀᴠɪs activated special effects →
  Sᴇʀᴀᴘʜɪɴᴀ's magical defense greatly increased
> ?Iɴᴛᴇʟʟɪɢᴇɴᴛ Vᴇʜɪᴄʟᴇ attacked → Hit Sᴇʀᴀᴘʜɪɴᴀ

"Grr...ugh...uaaagh—!"

Seraphina met the chariot's attack head-on with her shield. She activated a skill to ensure she would not be pushed backward, but the powerful blunt force very nearly broke through. Yet she stood her ground—as if forcing the chariot to a halt would in itself seal our victory.

"Seraphina—!"

"—Haaaaaah—!"

◆Current Status◆
> Aʀɪʜɪᴛᴏ activated Aᴛᴛᴀᴄᴋ Sᴜᴘᴘᴏʀᴛ 1
> Sᴇʀᴀᴘʜɪɴᴀ activated Fᴀɴᴀᴛɪᴄ → Abilities improved
> Sᴇʀᴀᴘʜɪɴᴀ activated Sʜɪᴇʟᴅ Pᴀʀʀʏ → ?Iɴᴛᴇʟʟɪɢᴇɴᴛ
  Vᴇʜɪᴄʟᴇ's actions were temporarily halted
> Sᴇʀᴀᴘʜɪɴᴀ activated Sʜɪᴇʟᴅ Sʟᴀᴍ → Hit ?Iɴᴛᴇʟʟɪɢᴇɴᴛ
  Vᴇʜɪᴄʟᴇ
13 support damage
> 1 ?Iɴᴛᴇʟʟɪɢᴇɴᴛ Vᴇʜɪᴄʟᴇ defeated

The chariot powered round and round by an infinite magic supply, the one that seemed it would never stop, screeched at last to a halt.

"Haaah, haaah..." Seraphina hung on to her shield and caught her breath. We'd all given everything we had to the battle, and none of us could speak right away. The spikes of light that had radiated from the chariot began to disappear. I cautiously approached, but the chariot showed no signs of moving again.

◆?Intelligent Vehicle◆
> SELF-DEFENSE MECHANISM is dormant

The apparition driving the chariot had also disappeared, though I imagined it still resided within the chariot itself. Up close, it seemed quite large for a chariot and was about my height in diameter. Still in her material form, Murakumo gripped her sword and pointed it at me. She walked closer and disappeared just as she was about to make contact.

"...I must rest. Master, this place...it leads to Mechanical God Ariadne's Sanctuary."

"It what...? Murakumo, what do you—?" But Murakumo fell asleep before she could answer my question. Her new attack had probably depleted all her strength.

"All devotees of a Hidden God will be called to wherever armaments for that god lie. I have never before been blessed with a devotee, so I was unable to predict this would happen," said Ariadne, taking over for Murakumo. Her dispassionate voice seemed to lack some of its usual strength; she must have been trying to apologize. If so, I could only say she owed us nothing. We'd chosen to bind ourselves to her and had only gotten this far because she'd saved us time and time again.

"I can sense the armament controller is near. Once you find it, it will react to the chariot, and you will be able to clear the path now *sealed by thorns. You may choose to destroy the chariot, but I advise you place it under your control.*"

"All right, I'll look for it. Hey, everyone, could you rest here for a minute?"

"Sure... Arihito, where are you going?" asked Elitia.

"There's apparently something like the sacred operation crystal we used when we had Murakumo join our group around here somewhere. We can use it to remove these thorns blocking our path."

"In that case, we'll all help you look. Ah—!" Igarashi lost her balance as she walked toward me. She seemed a little unsteady after putting such a strain on her magic.

"Please take a breather, Igarashi. You worked so hard to draw the chariot's fire."

"...I guess it's easy to faint all of a sudden when you lose magic that quickly... But I'm glad I did it. I managed to do my part."

"I think you went a little overboard... You've got some luck, and it sounds like you've always been pretty athletic, so you didn't get caught this time, but that skill doesn't guarantee you'll be able to dodge anything, you knooow," Misaki pointed out.

Igarashi clutched my arm to steady herself, then painfully shifted her weight to stand on her own. I went around behind her and used Charge Assist once more, but only after taking a sip of a mana potion since my magic was running dangerously low, too.

"...Th-thank you. Just when I thought I was almost out of magic, you restored it for me... I knew I could count on you to back me up while I fought."

"Well, that's me doing my part, so don't worry about it. I may need to

ask you to take on that role and draw enemy attacks again in the future…
but if possible, I want to find a way that doesn't put you at such risk."

"Thanks. But we all put ourselves at risk, so you don't have to
concern yourself with that too much."

"You showed up right behind me out of nowhere. That's the
only reason we made it through…," said Misaki.

"I think that rubble would have trapped us if it weren't for you,
Arihito," added Suzuna.

My skills wouldn't necessarily stop working even if we fell out
of formation since I could still technically be "behind" someone
depending on where we stood. But it was definitely good experience fighting an enemy that stood directly above us; it forced me
to analyze the situation in three dimensions.

"I'd like Igarashi and everyone else who's out of magic to rest
here. Theresia, are you all right?"

"……"

"Hmm… You mean the mana potion's enough for you? All right."

I handed Theresia the potion in my hand, which she'd been
looking at. I could restore my own magic, too, if I used Charge
Assist, but we didn't really need to worry about that then.

"…Ngh…"

Theresia took a sip of the potion. She'd never give away how
badly it tasted—or so I'd thought, but she did stick out her tongue
a bit for one second.

"…Too bitter?"

"……!"

She shook her head. Maybe she thought she shouldn't complain about the taste, or maybe all demi-humans felt that way. I could just be partial, but I didn't think it was the former. Melissa was also running low, so she took the potion next and drank a sip.

"Wooow, Arihito you're sooo... I'd have to reeeally work myself up before I shared an indirect kiss with someone like that, you knooow?"

"...I don't think Theresia sees it like that... Actually, m-maybe she does a little...?" said Melissa.

"We have exhausted our magic, but none of us has lost hardly any vitality. This is yet another indication of how peculiar your party is, Mr. Atobe... Of course, in a wonderful way."

"...Seraphina, you have the least magic left. Here," said Melissa as she handed over the bottle.

"Thank you. But I have my own potion, so I should be fine. It's very difficult to find a second during battle to drink them, though. That's the biggest drawback to these kinds of potable medicines," replied Seraphina and took out the bottle she'd brought with her... only to find the glass had shattered in battle.

"...Here."

"...Thank you kindly."

Seraphina blushed a bit, took the potion from Melissa once more, and brought it to her lips. She had a point; the fact we had all come out virtually unscathed from an intense battle with a surprisingly fierce enemy was truly exceptional.

I doubled back to the weathered Seeker skeletons we'd passed before and found a stone buried beneath them.

```
◆Alioth Crystal◆
> Unknown application. No information to
  display.
> Cannot be appraised.
```

It had a different name than the alkaid crystal, but I could tell from one look that it was made of the same material. It had the same shape and only slightly differed in color. This was still just a theory, but I was pretty sure some of the Seekers in the party who'd come here first had brought this armament controller with them. The chariot put them through the test—and cost them their lives.

Who created the Hidden Gods and their parts? Speculation surrounding those mysteries could at times tantalize Seekers who ventured to investigate and even drive them to their deaths. Other times, that search could reward Seekers who withstood trying crucibles with phenomenal powers. At any rate, we were only getting closer to the truth behind these Hidden Gods, behind Ariadne, because we'd managed to survive. We needed to persevere until we found the truth, no matter what it took.

These armament controllers revealed no secrets through appraisal and displayed no information on our licenses; not even the Guild fully understood them. Yet we'd already surpassed by far what most Seekers would ever experience. We needed to keep that fact close to the chest and tread very carefully.

I returned to the room where the chariot stood and told the others I'd found the alioth crystal. Then I inserted it into a depression on the chariot and—

◆Current Status◆

> Arihito is now owner of ?Intelligent Vehicle
> ?Intelligent Vehicle's first Inscription is
  revealed to be Alphecca

"Alphecca… Is that this chariot's name?"

"She looked like a princess or a queen… Do you think she'll materialize once again like Murakumo?" wondered Igarashi.

"Mr. Atobe, the thorns are shifting…," said Seraphina. "We should be able to proceed in that direction."

"Arihito, I found this while I was looking around this room…," started Misaki.

"This Black Box was lying on the ground. What do you think this means…?" asked Suzuna. We'd disabled the trap on a Black Box to reveal the trap cube—and found another Black Box within it. Something definitely didn't add up. We still hadn't found many possessions the defeated Seekers had lost, so there was a chance they could be inside this Black Box. But then why wasn't the alioth crystal in there, too? Could it be the armament controller wouldn't go in a Black Box while it lay on the same floor as the chariot?

"Armaments must long for Hidden God devotees to find them… It doesn't really make sense they'd then put those devotees through the wringer, but I'll bet that's what happened here."

"I did get the feeling she was kinda like, if you want me, you gotta beat me fiiirst! Maybe they're only supposed to obey really strong people?" suggested Misaki.

"Possibly… They're definitely powerful enough to have that

choice. I think even we would have had a hard time defeating this one without Murakumo," added Igarashi. In other words, we'd need one armament to obtain another. But I didn't think it'd necessarily get easier as we collected more armaments. The whole situation reaffirmed my belief there really were no shortcuts here.

"In any case, we need to get out of here… Shall we?"

We headed for the pathway once sealed off by a thorny blockade. I didn't even have a chance to wonder how I'd carry the chariot back with me before it started to fade away and eventually disappeared from sight.

"I have the power to summon armaments to my side. They can also materialize as an ether apparition and accompany you…as can Murakumo. I'd like you all to come to me. I can create a teleportation pathway from there to my chambers," Ariadne whispered in my ear.

It'd been a long time since I'd last seen Ariadne, and now we'd found a way to teleport to her. While I had spoken to her through Suzuna's Medium, I hadn't expected to return to District Eight for a long time still. Teleporting would make the trip much easier.

I told everyone the gist of what Ariadne had said. I was excited to introduce our newest members to her, our protective deity who always came to our rescue.

CHAPTER 5

Admiration and Stealthy Malice

Part I: Temptation

"Kaede, be careful!" Ryouko called out.

"Yeah, I know!" I replied, jumping back to avoid the clump of mud this ginormous caterpillar monster shot at me.

We'd started seeking in a new labyrinth so we could catch up with Arihito and the others. One of the Guild officers told us that out of all the labyrinths in District Seven, we could probably hold our own raiding this one, the Plateau of Primary Colors, even if it was just the four of us. I had no clue what kind of place it'd be from its name, but it turned out to be kinda like the reddish-brown Australian wilderness or Andes mountain range landscapes I'd seen before reincarnating. I guess maybe the Primary Color bit of the name had something to do with colors found in nature.

"—Anna, let's go!"

"Okay—!"

```
◆Current Status◆
> Ryouko activated Bubble Spray ⟶ 3 stages hit Mud
  Crawler
Weak spot attack
Removed Mud Armor
Reduced resistance to electrical attacks
> Anna activated Thunder Shot ⟶ Hit Mud Crawler
Caused Electrocution
```

Ryouko used water from this nearby puddle to make all these huge water balls and hurled them at the caterpillar's full-body mud armor. For something that cute, it could be a real pain since pretty much nothing could get through to it once it smeared mud all over itself. I'd heard it was pretty hard to beat if your party didn't have any aquatic attacks.

Ryouko'd drenched it in water and left it wide open to electrical attacks. The shock hit it so bad, for a split second, we could see its bones. I'm pretty sure regular caterpillars don't have bones or anything, but this one had a real clunker for a skull and even had bones running through the poison spike on its tail.

"—BEGYEEEE!"

"Hyaaaa!!"

```
◆Current Status◆
> Kaede activated Kakegoe ⟶ Intimidated Mud Crawler
Canceled action
> Kaede activated Ki-Ken-Tai
> Kaede activated Enhi ⟶ Hit Mud Crawler
Critical hit
```

```
> IBUKI activated CRESCENT KICK ──→ Hit MUD CRAWLER
> 1 MUD CRAWLER defeated
```

I bashed the sucker and ran past it just as Ibuki kicked out the final blow.

"BEGYEEEE..."

Someone in the party I joined when I first got to the Labyrinth Country once told me you should basically wipe out your enemy before they get a chance to hit you back. Those guys are still stuck back in District Eight. They said it's pretty common for people to call it quits if they lose to a monster even just the once, and I couldn't do a thing about it when the party decided to split up. But it was gonna take more than that to keep me down. I went off hunting Cotton Balls on my own and waited till I could find my own party. That's when I found Ibuki—and not too long after that, Ryouko and Anna.

"Phew... It would be lovely if we could stop at one, but these caterpillars aren't worth many contribution points," said Ryouko.

"The materials we could harvest from it don't garner a very high price on the market, either. I suppose most people prioritize hunting the more time-efficient monsters first," added Anna.

"All we can do is take it step by step," said Ibuki. "We fought with Teacher and his group, so we got credit for taking down two Named Monsters... Just one more, and we can check off that box."

Our situation did a total one-eighty after we met Arihito and his party. Until then, we hadn't met a single Named Monster since we got to District Seven, and some jerks had monopolized Beach of the Setting Sun, the labyrinth everyone said was the most efficient place to hunt. Plus, there was a ton of competition, and sometimes other Seekers would even steal monsters right out from under our noses.

We'd sometimes talk about how it could take us a whole year to move up to District Six. But even I knew deep down nothing mattered if we wound up dead, so we decided as a group that we'd make a run for it at the first sign of trouble if we went up against a really dangerous Named Monster.

"...Kaede?"

"Kaede, you seem a bit distracted today... Do you want to call it a day and head back to town?" offered Ryouko.

"Oh, uh, n-no... Sorry, I just got somethin' on my mind. But I'll be on it if we start fightin', don't worry."

"...Are you perhaps thinking about Arihito and the others?"

Anna really doesn't hold her punches with this kinda thing. I mean, it's better for me, too, if someone else can say what I'm thinking, but I know I shouldn't let her do all the hard work for me. She tries to sound all mature, but she's the youngest one here for cryin' out loud.

"...I was just wonderin' if we'd ever catch up if all we do is go at it like we did before we met those guys. We're all doin' our best, and I know *some* people do make it up to higher districts, but..."

"But...we don't have any other choice. We can't ask them to slow down for us... We just have to try our hardest, and we'll catch up," said Ibuki.

"...Whether we find another Named Monster will be up to fate, of course. The ones we all know how to find are fair game for everyone," Ryouko pointed out.

I had no idea if we'd ever get a shot at another one. Named

Monsters do show up again after they're taken down, but that could take a week or even a month. Unless we got real lucky, we'd never get that third Named Monster. And unless we basically killed ourselves, we'd never meet that twenty thousand monthly contribution points.

We had no choice but to go for it if we wanted to get those points. We'd get there eventually if we could hunt seven hundred points' worth of monsters a day like we were.

But the cold hard truth was I knew that meant we'd have to take down monster after stupid monster until we were sick and tired of it. We had no business moving up to District Six if we couldn't even get that strong. At the same time, I couldn't help but suspect the Guild wanted to keep us all from movin' up. Just thinking about that made me queasy.

I never felt that way when I was with Arihito, though, not even once. I always felt so pumped, like I could take on the nastiest monster as long as I could do it with him.

"Hey... You guys reach a dead end?"

"...Oh, h-hello... No, we were just fighting a monster here."

Some pretty girl wearing sunglasses we almost never saw even around town and a white cloak had been watching us for who knows how long. It didn't take me long to remember. Not many girls walking around in that getup.

She had hair a little whiter than gray and lots of white in everything from her weapons to her armor. I remember thinking she must really have a thing for the color white. Her armor was obviously loads better than anything you could get your hands on

in District Seven. I wondered what the hell someone like her was doing all the way down here by herself. It was weird.

"Need something from us?" I asked, kinda skeptically. I remembered Arihito had warned us to be careful around this girl.

"I got here just in time to see you finish that Mud Crawler off. You hit him first with water and lightning, then the last two of you went in and cornered him perfectly. That kind of coordination should work even up in District Six, don't you think?"

She said it so easily, like it was the most obvious thing in the world. I couldn't believe it.

I'd thought we had so far left to go, that we had so much more to do.

But—actually, I agreed with her.

We did our part just as good as anybody when we fought on Arihito's team. Didn't we deserve to go up to District Six with them, too? It's not like I was jealous of those girls. It's just, we'd promised to meet up again in the upper districts, and I was nervous 'cause I didn't know if we were gonna get to keep that promise.

"It's quite difficult to meet all the requirements for advancing to District Six... And we're still a bit..." Anna trailed off.

"It's definitely easier if you hunt a Named Monster. But if you guys can take down a level-five Mud Crawler that easily, I'm sure you can get the contribution points as long as you work at it. The Guild doesn't regulate points for the less popular monsters, so you can get fifty points for each one, no matter how many you hunt."

But what if that took us a week, or a month—or even longer? By the time we finally did catch up, we'd be old news.

They're gonna get close to another party and blow up even more, and we'll end up being that party they fought with one time way back when...

I knew he was never gonna forget us. But it'd suck just as bad if we never caught up.

"But you know, the Named Monster on the first floor here's already got its eye on another party, so I think it's going to be pretty hard to find. If you go to the second floor, though, I'm sure it'll come out right away—as long the conditions are right."

I could hear my heart thumping loud as hell.

I thought maybe, just maybe... This girl looked super high level, like she knew lots of stuff we didn't know. What if she knew something about Named Monsters?

"Do you want me to lead you to it? I won't ask for much in return. There's this one kind of monster on the second floor that tends to drop a certain item I'm looking for. We could call it even if you let me have them. Don't worry, it's not worth much to anyone but me really, and I'd pay you a fair price for it."

"Why would you go that far to help us...?" I asked.

"U-um... Would you really show us where to find it?" Ibuki asked the woman in white. "If you promise, then I guess..."

"Ibuki, we mustn't ask such questions... That's really valuable information for Seekers."

Ibuki'd basically read my mind, but Anna said we shouldn't ask that kind of thing—I got where they were both coming from. Ryouko had been the one who decided what we did ever since she joined the group. But now that same Ryouko stood speechless. I could see the hope in her eyes as she looked at the woman in white. I felt like it was my turn to stand in for Ryouko and talk for us, just this once. There were some things adults couldn't come out and say.

"...If you really think we've got what it takes...if you know what we'd need to do to get to that Named Monster...please. Could you please tell us?"

"...Kaede," said Ryouko, but it didn't sound like she was calling me out at all.

The woman in white smiled with this super-innocent look, like she'd been waiting for us to say exactly that.

"I'll say it again, but I think you've got what it takes to go up to District Six. So let me give you a little advice."

Part II: A Momentary Return Home

We left the scene of our fierce battle with the chariot through a pathway that opened in the back corner. Unlike on our journey here, this time we didn't see a single skeleton. No one had ever come this far. Who made this labyrinth and why? I didn't want to believe its sole purpose was to massacre Seekers.

Elitia led the way and stopped at the entrance to the next room. A teleportation pad like the one we'd used to come here lay in the middle of the circular room. "So we can use this to teleport home...?" she asked.

"Probably, but first we're going to stop at Ariadne's. It seems like we can set that destination into this pad."

"I guess it's no surprise this place would have something to do with Hidden Gods. We did find an armament here, after all," said Igarashi.

"I poked around the areas that stood out to me, but I wonder if we've missed some secrets...," continued Elitia.

"I performed Exorcism on the wandering spirits here. I felt it was the least I could do to ease their pain..." Suzuna glanced behind her. It looked like nothing to me, but she could probably see the ghosts of the Seekers who'd lost their lives in battle against the chariot. I turned around, closed my eyes, and offered them a prayer in consolation.

I know this kind of thing is fairly common in the Labyrinth Country. But I can't shake the thought we might have made it in time to see at least some of them alive if only we'd gotten here sooner.

"*...Sparing such thoughts for these lost souls helps deliver them some comfort. Your prayers are not in vain,*" I heard Ariadne say. No one said anything out loud; we were all silently praying. Suddenly, the pad beneath our feet began to radiate light and whisked us away, back to Ariadne's Sanctuary.

When I opened my eyes, we were already in the room where Ariadne's reliquary lay. We hadn't gotten a chance to look all around the last time we were here, but this time I saw there was a teleportation pad set up in the room.

But Ariadne has the power to teleport us back to the first floor of the labyrinth just by placing her hand on our heads, so this pad must be different, special in some way.

"…I have the power to exercise Return magic. It is similar to a Return Scroll, but from here, I can only send you to the first floor in the Field of Dawn," said Ariadne. For once, her voice did not echo in my mind.

Ariadne lay flat on the reliquary and was trying to sit herself up. However, it looked like she could only move her upper body. She managed to place her hands on the side of the reliquary but could not stand up.

"—Ariadne!" Igarashi cried out and rushed over. She raced up the steps and held out her hand to Ariadne, who still sat in the reliquary—but Ariadne didn't take it.

"…I can operate a greater range of movement now that I have collected two Mechanical God parts. This was merely a trial… I have not yet gained the ability to walk autonomously." Ariadne had mentioned before she would one day be able to move outside of the Sanctuary for limited periods of time if we collected all her parts. Adding the chariot to her collection had restored movement to her upper body.

"This room…and this young girl…" Seraphina trailed off.

I quickly explained who Ariadne was to Seraphina and Melissa. I told them it was her Guard Arm we summoned in battle and about how we'd signed a contract and officially gained her protection.

"...Your sword... Ever since our battle against Murakumo, I sensed something. You and your party have touched upon untold secrets in the Labyrinth Country that not even the Guild fully understands."

"I'm sorry I wasn't able to share these details with you until now. You've fought alongside us twice against Ariadne's different parts, and I can't even begin to thank you for everything else you've done for us... That's why I wanted you to know."

Seraphina didn't answer right away. She looked at us, closed her eyes, and took a deep breath.

"I am deeply humbled you would share such valuable information with me. All this time, I hoped for nothing more than to assist you. But now, I...I wonder if I might consider myself a member of your party?"

"Me too... I'm glad you told me. I've gotta tell Madoka."

"Yeah, we'll have to bring her here, too, one day. I was sure it'd be kind of hard for us to come back to District Eight...but I suppose that's all changed, hasn't it, Ariadne?" It was just as Ariadne said: If we made offerings to her, we could power the Sanctuary and eventually set a teleportation pad leading here somewhere outside.

"...I meant to explain this sooner. Offerings encompass more than simply material items... They can also be devotion itself. Your devotion level has increased, expanding the extent to which I can intervene in matters outside of this Sanctuary. That is why I am now able to operate on teleportation pads and the like and redirect their destination here."

"Does that mean we can come here, like, all the time?" asked

Misaki. "That's super exciting—it's like we have our own secret hideout! Don't you think, Arihito?"

"I must each time convert your devotion into energy in order to redirect your teleportation destination; therefore, I cannot use this power indiscriminately. You should come to my side only when truly in need." What did Ariadne use to power her other skills? Probably the same devotion level. If so, we needed to make sure we increased it as much as possible.

I don't see a problem in asking for Suzuna's help if we can do that with Medium. But would it also work if I use Charge Assist directly on Ariadne? Maybe we can try it out now that she can sit up—

But I realized what that meant as soon as the thought crossed my mind.

"Oh…A-Arihito, you really shouldn't look that much. She's…," started Suzuna.

"…Y-yes, good point. Things may be different for Hidden Gods, but I really do think you should wear something…," continued Igarashi.

"…I will be able to generate clothing once I recover my parts. I have no need of it now." I understood what she meant, but she had nothing except her long hair covering her chest, and I wasn't sure what to think. As these thoughts played around in my mind, Ariadne lay back down in the reliquary. "The Silver Chariot will need some time to repair itself. I will tell you once it regains functionality, Arihito."

"The Silver Chariot…? But, Ariadne, that chariot…"

It was not silver. But Ariadne closed her eyes before I could tell her. Perhaps she was not yet used to the strain of moving her body.

"...I shall transport you...back to the Guild...in District Seven..."

"Yeah... Okay. Ariadne, I'm glad we could come see you again. Sleep well."

"......"

Ariadne did not answer. Only her lips moved slightly, and we began to teleport once again.

When I opened my eyes this time, I saw we stood in a familiar place: the teleportation center near Green Hall. We opened the door and walked out onto the street. I thought we might stop by Green Hall and check in with Louisa since it was still around noon.

"Mr. Atobe... Look at this. We were right; the days do appear to pass more quickly in that labyrinth," said Seraphina.

By *the days*, she meant time flowed in days there, not hours. Seraphina bought a kind of simplified newspaper at a stall nearby and showed me the date at the top—several days had already passed since we teleported to the treasure labyrinth.

"—Mr. Atobe...! Thank goodness, you've all returned safely...!" Louisa came running out of Green Hall and straight for us. She looked unusually flustered, even considering our extended absence.

"Haaah, haaah... I'm terribly sorry, I saw you from my office and rushed out as fast as I could..."

"I'm sorry to make you worry so much. We ran into some

unexpected complications... I'm sure Madoka and the others are worried, too. Are they all right...?"

"Yes, they're fine. Ceres and Steiner returned as well, and I've been sharing a room with Madoka. We all discussed it and agreed you must be running a little late but that you would certainly come back to us."

So you can end up spending several days in a labyrinth, even if you mean to come back the same day—I'll need to bear that in mind. I should apologize to Madoka and the others later.

"More importantly, and I do apologize for bringing this up as soon as you've just returned...but I have something important to discuss with you," Louisa said.

"That's no problem; it's only felt like half a day for us. Is something wrong?"

"The thing is...my coworker told me Four Seasons went out on a seeking expedition yesterday but haven't returned yet. I know they practice great caution as a rule, and my coworker said they never stay overnight unless they plan it ahead of time..."

Memories of what to me felt like mere hours ago flashed through my mind. I'd seen the four ladies of Four Seasons heading toward a labyrinth...but we'd been on our own way to the teleportation center ourselves and hadn't spoken with them.

"Louisa, did those four go to the Plateau of Primary Colors?"

"Y-yes...that is what I've heard. They had been raiding it little by little, and apparently they told my coworker they expected to descend to the second floor yesterday. The first floor of that labyrinth is incredibly vast, so it took them a long time to discover the entrance to the second floor, but it seems they'd finally found it..."

So they'd started off carefully making progress. Then something unexpected happened on the second floor, or maybe they needed to camp overnight for some reason. I found it hard to believe they meant to camp overnight going into it, given the fact they'd explained their plans to their caseworker ahead of time. If that were true, though, it meant something had happened to them.

"It's entirely possible they've simply been delayed, but...Arihito, I think we should go look for them, just in case," said Elitia.

"I'm afraid the Guild Saviors cannot respond unless they can confirm the situation requires their assistance...and Ms. Adeline is now leading a follow-up investigation as a member of the Five Hundred and Thirteenth Guild Savior Corps into the events that occurred at the Beach of the Setting Sun."

"Thank you for the report. I had instructed my subordinates to carry out any commands from headquarters during my absence. Adeline is aware of what occurred at the Beach of the Setting Sun, so the investigation is in good hands." I was sure the corps weighed heavily on Seraphina's mind, but she said she'd come with us to search for Four Seasons. She must have been concerned the worst had happened to them.

"Listen, everyone, I'm sorry, but...I think we should go to the Plateau of Primary Colors. It looks like it's going to be a really big labyrinth, so if you're tired, please stay back and rest up," I said to the group.

"—Bow!"

"It's Cion! And Madoka—!"

Cion walked toward us with Madoka on her back. I looked over and saw Louisa had pulled out her license and smiled. Madoka had sent her a message saying she'd spotted us.

"Arihito! You guys—! I'm so glad you're back—!"

"I'm sorry, Madoka... You must have been worried," I told her.

"No, it's all right. All I wanted was to know you're all okay..." Madoka wiped her eyes with the handkerchief in her hand. We all gathered joyfully around Madoka and Cion—but we couldn't stay long.

"I think I'd like only our fastest members to come on this raid. We need to get to them as quick as we can."

"I—I get it. Even if I sprinted with all I've got, I'd never catch up to our suuuper speedy Ellie or Theresia," said Misaki.

"And I...well, I have Wolf Pack, so if Cion comes with us, I can run pretty quickly."

"I can also carry my shield without sacrificing speed if need be. I'd greatly appreciate if you would allow me to join you."

I'm probably the slowest one here. But if I use Yoshitsune's Leap at key points, I should be able to get over obstacles and things without much trouble.

```
◆Current Party◆
1: Arihito    X★o※          Level 6
2: Theresia   Rogue         Level 6
3: Kyouka     Valkyrie      Level 5
4: Elitia     Cursed Blade  Level 10
5: Cion       Silver Hound  Level 6
```

```
6: Melissa    Dissector    Level 6
7: Seraphina  Riot Soldier Level 11


Standby Party Member 1: Misaki    Gambler
   Level 5
Standby Party Member 2: Suzuna    Shrine Maiden
   Level 5
Standby Party Member 3: Madoka    Merchant
   Level 4
Standby Party Member 4: Louisa    Receptionist
   Level 4
```

"Arihito, please be careful... Next time you come back, we'll all...," said Madoka.

"We're gonna jump in the bath with youuu! And no sleeping on the first floor!" cut in Misaki.

"Please...we're counting on you to help the members of Four Seasons," added Louisa.

"Of course, I promise we'll all come back safely. All right, let's move!"

We set off running full speed toward the entrance to the Plateau of Primary Colors.

Once inside, we saw a vast, reddish-brown wilderness; large puddles dotted the terrain sparsely populated by green, leafy trees.

◆Monsters Encountered◆

Mud Crawler A

```
Level 5
Hostile
Dropped Loot: ???
Mud Crawler B
Level 5
Hostile
Dropped Loot: ???
Bluff Frog
Level 5
Hostile
Dropped Loot: ???
```

""BEGYEEEE—!""

A caterpillar monster saw us furiously racing by, hurled up thread, and shot it at us. But we stayed out of its attack range and pressed on without missing a beat.

"You can see a few of these monsters were defeated here... But there's no way to tell if Four Seasons took them down—!" shouted Igarashi.

"Let's keep going until we get to the second-floor entrance... Wow, this labyrinth is huge—!" I called back.

"......!!"

"Mr. Atobe, I can switch with you at any time! Please tell me before you get tired!" We had Seraphina riding on Cion's back so we could move as quickly as possible. I was sprinting with all I had but could still just barely keep up.

"...Arihito, want me to carry you? I'm actually pretty strong," offered Elitia.

"That's okay... I've also got a little something up my sleeve—!"

Each leap flung me from ship to ship, like the legendary warrior Minamoto no Yoshitsune had in battle against the Heike. I definitely did not have the strength to move that way on my own but could fly through the air like a natural as long as I wore Hannya's Greaves.

Still...this labyrinth is enormous. Is that why there are so few Seekers...? I would like to know more about the materials we could get from the monsters we've spotted. They're so spaced out, though; it must be hard to earn many contribution points here.

Even with the Alliance's monopoly out of the picture, we all still strived as a basic rule to choose labyrinths where we wouldn't encroach on other Seekers' hunting grounds, and vice versa. That was probably a big reason Four Seasons chose to come here. Lighter competition also meant they had better odds of finding a Named Monster. And if the Named Monster on the second floor of this labyrinth hadn't been defeated yet, there was a chance they'd run into it, albeit a very small chance.

Those four were very brave Seekers. At the same time, they strongly believed in taking every precaution they could, or at least that's what I'd thought. What would make them go hunting down on the second floor when getting there in itself took so much out of you?

"...I imagine...they were in a rush. They wouldn't have come so far without good reason. We should never criticize them for that," said Seraphina.

"Yes...I know. And I wouldn't be surprised if they told us to mind our own business. We don't even have the right to think of ourselves as overprotective; that's far too patronizing," I replied.

"It's fine... The truth is we *are* worried... If we don't act now, we'll regret it later—!" said Igarashi.

"Awoooo!!" In one valiant bark, Cion put it better than my clumsy comment ever could.

I took a sip of the mana potion just as I was about to run out of magic. I'd been trying my best not to use too much of it, but with that, I drained the dregs of another bottle.

Part III: Trap

An enormous stone edifice marked the entrance to the second floor. Large boulders had been fit together to create the almost primitive man-made structure; once we passed beneath it, the scenery around us changed completely.

It had taken us maybe two hours to reach that point, but we'd seen almost no other Seekers on our way. The labyrinth also had very few monsters and therefore a reduced risk of a stampede occurring; I figured most people probably left it alone for that same reason. However, we noticed something unusual as soon as we stepped into the second floor.

"Look... Do these clumps of mud have arms?" asked Igarashi.

"...It looks like they have faces. Someone wet these clay

golems...made them soft, then beat them down," explained Melissa. She and Igarashi examined the defeated monsters' remains that had been left strewn all over the ground. Theresia didn't respond in any way, so unless there was something Trap Detection 1 couldn't catch, we were safe to look around.

The same large puddles we'd seen before dotted the landscape here as well. Except here, an unnaturally steep kind of wall towered overhead and cut off our line of sight. But that wasn't what surprised us; we'd seen something similar in the Beach of the Setting Sun. What did set off alarm bells was the fact that none of the monsters defeated here had been retrieved by a Carrier.

"A water skill... Ryouko and the others fought here a few hours ago..." It seemed Melissa's Appraise 1 allowed her to examine defeated monsters—or rather, the materials they were made of—and detect some other bits of information.

"...What are these...?"

I noticed a depression in each of the monsters' foreheads. Every one looked like it'd held something at one point. We kept going a bit farther and found even more carcasses; these also bore the same empty dents barely large enough for a magic stone to fit into.

Did they...just harvest the magic stones and keep going...? There are some gaps between the monsters, but they clearly defeated every one they came across. But what does that mean? Also, is it possible that every single one of these monsters had a magic stone? Does that kind of monster even exist? What were they collecting? And why? Or did they just happen to pick up whatever it was?

"...Arihito—! I can hear someth—"

"Let them go—! Please, give them back—!"

"Anna—?!"

"......!"

Igarashi cried out, and Theresia raced off, the rest of us close on her heels. We had no time left to think and not a second to waste. Anna's voice echoed over the whole area from the other side of the wall looming over us; we had to get to her as quickly as possible.

We saw a few more mud creatures as we ran. They looked to be around level-5 or level-6 monsters. Four Seasons had most likely worked together to defeat a few of them, but some corpses mixed in among the remains bore markings hinting at a totally different hunting style. Some kind of sword had sliced these carcasses to shreds. Four Seasons never used more force than necessary to defeat an opponent, yet these monsters had clearly been on the receiving end of an overwhelmingly powerful attack.

None of the District Seven Seekers we'd seen so far could even begin to compare to the force this person commanded—but I knew one person with the weapons to leave such marks. A young girl with two short swords hung about her hips: Shirone.

"I'll give you until the next time we meet to think it over."

"If you have a change of heart, come find me anytime."

If it really was her, what was she doing with Four Seasons...?

"—Anna!"

We sprinted around to the other side of the wall blocking our sight. That's where we saw her: Anna, cornered up against the wall, gripping her racket tightly in both hands. A clay golem so enormous we had to crane our necks to see all of it stood before her, raising its fists in the air.

"Run, Anna—!"

Elitia activated Sonic Raid and sped up; she didn't waste a single breath and went straight in for the kill.

"—Stop—! You can't attack him! They're all—!"

"......!!"

It all clicked as soon as I heard Anna's anguished cry.

◆Monster Encountered◆

★Cursed Tri-Masked Clay Giant

Level 9

In Combat

Absorbs water and electricity

Dropped Loot: ???

◆Current Status◆

> ★Cursed Tri-Masked Clay Giant captured Kaede, Ibuki, and Ryouko

> Elitia canceled Lighting Bolt

> Arihito activated Defense Support 1 ⟶ Target: Elitia

> ★Cursed Tri-Masked Clay Giant attacked ⟶ Hit Elitia

"—OOOUGHHH—!!"

"Shit—!!"

Once we realized what Anna had meant when she screamed *Give them back!* we could think of nothing but to avoid attacking the three ladies who had been captured. The golem slammed its fist down on Elitia, but she somersaulted in midair, landed, and immediately raised her sword.

"...I've never even heard of such a vicious monster...!"

This Clay Giant looked like an enormous version of the golems we'd just seen. It'd buried Kaede, Ibuki, and Ryouko in its chest. Only their heads stuck out, but we could see the outline of their bodies underneath the clay.

"Ugh... Aah—!"

"...Anna... Everybody, run—!"

"Please...save Kaede, Ibuki...and yourselves...!"

Anger boiled up within me. I wanted with everything in my body to scream out of rage, but that wasn't going to help anyone.

We need to find a way to attack without hurting them... Show me its weak spot...!

◆Current Status◆

> Arihito used Hawk Eyes to perceive ★Cursed Tri-Masked Clay Giant's weak spot

Buried underneath its head—or rather, the bulge sticking up out of its body in place of a clearly defined head—were three masks of different colors and bizarre expressions. The blue and yellow ones were glowing; only the red one remained unlit. I glanced at my license and tried to guess what the colors represented.

The blue one is probably for water, and the yellow, electricity—those are the ones it says the monster can "absorb" now. In other words, it absorbs attacks of the same type of whatever masks are lit... So right now, only fire attacks will work on this thing. That's got to be its weak point—!

"Theresia, get the red mask—!"

I'll get her to attack that red one with the fiery Azure Slash. First, I'll use Command Support to pinpoint her target, then I'll add on either Attack Support 1 or 2. We'll wait to see how it reacts once we get that out and either decide to go in for another attack or take a defensive stance.

I decided our course of action—but never got the chance to call out the full command.

"Good work coming all the way out here, rearguard. But this is where you take your leave."

"Shirone—!!"

Where was she hiding? Is this what she'd been waiting for?

No. She'd been planning this for a long, long time.

◆Current Status◆
> Conditions for SHIRONE'S MAGIC MARKING placed on ARIHITO were met
> SHIRONE restricted scroll effects to ARIHITO
> SHIRONE used RETURN SCROLL ⟶ Target: ARIHITO

Anna and the rest of my party turned back to look at me and stared wide-eyed. The world around me started to recede, and there was nothing I could do to fight it. A split second later, I was once again looking upon the scenery we'd seen two hours prior at the entrance to the Plateau of Primary Colors. I checked my license. Shirone had activated her skill, torn me alone away from the group, and teleported me back to the start.

I ran—if only I had a little time to think. District Seven had another unusually powerful level-9 Named Monster: Merciless Mourner. This labyrinth should have been classified as much more dangerous if it had a Named Monster that was just as strong. Shirone very likely had some background on this Named Monster. Maybe she'd gotten it through raiding this place with the White Night Brigade, but that was all I really knew. She'd realized Four Seasons and I were close and lured them to the Named Monster. Or maybe she'd had them help her create the conditions to make it appear. But the clay golems she'd decimated with techniques unlike anything Four Seasons used proved she had not merely sat by and watched.

◆Current Status◆
> Arihito activated Yoshitsune's Leap

I chose the fastest way I knew how to move and leaped up and down through the air without stopping. I took out the other mana potion I had as I was about to run out of magic—but it did not go as planned.

I tried to drink the potion only to feel my body reject the liquid. I lost control of my body, crashed down into the reddish-brown earth, and rolled down a slope.

"...Gak—!"

◆Current Status◆
> ★SCHOLAR'S ANKH activated ⟶ Converted vitality
  into magic

Wow...was I that low on magic already? I don't have time for this...

I started running again. But my legs felt as heavy as lead, and I couldn't run as easily as I had the first time. Mud Crawlers I should have been able to shake off blocked my path. I could have jumped over and ignored them with Yoshitsune's Leap, but I no longer had that option.

""""BEGYEEEE—!!"""" they cried, calling over more of their mates. The next thing I knew, I was loosely but unmistakably surrounded by monsters.

How did we get here? I could think of two reasons: I knew Shirone harbored nothing but ill will for me yet still neglected to investigate what had happened when she touched me. That was probably how she had secured the conditions for her Magic Marking to work.

The other reason: I had fought alongside Four Seasons and promised to see them again in a higher district. I meant every word, but I never should have said something that would pressure them to rush.

But I had other things to worry about. There I was, covered in mud, at a standstill, completely hopeless.

"I can't let it end here...not like this..."

As a rearguard, I had only one way to break through when surrounded on all sides: I had to call on Murakumo.

I still have the power to change my vitality into magic. I'm completely drained now, but I don't care if it means chiseling away at my life, I have to—

"*My dear devotee. Should you wish it, I shall grant you the power to protect your friends.*"

"...Ariadne... Could you teleport me to where they are...?
"*That I cannot do. However, I can take you to them.*"

She was going give me the power to go back over this wasteland, back to where my friends were fighting the Clay Giant. "...I beg you...lend me your strength. Ariadne—!"

"*Unwavering rearguard, I shall reward your devotion and guide you—on the Silver Chariot, which races over roads of light.*"

◆Current Status◆
> Arihito requested temporary support from Ariadne
> Ariadne summoned Alphecca

"*—In the name of mine Hidden God Ariadne, we shall lead her beloved devotee. We are Alphecca...the incarnation of Arianrhod.*"
"Arianrhod...the Silver Chariot..."

A silver-colored chariot materialized around me, and I found myself sitting on the carriage between its wheels. Alphecca had manifested and pulled me on board.

"*Remain seated, Master. We shall arrive in but a flash.*"

Neither Ariadne nor Murakumo said anything. They, and Alphecca, were waiting for my command.

"Full speed ahead, Alphecca!"

"*As you wish.*"

◆Current Status◆
> Ariadne converted Arihito's devotion level to
  magic
> Alphecca activated Endless Loop ⟶ Alphecca stopped
  consuming magic
> Alphecca activated Rose Spike ⟶ Will absorb
  vitality and magic when attacking and
  distribute to passengers
> Alphecca activated Floating ⟶ Bypassed obstacles
  and gained ability to fly at will

The Mud Crawlers slithering after us pounced all at once—but the chariot had already started moving and didn't give them the chance to get close.

The chariot is floating...and flying through the air—!

"—BEGYEEEE!"

◆Current Status◆
> Alphecca attacked ⟶ Hit 3 Mud Crawlers
Large knockback
> Rose Spike activated ⟶ Arihito recovered
  vitality and magic

The monsters hit the chariot, now strengthened by Rose Spike, and got blown back. I'd never seen anything get flung that far. The instant they collided with the chariot, I could feel power surge up within me. Magic flowed into my body that had refused the restorative powers of the mana potion. The ghostly apparition at my side looked over at me and checked how I was doing. Her face was almost entirely translucent and difficult to see, but I thought I saw her smile.

"Healing our passengers falls under our sworn duty. We shall deliver you in perfect condition."

"Yeah...please do. You're a huge help—!"

Alphecca rose up from the ground and slid through the air, racing along the undulating currents. We raced not quite as quickly as Sonic Raid but at a steady and furious pace, one exponentially faster than the first trip down this road.

Part IV: The Clay Giant

Shirone had teleported Arihito away, forcing the rest of us into fierce battle with the Clay Giant. We still hadn't found any effective method of attack, leaving us only capable of defending.

"Ellie—!"

"Agh—!"

The Clay Giant raised its fists and slammed them down—the attack reached far and wide. I heard Kyouka's warning cry as I leaped through the air and dodged it. Evading large-scale attacks, even powerful ones, isn't very challenging in and of itself. But we had a very clear reason why we couldn't afford to put space between us and the monster—or run away entirely.

"Grr...... Grrrr..."

Cion had bravely attacked the giant, but it covered her in mud and left her unable to move. Seraphina ran over to protect her.

"I'm your opponent, not her—!" she screamed.

◆Current Status◆
> ★CURSED TRI-MASKED CLAY GIANT activated MUD FIST ⟶ ELITIA dodged
> ★CURSED TRI-MASKED CLAY GIANT activated CLAY CAGE ⟶ Restraints on KAEDE, IBUKI, and RYOUKO strengthened Stole vitality and magic

The Clay Giant used the mud that splashed up every time it smashed its fists into the ground to trap the three girls ever deeper. Each time, the monster drained more and more power from them.

"You coward—! Release them—!"

◆Current Status◆
> ELITIA activated BLADE ROLL ⟶ Hit ★CURSED TRI-MASKED CLAY GIANT
> ★CURSED TRI-MASKED CLAY GIANT activated DESTROY ARMOR ⟶ ★CURSED TRI-MASKED CLAY GIANT destroyed damaged armor and restored durability

If we break only the surface of its armor, the Clay Giant restores it by adding on more mud... Does this mean we can't beat this enemy unless we figure out its weak spot...?!

Arihito had started saying something—I'm sure he meant the three masks on the bulge the giant had for a head were his weak spot. But I'd run the risk of inflicting collateral damage on the Four Seasons girls trapped in his chest if I were to try to take the masks out with Blossom Blade. My attacks were never meant for precise targets. And they were most powerful when Arihito supported me and told me how and where I should strike to make the biggest impact.

But Arihito wasn't here. We had to get through this on our own. Shirone had been observing us ever since she'd appeared. If we didn't survive this, we'd never get the chance to make her pay for what she'd done.

"Look, Ellie, here it comes again! If you're having trouble with that sword, want me to use it for you?!"

"...Shirone...you little...!"

She taunted me, knowing very well I could never let go of this cursed blade.

...Or maybe she's thinking if I die here, she can take it back...?

◆Current Status◆
> ★Cursed Tri-Masked Clay Giant activated Mud Fist ⟶ Elitia dodged
> ★Cursed Tri-Masked Clay Giant activated Muddy Rope ⟶ Reduced Elitia's speed

"—Curses—!"

"—Hyaaaaa!"

◆Current Status◆

> ★Cursed Tri-Masked Clay Giant activated Mud Fist
> Seraphina activated Shield Parry ⟶ Nullified Mud Fist
> ★Cursed Tri-Masked Clay Giant was temporarily
  rendered immobile
> ★Cursed Tri-Masked Clay Giant activated Mud Rain ⟶
  Cast mud on Seraphina

"Ugh—!"

"—Seraphina!"

"That mud is dangerous—! Once that giant gets it on you, it can pull you in—!"

◆Current Status◆

> ★Cursed Tri-Masked Clay Giant activated Mud Lure
> Theresia activated Accel Dash
> Theresia activated Double Throw
Threw two small dirks
> 2 stages hit ★Cursed Tri-Masked Clay Giant
No damage
> Melissa activated Helm Splitter ⟶ Hit ★Cursed Tri-
  Masked Clay Giant
No damage
> Kyouka activated Double Attack ⟶ 2 stages hit
  ★Cursed Tri-Masked Clay Giant
No damage

Seraphina was about to get captured. The three of us attacked to prevent that from happening, but none of our attacks made any dent on the giant.

"……!!"

"…We can't stop it—!"

"We have to do something about those masks… But what kind of attacks will work on them…?!"

If the shining masks represented the types of attacks our enemy could resist, then… The red one was the only one unlit, meaning its weak spot was probably fire. I wished Ceres were here, so she could attack with her Fire Text. But there was no use asking for the moon. Seekers should always strive to have attacks with as many different properties as possible. Theresia had her own fire attack, but even with that, our enemy wasn't going to make it easy for us.

"……!"

"—Theresia!"

◆Current Status◆
> ★Cursed Tri-Masked Clay Giant activated Mud Rain ⟶ Cast mud on Theresia
> Theresia activated Accel Slash ⟶ Hit ★Cursed Tri-Masked Clay Giant
No damage
> ★Cursed Tri-Masked Clay giant activated Mud Lure ⟶ Captured Theresia

"……!!"

The Clay Giant shifted targets from Seraphina to Theresia. Theresia flailed in the creature's enormous hand, unable to escape. Not only had we failed to save anyone, we'd actually added to the number of hostages. They could breathe now, but every time it used Mud Cage, they got buried further and further into its chest and would eventually completely disappear. If that happened... we'd be letting them die. I'd watch it happen once again, right before my eyes, helpless.

"...If I...bathe in blood..."

"—Ellie, no! You can't!" Kyouka cried out. She sounded so very far away.

I looked at my blade. Once blood landed on me, I would activate that abominable skill—and lose control.

But I don't care, as long as it means we can defeat this giant. Nothing should be able to resist the Death Sword.

"...I'm sorry... This is all my fault for being so weak..."

"—Raaaaaaaaah!!"

I heard it just as I clenched my sword: the voice I'd been waiting for all this time. His voice, the one I believed would come back for us. There was no mistaking it.

Part IV: The Silver Chariot

We bounded into the second floor and continued forward at full speed. Finally, we came upon a terrible, but not entirely hopeless, scene. The Clay Giant was clutching Theresia in its hand. I needed to get her free first, before anything else.

"Let's go straight in for the attack... Can you find a way to blast that thing's arm off?"

"*We can charge at maximum speed if we should burn all the magic we currently possess.*"

"All right... Give it all you got—!"

"*—As you wish.*"

The Clay Giant turned toward us. In that split second, the chariot rose up and floored it.

◆Current Status◆
> ALPHECCA activated AURA SPIKE ⟶ Strengthened physical attack power and expanded attack range
> ALPHECCA activated BANISH BURST ⟶ Speed increased Limit break
> FLOATING SPECTER added
> ALPHECCA activated SILVER TRACES ⟶ Hit ★CURSED TRI-MASKED CLAY GIANT
> Destroyed section of ★CURSED TRI-MASKED CLAY GIANT ⟶ ★CURSED TRI-MASKED CLAY GIANT dropped loot

The next instant, I was floating in midair. I looked back and saw traces of the Silver Chariot's light along the path we'd flown.

"—OOUGHH—!! —OOOUGHHH—!!"

The Clay Giant's right arm had ripped clean off. Its grip loosened, and Theresia immediately escaped its clutches—but the enemy still had one good arm left.

"—Theresia, aim for the red mask with your sword!" I yelled.

Normally, she would have a tough time aiming for something that high up—but not this time.

"......!"

"—Get hiiim!!"

```
◆Current Status◆
> Arihito activated Command Support 1 —→ Now capable
  of guiding party members' target
> Theresia activated Azure Weapon —→ Added fire
  property to Elluminate Razor Sword +6
> Theresia activated Double Throw
Threw Elluminate Razor Sword and small dirk
```

Theresia's blade, imbued with fire properties by the blue flame stone, radiated blue light as it hurled through the air—and thrust straight into the Clay Giant's red mask.

"—OOOUGHHH—!!"

```
◆Current Status◆
> 2 stages hit ★Cursed Tri-Masked Clay Giant
Weak spot effect
Weakness altered
Defenses lowered
Critical hit
```

That one blow turned the tide of the battle. The Clay Giant reeled, lost its balance, and steadied itself with its left hand against the ground.

"...What do you think you're doing? This is where you lose, you know..."

"Shirone, we will never let you have your way...never—!" Elitia screamed. She had no idea how much her voice, her fighting spirit, emboldened the rest of us.

"—Igarashi, Anna!"

""Okay!""

Water and thunder: Four Seasons' attacks were not necessarily useless against the Clay Giant. It's just that without fire, we would not have managed to force its weakness to shift.

We haven't done anything wrong. We can definitely turn this around...!

With the red mask crushed, the yellow mask faded and went dark. That meant a different type of attack would hurt him now: electric.

```
◆Current Status◆
> Anna activated Thunder Shot ⟶ Hit ★Cursed
  Tri-Masked Clay Giant
Weak spot effect
> ★Cursed Tri-Masked Clay Giant was Stunned
No Electrocution caused
> Kyouka activated Lightning Rage ⟶ Hit ★Cursed
  Tri-Masked Clay Giant
Weak spot effect
No Electrocution caused
> Lightning Rage activated additional attack ⟶ 3
  stages hit ★Cursed Tri-Masked Clay Giant
Weakness altered
Defenses lowered further
```

The yellow mask shattered beneath Igarashi's and Anna's attacks, and then we were down to one: the blue mask.

"Ugh…uhhh…"

Ryouko was the only one who could use water attacks, but she was still suffering, trapped inside the Clay Giant. I kicked myself for not buying another tide stone, then shook that off and tried to think of another plan.

"*—Master, of what material is that giant composed?*" Alphecca asked me. A Clay Giant; was that some kid of hint?

Clay… It's made of clay. What works against that…?

"*Not an attack—divine providence. What plunders strength and grows…from clay?*"

"…Plant roots… Your vines might be able to break that cage—!"

"*A crown of thorns adorns our brow. We are the chariot racing to battle, and she who harbors the power to bend vines to her will—!*"

"—That could work—!"

◆Current Status◆
> Arihito activated Vine Shot ⟶ Hit ★Cursed Tri-Masked Clay Giant
> Ryouko was caught by Vines ⟶ Released from Mud capture
> ★Cursed Tri-Masked Clay Giant fell by 1 level

Vines flew out of my slingshot fitted with the living young vine, the material we'd taken from the Vine Puppeteer, for a bowstring. They effortlessly pierced through the giant's clay crust and dug into its body. Alphecca wound the vines around Ryouko's body and tore her away from the clay restraints. The Clay Giant was instantly weakened. It had only reached a high level so out of place for this labyrinth because it had captured Seekers and, in that, accumulated strength.

"—Ryouko! Please aim a water attack at the last mask!" I shouted to her.

I knew I shouldn't force her to do that the second she recovered her freedom, but someone else might fall into the giant's clutches again if we let our guard down.

"...Let my friends...gooo—!!"

◆Current Status◆
> Ryouko activated Aqua Dolphin
> Hit ★Cursed Tri-Masked Clay Giant
Weak spot effect
Defenses lowered further
Critical hit

The last mask cracked open. I immediately pummeled the giant with two vine shots, which Alphecca then took over. The Clay Giant dropped another two levels and shrunk by about a third of its original size.

"You're joking... This can't...be happening...," protested Shirone.

"—It's no joke. This is how...we and Arihito have come so far...!"

"—NOOOOOOOOOO!!" Shirone howled. She'd been so sure the Clay Giant would win and finally lost all composure.

"Elitia...I'll support you!"

"Scatter like flower petals... *Blossom Blade!*"

◆Current Status◆

> Arihito activated Attack Support 2 ⟶ Target: Vine Shot
> Elitia activated Blossom Blade ⟶ 12 stages hit
  ★Cursed Tri-Masked Clay Giant
Critical hit
> Elitia activated additional attack ⟶ 8 stages
  hit ★Cursed Tri-Masked Clay Giant
Critical hit
> Elitia's Unicorn Ribbon +2 activated ⟶ A portion
  of critical hits will pierce the target's
  defense
> Attack Support 2 activated 20 times ⟶ ★Cursed Tri-
  Masked Clay Giant was completely captured by Vines
> Shirone's Manipulation Spell was destroyed ⟶
  Attack that hit ★Cursed Tri-Masked Clay Giant
  backfired on Shirone
> 1 ★Cursed Tri-Masked Clay Giant defeated

Elitia swung her sword in a frenzied dance—vines sprouted at every blow and shackled the Clay Giant, imprisoning it.

"...That's much better. Now you look the part for the Plateau of Primary Colors."

Elitia sheathed her sword and turned her back to what was once the Clay Giant. Vines coiled around its entire body and made it look like a huge sculpture.

"—Shirone!"

Elitia had without a doubt unleashed her strikes on the Clay Giant. However, Shirone's cape was now torn to shreds and her body covered in wounds, as if she had borne the brunt of Blossom Blade herself. The sheaths holding her swords had broken and fallen on the ground, but she was so depleted, she didn't even have the strength to pick them up.

"Ugh—!"

She staggered as she stood up but used a skill to recover some vitality, then made a run for it, heading deeper into the labyrinth, all by herself.

"...What she did was against Guild law. Her information will be sent to every district, and she'll get arrested at some point," Elitia said, her eyes downcast. It would be flippant to say I knew exactly how she was feeling—however.

"I know she's a very high-level Seeker, but there's no telling what might happen if she comes upon a group of monsters. If she has a Return Scroll but chose not to use it, that means..."

"...I don't know. I have no idea what she's thinking. She was never the kind of evil person who'd go around deceiving people before." It wasn't going to be easy to decide what we should do. But first, we needed to get the Four Seasons members back to town.

"Kaede, Ibuki...Arihito...and everyone else saved us..."

Igarashi was looking after Kaede, and Melissa was tending to Ibuki. The girls still seemed to be fading in and out of consciousness, but they both managed to squeeze the hand of the person caring for them. They were all alive.

"Thank you, Cion...for jumping in to protect us," said Ryouko, pouring water over Cion.

"Bow!"

Ryouko washed away the hardened clay that immobilized Cion and set her free. Fortunately, she looked otherwise unharmed.

"......"

Theresia went over to retrieve her sword from the Clay Giant carcass and then walked up to me.

"You did a great job... Theresia. I'm so sorry, everyone," I said.

"You have nothing to apologize for... But I will say, I never imagined you'd come back on that Silver Chariot," responded Elitia, smiling grimly. She was also covered in mud head to toe, but none of that mattered. These were the best friends I could ever ask for.

Relief spread across their faces and turned into smiles, but I knew I probably never would have made it back by myself. I could have been stranded, completely drained of magic, unable to move an inch. A renewed sense of appreciation welled up within me for the Silver Chariot that guided me here and my friends who stuck it out, believing I would come back for them. Georg of Polaris had said he and his party would be done for if they lost even one member, and I couldn't agree with him more. We had to keep pushing forward, but I would never allow us to lose anyone along the way. I vowed I would continue to protect everyone I held dear.

Seraphina, who had been staring out into the direction Shirone ran, approached us. The first words out of her mouth were full of appreciation for what we had done. "I cannot help but admire the bonds you share. Everyone firmly believed you would return, Mr. Atobe...myself included."

"Shirone used her special skill on me, but I didn't even realize. All this has taught me I need to pay much closer attention."

Seraphina nodded and grinned slightly. But she still had more she needed to say.

"Based on the record on my license, I believe that woman... Shirone was the one controlling the Clay Giant. Why would she have done such a thing? She must have known she would pay dearly for this in karma..."

"...Do you think she ran deeper into the labyrinth because she knew she would be arrested as soon as she left?"

"Most likely. Inciting a monster to attack other Seekers is a crime, but the perpetrator's karma will only increase if there is evidence to prove the claim... However, we have many witnesses here, as well as tangible proof. I have already sent a preliminary report to the Guild Saviors headquarters. As of this moment, Shirone Kuzunoha is a wanted criminal."

Shirone had lost any chance of returning to the White Night Brigade. Had she disappeared so she could shake off the Guild and find a way to escape this labyrinth? Or—

"...I'm sorry, but could you tell me what happened to your party—and what Shirone did?" I asked Anna, who had escaped capture from the Clay Giant. She looked over at her companions. Igarashi was still tending to Kaede, who painfully struggled to sit up, then said, "It's my... It's all my fault. I was in such a rush... She said she would tell us how to find a Named Monster, that we could all take it down together..."

"That's not true… We decided to do that as a group. I think Shirone didn't actually believe we could defeat that Clay Giant, but…she promised she would tell us about it, and she kept her word. Mr. Atobe, I cannot apologize enough. You've come to our rescue so many times, and now we've kept you from moving up to District Six…"

Tears streamed down Ryouko's cheeks as she spoke. Ibuki had her head resting on Melissa's lap and covered her eyes with her arm to hide her own tears as well.

"I'm so sorry, Teacher… We all just really wanted to…be with you…and everyone again…"

They had no reason to apologize. They'd worked so hard to advance to the next district so they could catch up to us as quickly as possible. If that was why they'd gone a bit overboard, there was only one thing I could say.

"Thank you. You've all worked so hard so we could go seeking together again… It's that kind of care that inspires us to keep doing all we can, too."

"I know normally parties compete with one another, but…I would love if we could build a relationship where we support one another instead," said Igarashi.

She was exactly right. Anna was silently crying, and Ibuki sobbed like a child. Theresia placed her hand on Anna's shoulder and softly patted it to soothe her, while Melissa handed Ibuki a handkerchief and stroked her head to calm her down.

"We bear some of the responsibility for accepting Shirone's proposition. But…"

"...Elitia. You said there's more to Shirone than plotting against other Seekers. Do you think there might have been another reason for what she did?"

"I..."

I knew it wouldn't be an easy question for Elitia to answer. I could see the hesitation in her eyes; she didn't know what we should do for Shirone, who had ventured off deeper into the labyrinth, alone and unarmed.

"I...I know this will sound naive. But I can't just leave her alone in good conscience. I'll admit, I was definitely angry at her when she sent me flying back to the entrance. But I don't think we should let her go into the labyrinth on her own... That's not how she should pay for her crimes."

"...Arihito."

There was no denying the fact Shirone had led the members of Four Seasons into a trap. And we couldn't simply forgive what she'd done. But at the same time, not even her victims wanted to leave her to fend for herself. If that's where they stood, I had to respect their wishes.

"That's true... Even if you trust you can make do on your own, you could be hard-pressed to handle unexpected situations if you're not with a party."

The rest of the group agreed with Igarashi's sentiments. Cion also barked softly to signal she was on board, too.

"Seraphina, could I leave the ladies of Four Seasons in your hands?"

"Understood. In that case, I shall use a Return Scroll to retreat for the moment and take the opportunity to file a complete report at headquarters… Please do be very careful."

"…Arihito, thank you…thank you so, so much…!" said Kaede, fat tears spilling down her cheeks. Her sincere gratitude tugged at my heartstrings.

"We'd better brace ourselves, Atobe… Also, I can't believe it—it looks like you've completely recovered. And that was such a fierce battle."

"It's all thanks to the chariot. It really put us through the wringer as an enemy, but it's an incredibly reliable ally to have on our side."

"*Master, you are enamored with the Stellar Vehicle. I shall endeavor to prove even more useful to you.*"

"*Weapons and vehicles fulfill different roles. Should we ring our voices out in chorus, we shall surely exalt one another.*"

Murakumo had materialized and was now speaking with Alphecca, who sat atop the chariot. Seraphina saw them and said, "The Silver Chariot… I wonder how far it will take you. I only hope I can see for myself at your side."

We proceeded to decide who would sit on the chariot as we went after Shirone. It held three people at most. Theresia sat on my lap because of her contributions to the fight while Elitia and Melissa stood behind us and held on tight.

"……"

Theresia had fought so valiantly, yet now she was sitting prim and proper on my lap. I felt a little embarrassed but didn't have time to be worrying about that.

"…*Master, your orders*," said Murakumo.

"All right. Onward, Alphecca…after Shirone."

"—*As you wish.*"

The chariot's wheels slowly began to turn. Four Seasons and Seraphina saw us off as we started our journey, down to the third floor of the Plateau of Primary Colors.

For anyone who is just joining us, it's a pleasure to meet you. For those of you picking up where you left off in Volume 4, thank you very much for your continued patronage. We've been fortunate enough to make it to the fifth volume with your help and warm support. I thank you from the bottom of my heart.

I'd like to jump right into the topics touched on in this volume, so I'd gently advise you to read it first before continuing here.

Are you ready? All right, let's do this.

In the last volume, Arihito and the gang had no time to rest. This time, though, I was able to include an episode at a resort, as promised. However, I imagine a few of you may be wondering, *Did they actually do any relaxing?*

But accidents are bound to happen once you step foot into a labyrinth. Arihito could not avoid raiding a labyrinth; his fate was sealed by the very fact the Guild's health resort was located in one—though I'll admit that's a bit of an excuse. At the same time, I wanted to include the heartwarming story, the likes of which we may or may not see again, of how an enormous penguin joined the party on their journey. I suggest everyone cling to a large penguin stuffed animal, or if you don't have one, fluff up the nearest bean-bag chair, or even put some penguin videos on in the background while you read that part of the story. These methods are sure to enhance your relaxation.

Sadly, real penguins abound with natural enemies. I cannot help but mention their love-hate relationship with seals in particular brings some very mixed feelings. Even the cutest penguins are in a constant battle for life or death. Meanwhile, Snow (Arihito's Jeweled Wings) and the Coral Peigoes will almost certainly live out their days peacefully in the ranch, free from intruding enemies. I hope this can convey in even the smallest way my wish to protect all the lovely penguins out there.

By the way, the battle against Jeweled Wings in this book differs greatly from the web novel version. If you were to ask, *What kind of penguins look most like the Coral Peigoes?* I would have to say it's the southern rockhopper penguin. I think that may really help you picture these little guys in your mind. I'd like to thank my editor once again for this piece of advice.

In any event, I myself would love to visit the warm, thickly forested island the Coral Peigoes call home, especially at night. I can just imagine the crystal-clear spring with its shining bed illuminating everything in the water around me. It's like something straight out of a movie or an RPG cut scene, don't you think?

No one in the party has to worry about running out of breath while swimming as long as Ryouko goes along. Maybe one day they'll raid an underwater labyrinth... That being said, the labyrinths they visit will change depending on what the group decides to do. So not all the labyrinths that lie in wait for them will make an appearance in this story. We have already heard of the Sleeping Marshes, whose idyllic-sounding name belies the deep connection it shares with Theresia. There is a chance the group may double back to labyrinths in districts they've already left, but in any case, I'd like to depict their journeys into as many labyrinths as possible.

However, as described in the prologue this time, the situation surrounding Shirone will also raise tensions between Arihito and the White Night Brigade. I imagine Arihito and company will continue pressing on in their quest to save Elitia's friend, after perhaps a short break, and eventually collide with the Brigade head-on.

But look at me, spending so much time on all the serious aspects of this story. I do want to share one regret I have about this fifth volume. That is: I could not find a way to include the nighttime bits we've all come to expect.

Now you may be thinking, *What is he going on about all of a sudden?* Nevertheless, the interpersonal aspects of the group are just as important as the seeking they do, and I have a duty to gradually reveal what the party members are doing to Arihito in his sleep night after night. Spelling even that much out risks exposing too much of what yours truly intends for the series, so I'll hold my tongue about what will happen next or what new details I want to add to this book version of the story.

Ideally, I would love to use these portions to incorporate my readers' requests as well. As an author, you more or less have a general idea of which characters readers prefer. But once you can clearly see which characters your audience wants to see more of, you're left with an ever-present reminder, and desire, to do everything you can to fulfill those wishes.

I'd like to start by adding new episodes I think need to be included for the moment. We left our heroes at the end of this volume heading off into the depths of the labyrinth, so I'll do my best to work those into the next volume. They'll mostly be calm scenes to help alleviate some of the building tension or stories of antics that can only truly come alive after nightfall. However, please feel free to write a letter to the editor or otherwise leave a comment on the web novel or on the forum if you'd like to read about any other kinds of anecdotes.

The etymology of the chariot's name as well as the appearance of the alioth crystal are both pretty big hints as to the worldview in the Labyrinth Country. But I'll hold off on saying more about that until we get a little further into the story. Of course, the nine stars on the Guild's door are another big hint. You can see a panoramic overview map of all of the Labyrinth Country in the manga version by Rikizou. You may discover something if you look at all these factors together.

The manga version is based on the light novels, but it's also Rikizou's fresh interpretation of the story, so I'd definitely recommend it to those who have already read the original work as well. If you haven't had the chance to read the manga yet, the first, second, and penultimate chapters are available online. I do hope you take a look whenever you have a moment.

I'm almost out of space, so I'd like to switch over to expressions of gratitude.

To my editor, for whom I caused a whole world of trouble this time, I promise to do my utmost in the next volume to ensure this will not happen again. Thank you for thoroughly examining the fine details and for all your suggestions on how to improve the work. These pieces of advice at times focus on the content or expressions used, but most serve to strengthen the story's foundations and sometimes even alter it in a major fashion. All your careful consideration ensures the series is headed in the right direction. I look forward to continuing to work under your guidance so I can deliver even better versions of *World's Strongest Rearguard* to my readers.

To the illustrator, Huuka Kazabana, thank you once again for your wonderful artwork!

Your spectacular illustrations paint our heroines in the cutest light and make the battle scenes seem larger than life, while your depictions of Arihito are faithful to the finest detail. All of your invaluable work helps tremendously in bringing the world and atmosphere of *World's Strongest Rearguard* to life for readers. This volume also had some swimsuit scenes, and I'm sure readers will look forward to those illustrations. I know I am.

To the team of proofreaders who work tirelessly to maintain accuracy and consistency throughout the text, I pledge to do all in my power to lighten your load going forward. Thank you for all your hard work in this volume. Every time I read a comment you kindly point out, I gain a better understanding of the things I tend to overlook. It is all thanks to you that this book made it out into the world. My devotion level for you is off the charts.

As I mentioned briefly earlier, Rikizou has taken over an extremely dense project with the manga serialization. Thank you for putting so much strength, figuratively and literally, into your artwork. Please do take good care of yourself so as not to over-exert your masterful hands. As a fan of your work, I look forward to reading the series.

Above all, to the bookstores, ebook publishers, and everyone else who has been a part of this project in one form or another, you have my sincere gratitude. Thank you all very much.

By the time you have this book in your hands, summer will most likely be upon us. I think I'd like to go to an aquarium if I ever have a moment. I want to see the crabs—but, more importantly, the penguins.

I wish you all good health and cool moments in the midst of the summer heat.

Happy Reiwa,
Tôwa